PENGUIN BOOKS

SECRET SON

Moroccan-born Laila Lalami is known internationally for her blog, www.moorishgirl.com, and is author of the acclaimed short-story collection *Hope and Other Dangerous Pursuits*. Shortlisted for the Caine Prize for African Writing and recipient of an Oregon Literary Arts grant and Fulbright Fellowship, her work has appeared in *The New York Times*, the *Washington Post* and the *Boston Globe*.

Secret Son

LAILA LALAMI

Printed in Great Britain by Clays Ltd, St Ives plc

A CIP catalogue record for this book is available from the British Library

PENGUIN BOOKS

PENGUIN BOOKS

Published by the Penguin Group
Penguin Books Ltd, 80 Strand, London WC2R ORL, England
Penguin Group (USA), Inc., 375 Hudson Street, New York, New York 10014, USA
Penguin Group (Canada), 90 Eglinton Avenue East, Suite 700, Toronto, Ontario, Canada M4P 2Y3
(a division of Pearson Penguin Canada Inc.)
Penguin Ireland, 25 St Stephen's Green, Dublin 2, Ireland (a division of Penguin Books Ltd)
Penguin Group (Australia), 250 Camberwell Road, Camberwell, Victoria 3124, Australia
(a division of Pearson Australia Group Pty Ltd)
Penguin Books India Pvt Ltd, 11 Community Centre, Panchsheel Park, New Delhi – 110 017, India
Penguin Group (NZ), 67 Apollo Drive, Rosedale, Auckland 0632, New Zealand
(a division of Pearson New Zealand Ltd)
Penguin Books (South Africa) (Pty) Ltd, 24 Sturdee Avenue, Rosebank,
Johannesburg 2196, South Africa

Penguin Books Ltd, Registered Offices: 80 Strand, London WC2R ORL, England

www.penguin.com

First published in the United States of America by Algonquin Books of Chapel Hill,
a division of Workman Publishing 2009
First published in Great Britain by Viking 2010
Published in Penguin Books 2011

004

This is a work of fiction. While, as in all fiction, the literary perceptions and insights
are based on experience, all names, characters, places and incidents either are products

ISBN: 978-0-141-04273-2

www.greenpenguin.co.uk

MIX
Paper from
responsible sources
FSC™ C018179

Penguin Books is committed to a sustainable
future for our business, our readers and our planet.
This book is made from Forest Stewardship
Council™ certified paper.

For my father and for my mother

Silence is death
And you, if you speak, you die
If you are silent you die
So, speak and die.

TAHAR DJAOUT

The fact that I
am writing to you
in English
already falsifies what I
wanted to tell you.

GUSTAVO PÉREZ FIRMAT, 'Dedication'

SECRET SON

PART I

The Year of the Flood

The rain came unexpectedly, after nearly three years of drought. In those days, Youssef still lived with his mother in a whitewashed house that huddled with others like it along a narrow dirt road. The house had one room with no windows, and a roof made of corrugated tin held down by rocks. The yard, where his mother did the cooking and the washing, was open to the sky. It was in the yard that she cleaned the sheep hides she took in on the day of Eid, and there Youssef received the rare friends who came to visit. The front door was painted blue, but over the years rust had eaten its edges, turning them reddish brown, so that holes had begun to appear at each of the four corners.

They were having lunch when it began to drizzle, the thin raindrops making craters as they landed on the fava bean soup. Youssef's mother looked up at the sky for a few surprised seconds, and then, as though a spark had ignited inside her, she jumped to her feet, grabbed the soup pot by its ears, and took it to the bedroom. Youssef's first thought was of the framed

black-and-white picture of his father, which hung on the yard
wall, above the divan. He took it inside, wiping the raindrops
off the glass with the hem of his shirt. His father gazed back
at him—a young man in his twenties, in a dark suit and gray
tie, with his hair combed back neatly, as if he were on his way
to an important appointment. His smile was timid, or perhaps
reluctant; Youssef had never been able to tell. He left the picture
next to his bed and went back outside.

His mother had already picked up the bowls and the loaf of
bread, so he grabbed the radio and carried it to the water closet.
He lifted the divan on which they had been sitting and posi-
tioned it on its side, under the green awning that ran from the
kitchen corner to the front door. There was just enough room
there for the table as well. His mother finished collecting the
laundry—now everything was safe.

They stood together at the door of the bedroom, arms folded,
watching the rain. "The year might turn out to be good,"
Youssef said. He was thinking of the farm laborers who had
been moving into the city, chased by the drought. They came
from the Gharb, from the Chaouïa, and even from as far south
as Marrakech, here to Casablanca, where their teenage children
crowded the markets and drove down wages for every kind of
labor. Maybe this year there would not be as many of them.

His mother looked up at him. "We're already in March," she
said. "It's too late for the rain to do most crops any good."

"Your flowers, at least, won't mind it," Youssef said, glancing at the row of potted roses, daisies, and gardenias under the
laundry lines. One by one, she had rescued the flowers from
the trash cans at the hospital where she worked, brought them

home, and nursed them back to health. It was a rare indulgence; she was a woman who valued work over pleasure, utility over beauty. And she was beautiful. The week before, she had turned thirty-nine, and though her hair was streaked with gray and her forehead lined with wrinkles, her green eyes and high cheekbones gave her a distinguished, almost aristocratic look.

At length, they sat down on the straw mat, facing the open door. Youssef's mother dipped her bread in the thick soup and tasted it. "It's all cold now," she said. "I'll reheat it for you."

"Don't trouble yourself, a-mmi," he said. Always, she doted on him like this, as though he were eight instead of eighteen. Even though he discouraged her constant attention, it never occurred to him to resent it. He was her only child.

When they finished eating, he put on his sneakers and checked his watch. He wondered what movie he would see this week at the Star Cinema, but even before he could ask his mother for ticket money, she was already sorting through her purse. She handed him a coin. "Don't forget your jacket," she said. He left the house, hunching his shoulders against the light rain, and headed for the theater.

THE STAR WAS NOT, strictly speaking, a cinema. This would have been obvious to anyone who visited the dilapidated building that stood across from a butcher and a tailor on one of the garbage-strewn alleyways of Hay An Najat. Nevertheless, that was the name that a Casablanca charitable association had given to the place where, every week, a new older movie was projected on a cracked screen, and where patrons competed with rats for space on the gutted seats. For five dirhams, Youssef could watch Hong Kong action films, Bollywood romances, Egyptian dramas, or American blockbusters. He never missed a show.

All his life, he had dreamed of becoming an actor. He had performed in the only play his high school had ever put on, a reenactment of the Green March, and he had spent long afternoons playing football, hoping to have the athletic chest that was appropriate for the moment when, shirtless, he would raise the Moroccan flag and lead his fellow civilians to reclaim the Spanish border post in the Sahara. He loved inhabiting the life of the hero, loved feeling his triumph, and when the audience applauded, a surge of euphoria, much like the one he had felt when he had tried hashish with Amin and Maati, ran through him. Of course, Youssef knew that his dream was unachievable — no different than wanting to win the lottery when you can't even afford to buy a ticket — but it provided a refuge from the more sobering turns he knew his life would, by necessity, have to take: finish high school, go to university, and, with any luck, find a steady job that would finally get his mother and him out of Hay An Najat.

This week, the Star Cinema was showing *Boyz N the Hood*. Right away Youssef knew that it would not be a big hit with his friends: there were no explosions, no car chases, and, most unforgivable of all, only one naked woman — and she didn't even face the camera. But he stayed glued to his seat because of Laurence Fishburne's fatherly presence, his smooth voice and limitless experience. Youssef had lost his own father at the age of two, so his memories were few, and also faint. He remembered a tall man walking through the doorway, a hand tousling his hair, the smell of a stuffed pipe at night, but, maddeningly, little else.

Whatever tangible knowledge he had of his father came to him at second hand, from his mother. Nabil El Mekki was a fourth-grade teacher, respected by colleagues and students alike for his dedication. Back then, the family lived in an apartment in the Fès medina, though Nabil often worked odd jobs at night or on weekends to save enough money for a house. Some neighbors who were preparing for a big Eid party asked him to hang lights on their roof. He tripped on a wire and fell down three floors, breaking his neck on a cart filled with roasted sheep heads. He died instantly. It was an accident, the doctors said, though everyone called it fate — mektub — for how else could one accept that such a young man had died so needlessly?

Of course, Youssef and his mother weren't the only people in Hay An Najat without a father or a husband, but they seemed to be the only ones without any family. She was an orphan, raised in the French orphanage at Bab Ziyyat. After her husband's death, she had moved from Fès to Casablanca but refused to stay in touch with Nabil's parents, who had cheated her out of the meager inheritance. This was why, growing up, Youssef had often felt that he and his mother were both unmoored, somehow.

AFTER THE MOVIE, Youssef walked out of the theater into the darkening afternoon, making his way around the puddles of water, heaps of trash, and pieces of metal. It was raining a little more steadily now, and the clouds hung low, shrinking the horizon in all directions. He always found it hard to go home after a movie. He needed time to adjust to real life, where heroes and villains could not be told apart by their looks or their accents, where women did not give themselves over on the first date, where there were no last-minute reversals of fortune.

He wanted to buy roasted sunflower seeds or chickpeas, but the cart vendors near the theater had all left because of the rain. Amin and Maati, who could usually be found at the street corner, had retreated under the blue awning of a hanout farther down the road. Standing between crates of wrinkled oranges and dark mint, they were arguing about the Widad and the Raja', the odds of either football team at the national championship.

"What's the difference between the Widadi goalkeeper and a taxi driver?" Maati asked, flashing a wide, gap-toothed smile. Even though it was cold, he wore a short-sleeved shirt. Youssef suspected it was because Maati liked to show off his biceps.

"What?" Youssef asked with a smile.

"The taxi driver only lets in three at a time."

Amin clicked his tongue. "You won't be joking like that when the Widad defeats the Raja'. And anyway, that's an old joke. Tell us one we haven't heard."

"All right," Maati said. "What's the difference between a girl-friend and a wife?"

"What?"

"Twenty-five kilos."

This time, Amin slapped his thighs and laughed.

"Here's another one," Maati continued. "What's the difference between a bucket of shit and the government?"

"What?"

"There isn't any."

Youssef and Amin chuckled. Maati lit a cigarette and passed it around. A girl none of them knew walked up the lane, carrying a bag. They watched her pass them by. Her wet sweater clung to her body, showing the faint lines of her bra and the tips of her nipples. "Come here, kitten," Amin said.

The kitten didn't acknowledge him.

"Hshouma," Youssef said. "You should respect the girl."

"Come on, my brother," Amin said. "Let us live a little. Didn't you see those breasts?"

"Her name's Soraya," Maati reported. "Her family just moved in, three streets up that way. Stay away from her, or her brother might come find you."

"Youssef's bringing us bad luck," Amin said. "She'd have talked to me if he wasn't around, looking so serious, wanting to respect her."

All three of them laughed. The year before, they had been taken by Amin's brother Fettah to visit a prostitute, where their Eid money had bought them ten minutes each. Now they dreamed of doing it with a girl their own age, someone who would, unimaginably, let them go all the way.

"She wouldn't have talked to you," Youssef said. "She's not the type."

"And how do you know this?" Amin asked, narrowing his eyes in a playful way, already sure of the answer.

Youssef shrugged.

"That's what I thought," Amin said, laughing. "So let me try my luck."

The rain grew heavy. Youssef walked hurriedly home and was soaked by the time he arrived. He found his mother struggling to move the divan, carefully covered with a plastic tablecloth, to the bedroom. "It's just some rain," he said. "Do we need to move everything inside?"

"It's going to flood," she replied. She had a habit of immediately thinking about the worst outcome to any situation, and Youssef had long ago learned not to argue when she got into one of these moods. He took the divan inside. "Can you put some more plastic on the roof?" she asked, and while he did that, she lined his side of the bedroom with pieces of cardboard to keep out the damp.

Inside, he changed out of his wet clothes. When he sat on his bed, his eye fell on his father's picture, and immediately he noticed that a drop of water had seeped in between the frame and the photograph, darkening the print. He grabbed the picture, running his palm over the spot — his father's forehead — as though he could dry it. In frustration, he put it back down on the floor and rummaged under his bed for his history textbook. His high school exams were just three months away. Amin and Maati always complained that they were required to learn things by rote, but Youssef told himself he was an actor. An actor could learn lines.

❖ ❖ ❖

The weather forecast had said that it would clear up late in the evening, but it rained furiously all night long. Youssef could not sleep for the sound of the water drumming the tin roof and the wind thrashing the bathroom door. Halfway through the night, just as he had begun to drift into slumber, he heard a group of men splashing down the alley, arguing loudly. He pulled his blankets up to his chin and turned to the wall, where the cardboard had begun to smell of ink.

In the morning, he could not go out to meet his friends because it was still pouring. He studied by the yellow light of the lamp, fiddled with the radio for a while, and then grew restless. His mother was knitting a sweater, her eyes fixed on the Mexican *telenovela* showing on television. She was different from the other women in Hay An Najat, he knew. *The widow,* he had heard some of them call her, a scornful look on their faces, as though his mother were a leper, as though widowhood were contagious. The fact that she could speak flawless French somehow exacerbated their resentment; they said she put on airs. And she was not given to large displays of emotion. Aside from a few photographs, she had not saved any of his father's relics — a ring, a watch, a book, some prayer beads.

Youssef, too, was different from the other boys. Until he was twelve or thirteen, he had never been left alone in the house while his mother was at work. Instead, his mother told him to play in the hospital garden or go across the street to the used-book store, whose cashier she knew. He spent all his summer days sitting between stacks of books, reading. He had grown five centimeters in the past year alone and towered over all his friends. And then there were his eyes — sky blue, bright turquoises — nearly out of place on his face, certainly out of place in Hay An Najat. You would expect his eyes on a Fassi, a descendant of the Moors, one of those pedigreed men who had for generations controlled the destiny of the nation. You might expect them on a tribal chieftain from the Atlas, though even there they might come with the freckled skin of Berber ancestors. You would not expect those eyes in the melting pot of misery and poverty that was Hay An Najat.

YOUSSEF HAD TO WRAP his shoes in plastic before going to school the next day, and in the unheated classrooms he regretted not wearing the additional pair of socks his mother had pressed into his hands that morning. When he came home, he found that water had trickled through an opening in the roof onto his mattress. He climbed back onto the roof to adjust the blocks of concrete, then stripped the sheets and blankets off the bed and set them to dry. But at least the television and the radio seemed to be in working order.

By the time his mother came home, the rain had at last faded to a drizzle. She asked him to go buy some flour, oil, and sugar, so he left the house and headed down the muddy road toward the hanout. At the first intersection, water pooled into a little pond, from which emerged a rusted old signpost, upright and persistent like a warning. In the next row of houses, the water ran into a rivulet. It quickly met with other tributaries to form a river, brown and fast and hungry. Youssef stopped at the bottom of the street. The river before him carried possessions away with it, like offerings to an ancient god—a suitcase, some tires, a broken bicycle, a few cinder blocks. A yelping dog swam helplessly in the middle of the debris.

Holding on to the wall, Youssef craned his neck to see if he could make it to the grocer's, but all along the little street, shops and houses were flooded. Hammad came out of his store, pushing a wheelbarrow stacked high with bags of flour. A group of boys splashed around in the dirty water. Standing where the water was shallow, the tailor yelled into his mobile phone, asking someone to come help him. Through the broken window of the beauty shop, a blond-wigged mannequin head with painted lips surveyed the scene dispassionately.

Across the street, three red cushions floated aimlessly outside the gaping doors of the Star Cinema. Youssef felt a pinch in his heart at the sight, though he had no time to dwell on the damage to the theater because, just a few feet away, knee-deep in the water, men and women were moving their belongings. A man and his two sons turned the corner toward him, carrying a chipped divan base, a torn mattress, and a table. In places where the mud was too slippery, they held on to house walls or laundry lines. Youssef ran up behind the smaller of the sons to help him with the table. They were moving to an uncle's house, the boy told him. It was the worst thing in the world, Youssef thought, to lose everything and, at the same time, to have everyone see that you did not own anything worth saving.

He continued walking toward the top of the hill, up to where the road was tarred. Rainwater filled potholes, and the bus stop sign was knocked out, but from this vantage point he had a full view of the neighborhood, of the streets that had been flooded and those that had been spared. This was another mektub. It would split someone's life into a Before and After, just as his father's death had done for him. Children born this year would be told that they came into the world during the Year of the Flood.

❖ ❖ ❖

The news spread quickly through the neighborhood: a city councilman was coming to Hay An Najat to inspect the damage. Because Youssef had never seen a government official except on TV, he went with Amin and Maati to the marketplace, where a small crowd had already gathered. The councilman climbed out of his chauffeur-driven Mercedes, while a dozen staffers carrying file folders and speaking on their mobile phones streamed out of a line of cars behind him. He wore a blue raincoat over a pin-striped suit, and eyeglasses that gave him an attentive air. He lifted his trousers and walked up the street, trailed by his assistants. Some people followed him, but Youssef and his friends stayed back to admire the Mercedes sport-utility vehicle — from a distance, since the driver chased away anyone who came too close.

The councilman was back in front of his car after five minutes, a constipated expression on his face. He spoke in a voice that sounded precious, as if it were reserved for special occasions. "We are monitoring the situation," he said. "I have given instructions to the emergency management office to send out tents and blankets. They should be here soon."

"When?" Amin asked.

A benevolent smile appeared on the councilman's face. "They're already on their way, my son. Tomorrow. Or the day after."

"Try spending the night under the rain," someone yelled. Youssef turned to see who had spoken; it was Bouazza, whose tin roof had collapsed, trapping his children for two hours before he and the neighbors rescued them.

"You have to be patient," the councilman said, a trace of impatience already apparent on his face. A sudden wind lifted a section of hair he had carefully combed over his balding head. He patted it back into place. "It takes time to get materials out here. There is flooding in other neighborhoods, and we're trying to help everyone."

"What about our businesses?" Hammad asked.

"You will get assistance, too," the councilman promised.

It started drizzling again. The water was so soft and thin it felt like dew on Youssef's face.

"We have helped you before," the councilman said. He opened his enormous umbrella and held it over his head. "Didn't we get you running water?"

Youssef laughed. "This guy doesn't even know where he is!"

"You're not in Qubbet Jjmel," Maati yelled.

"Qubbet Jjmel is just a few streets away," the councilman said quickly, catching himself. "You'll get running water here as well."

Youssef could hear the councilman's gaffe being repeated. He felt the crowd pressing closer behind him. "Where are the supplies?" he asked. "Tell us where they are and we'll get them ourselves."

The councilman smiled as though at a child. "It doesn't work that way," he replied.

"He's lying," Bouazza said. "There's no help. There's nothing."

Someone threw a tomato; another, a shoe. A rock smashed into the car's front light. The councilman tried to close his umbrella before climbing into the backseat of his car, but under the shower of random projectiles he abandoned it and jumped inside, closing the door behind him. Youssef and his friends joined the protesters, pounding windshields and kicking at tires as the procession of government cars made its way slowly, painfully, through the crowd. At last it extricated itself from the masses and sped away in a cloud of dark exhaust. Youssef picked up the councilman's umbrella, wanting to break it over his knee, but it would not snap in two. Instead, the braces came loose and cut him. On his left palm, four thick beads of blood appeared. He rubbed them away on his sleeve.

LATER, AS YOUSSEF was walking back home with Amin and Maati, they were nearly run over by a white Volkswagen van on which a loudspeaker had been mounted. At deafening volume, the driver announced that a representative from Al Hizb, the Party, would bring emergency supplies to the marketplace. Youssef had not heard of the Party before, and neither had the others, but the promise was tempting. They retraced their steps.

The white van pulled up in the little square at exactly three o'clock. A stocky man in a skullcap, a black leather jacket, and jeans brought out some wooden crates, which he stacked together. Then he introduced the speaker as Si Hatim, chairman of the Party. Hatim climbed onto the makeshift podium and stared thoughtfully at the crowd, as though he were appraising it. He was dressed in a crisp white jellaba, his head was turbaned, a white cloak floated over his shoulders. He had lively eyes, a neatly trimmed beard from which a few white hairs stood out, and big hands, with long fingers that spread out like the tines of a rake.

"My brothers and sisters in faith," Hatim said, "this flood is a big test of your faith. At a time of such suffering, the faithful

ask themselves why God let such a thing happen. I am here to
tell you that He let it happen for a reason. This flood is a warning to those who have cast aside their religion, to the men and
women who sin against our Lord, again and again and again."
Here he stared at the young people in the crowd. Two teenage
girls, perhaps not so willing to blame themselves for the fate of
the neighborhood, walked away, but Hatim went on. "Look at
what happened in Asia. For years and years, those people committed the kaba'ir, the sins of fornication and prostitution, so
in the end the Lord had enough. He sent them the tsunami to
punish them. Now He has sent *you* a warning, and we are here
to help you heed it."

Youssef was about to leave—he was in no mood for a sermon—when Hatim's speech took a different turn. "My brothers and sisters in faith, I have here in this van some tents and
blankets and food. You will get help today, not tomorrow, not
next week. Today!" he said triumphantly, his finger spearing the
air above him. People cheered, a few of them clapped; everyone
looked eagerly at the van.

"The government has abandoned the people," Hatim said,
"and so have all the parties. The socialists spent decades making
promises, but in the end they did nothing. The conservatives
praise the Makhzen and get rich on our taxes. The so-called Islamic parties don't want to risk their seats in Parliament or their
big salaries on fixing our problems. The people are alone. *We*
are alone. But *we* have the power to change things for ourselves.
And the only help we need is the Lord's help, may His name be
remembered on earth as it is in heaven. This is what the Party
stands for: Power to the people through God, with God, and

by God. *Through God,* because our program is simple: we, the Partisans, follow God's way in the knowledge that it is the best way. *With God,* because we know that the Lord is with us: He will help us and He will smite those who stand in our way. *By God,* because we have made this commitment to you and we will not waiver in our resolve to help you. Remember this: *Through God. With God. By God.*" He raised his finger upward again and looked sternly at the people.

As if a signal had been given, the driver slid open the van's doors and asked people to line up. He began handing out tents, blankets, sacks of flour, tins of sardines, tubes of toothpaste, packets of gum, bottles of cooking oil, rolls of masking tape, boxes of detergent, and canisters of propane gas. It looked like the loot from a corner-store robbery, but people fell on it, pushing and shoving to get their share. Hatim stood aside to watch. The white of his attire stood out against the dark sky above and the muddy ground below. He looked like an angel who had lost his big wings and fallen straight from the sky.

❖   ❖   ❖

The Star Cinema remained unoccupied until May, when Hatim returned to Hay An Najat with a team of construction workers. There were rumors that he had bought stolen cement from contractors who built homes for Moroccans working abroad. No one was sure. In truth, no one cared—a building being fixed up in Hay An Najat was too satisfying a sight. Hatim also hired some workers to repaint the walls, replace the wood, and retile the floors. The building was ready in just a few weeks: It

had a real roof, huge double doors, new glass windows. A sign
was hoisted over the entrance. In block letters it proclaimed,
HEADQUARTERS OF THE PARTY.

Youssef went with Amin and Maati to the grand opening.
On the ground floor, there was an infirmary, a meeting room
with rows of chairs, and a café named the Oasis (drinks were
free on Fridays). The notice board in the hall advertised a cul-
tural program: evenings of Qur'anic study, lectures by visiting
Partisans, and, miraculously it seemed, a movie every Thursday
night. Standing at the bottom of the stairs, they heard the beat
of a hip-hop song drifting down toward them. "That's where
Hatim's office is," Maati said, pointing.

"He has good taste in music," Youssef said. He wanted to
have a look upstairs, but a sign saying PRIVATE warned him
against it.

"I heard he studied in New York," Amin said.

"No, no," Maati countered. "The doorman said Hatim went
to school in Cairo."

"New York or Cairo," Youssef said, "what difference does it
make? The tea is free today. Let's go to the café." They sat in
front of the large TV and played chess until closing time, Amin
methodically defeating both Youssef and Maati in turn.

YOUSSEF WAS THE FIRST to arrive at the Party's headquarters for the picture show. He was expecting an action film,
but the movie turned out to be *Fatmah,* with Umm Kulthum
and Anwar Wajdi in the leading roles. Youssef had already seen
this tearjerker several times, but he had no other plans for the
evening and he loved the feeling of being in a darkened theater

once again. He watched as the righteous Umm Kulthum was seduced by the debonair Wajdi, who later abandoned her when she became pregnant.

When the lights were turned on, Hatim stood up and asked about the movie's "message." Everyone in the audience gave him a blank look. "This movie was made in 1947, my brothers and sisters, but it could have come out this year, so little seems to have changed. Wajdi's people spend their time drinking, dancing, and carousing, while the people of the Hara can barely find enough to feed themselves. Umm Kulthum's misery is her own fault. This is what happens when Muslim women engage in relations with dissolute men. *That* is the message of this movie. Let it be a warning to the sisters in the audience." And with this, he stared down the single teenage girl who was in attendance.

Youssef went home without getting a snack or lingering at the street corner with his friends. He found his mother bent over her embroidery. She was sometimes able to supplement her income by preparing trousseaux for brides. Without taking a break from the wedding sheet she was adorning in the Fassi style, she looked up and asked him to go buy a quarter kilo of flour.

"I was at the new cinema," he said, sitting down.

"How did you pay?" she asked, needle paused in midair. "You didn't ask me for money."

"It was free."

"Really? That's odd."

He shrugged. "They showed *Fatmah*."

She started again on her embroidery. He told her about the

movie, describing how Umm Kulthum had been deceived, how she had fallen in love with the handsome Anwar Wajdi, how she had had to go to court to prove the baby's paternity, how it had all been the fault of Wajdi's family. His mother remained silent, Youssef noticed. Even though she loved Umm Kulthum, she did not ask which songs had been performed in the film. And the way she kept her neck bent seemed slightly unnatural, as if she were making a special effort not to look at him. He waited.

At length, she set aside the wedding sheet, her eyes meeting his for the first time. "Why are you telling me this?" she asked.

In a way Youssef could not explain to himself, he had always felt that something was amiss in the stories she had told him. "I think you know why," he said softly.

"I don't know what you're talking about. What I do know is that you're going to the movies instead of studying for your final exams. You only have two weeks to go, my son. What are you going to do if you fail? You'd better go get the flour and come back and start studying."

He took the money she handed him and left, kicking at rocks on the road as he walked.

❖ ❖ ❖

Youssef took his final exams at the end of June, and on the day the results were to be announced, he made his way to school with Amin and Maati. He felt confident about his chances; he knew he was a good student, even if his mother seemed never to believe it. Maati, too, was not worried because, he said, he had "studied with the best," by which he meant that he had copied from Youssef. Only Amin was sure he would fail. He had nearly refused to come along.

The lists were posted just outside the gates. Youssef pushed his way through the crowd that circled the notice boards. He scanned the names quickly: Youssef El Mekki, Amin Chebana, but no Maati Aït-Said. "Maybe someone's taken one of the pages," Youssef said, turning around to look at Maati behind him. "Some people like to keep them as souvenirs."

Maati's jaw tightened. "Nothing's missing." He said he was going for a walk.

"Wait, my friend," Youssef said, but Maati did not look back.

Amin shook his head disbelievingly. He said he would go find his brother Fettah, and together they would ride the bus to the house in Anfa where their father worked as a gardener, to tell him the unexpected good news. Youssef walked back home alone. "I passed," he announced, as soon as he pushed the door open.

"Praise be to God," his mother said, rising from her seat and breaking into a series of high-pitched joy cries. She hugged him tightly, her head barely reaching his chest. She told him that she had asked God for good results every day for the past year, and that He had answered her prayers. "Now, everything is going to change."

Youssef had never seen his mother so happy. She looked years younger now, her eyes sparkling with joy. He smiled as he kissed her hand.

"I'm going to make something special for dinner tonight," she said. "What would you like?"

His thoughts drifted to his father, as they always did on special occasions. "If only he could have seen me," he said.

Her face returned to its usual cautious seriousness.

"What's wrong?" he asked.

She looked away. She picked up a shirt from the laundry pile and began to fold it.

"What is it that you're hiding from me?"

"Nothing."

Youssef took the shirt from her hand. "Tell me," he said.

There was no grand soliloquy—the sort of thing he had seen hundreds of times in the movies. His mother spoke very tersely about her life. The Franciscan nuns at the Bab Ziyyat orphanage had sent her to train as a nurse in a hospital. She had been there a few months when a young lawyer by the name of Nabil Amrani came in for a minor checkup. He had been involved in a scuffle with the police at a political rally. They started to see each other, and she quickly became pregnant. They planned to get married. The weekend before their wedding, Nabil went to Casablanca to pick up his brother from the airport, but in the morning fog his car collided with a truck and he died. Madame Amrani, Nabil's mother, had never approved of the marriage, and when she was told about the pregnancy, she accused Youssef's mother of sleeping with one of the doctors at work. Youssef's mother could not complete her training and went to live with a friend from the orphanage until after the birth. Then she left Fès and settled down in Casablanca.

"Amrani? Like the bus company?"

She shrugged. "It's a common name."

"What about my last name, El Mekki?"

She looked down. "I bribed an official to put that name on your birth certificate."

Youssef swallowed. Was that all there was to his story? It was a tale of outrageous misfortune, and yet it was utterly ordinary: he had been born an illegitimate child. That was why his mother had never stayed in touch with his father's family and why his father's family never came looking for him. He wanted to take her by the shoulders and shake her. Why had she kept the truth from him? Who was Nabil Amrani? Was there no hope that the Amranis would want to meet him? His head was filled with questions, but he was too angry to formulate them.

He walked out of the house, delivering himself to the scorching afternoon heat. As he made his way to the Oasis café, he realized with a mix of horror and delight that he had not been the only actor in the house. All his life, his mother had played the part of the respectable, grieving widow, talking frequently about the happiness that had been cut short by a terrible accident. She had told him that his father was a good teacher, that he loved to read books, that he always helped her with chores around the house. Those were all lies. And now she had burdened Youssef with her secret, so that he, too, had to play a role.

2

SENTIMENTAL EDUCATION

THAT SUMMER IN CASABLANCA was humid. The oppressive heat strangled hibiscus shrubs, leaving shriveled red and pink flowers on brittle branches. People drew their curtains to keep their homes dark and cool, but children still played football outside. The older of them took the bus to the beach, returning home with their noses red and their shoulders blistered. At the market, vendors hawked their homemade ice cream or fresh-squeezed orange juice ("'Asir, 'asir! Dirham, dirham wahed!"), their voices getting hoarse by the end of the afternoon. At night, turbaned old men ventured out to crowded cafés, where they drank glass after glass of mint tea and played endless rounds of Ronda.

Youssef spent all that time avoiding his mother. In the morning, he did not get out of bed until after she had already left for work; during the day, he went to the beach with Maati and Amin; at night, he played chess or watched TV at the Oasis. He could not bring himself to talk to her. Mothers were mothers; they were not supposed to have sexual lives. How could he talk to her about how he had been conceived? He also blamed mektub. Had his father not died in that car accident, the wedding would have taken place on schedule and no one would have known that his mother was already pregnant. Now *he* knew, and that brought him shame he could barely conceal and certainly never share. By avoiding his mother, he could perhaps forget the existence of her secret.

But it was difficult once September came and school started. He watched from his bed as his mother opened the armoire to pull out a button-down shirt for him to wear with his blue jeans. "Here," she said cheerfully. "I ironed it for you."

"Thank you," he said, looking away, unable to summon the same excitement. When he still believed he was the son of a respectable schoolteacher, he had modest but clear ambitions— to become a teacher himself or perhaps a civil servant. But now that he knew he was the illegitimate son of a community organizer, he felt somehow diminished, as though he were already marked for an unfavorable future.

They sat down to eat breakfast together. News on the radio was the usual: the king had met some foreign dignitaries; there was bloodshed in Palestine and Israel, in Iraq and the Congo; a French delegation had toured Moroccan companies and praised them, saying they were on "the right track"; a festival of music was set to open in Agadir; the Widad was on a losing streak. The bulletins compounded the sense of futility that had been growing inside him.

"It's going to be a beautiful day."

He did not answer.

"Are you ready for registration?"

He nodded.

"Do you have a copy of your *baccalauréat*?"

He patted the bag next to him.

"And the photographs for your ID card?"

"Yes."

"May God open all doors for you," she said.

She looked as if she were about to give him a hug; he dodged it by grabbing his bag and slinging the strap across his shoulders. He stuffed the hundred-dirham bill she gave him for his registration fee in his jeans pocket and left.

❖ ❖ ❖

Just three weeks into the school year, Youssef could already see clusters of students huddling together in distinct cliques. There was the Mercedes-and-Marlboro group, half a dozen spoiled kids who, for one reason or another, had not gone to college abroad like the rest of their friends. They spoke French, wore designer clothes and carried patent leather satchels, spent their time smoking expensive cigarettes and talking about holidays in Paris or weekends in the bars of Marrakech.

There was the headscarf-and-beard faction — girls who looked at once virtuous and threatening, and boys who had the same determined expressions as the Partisans. They organized strictly along gender lines, with the girls sitting on the stairs outside the building, chatting about which hadith recommended which manner of eating or drinking or sneezing, while the boys carried on their own quiet conversation, occasionally passing out leaflets that urged students to join their group, the Islamic Union of Students.

The Marx-and-Lenin group met at the other end of the main hall, right under the windows. There were only five or six of them, and they spent most of their time complaining about the condition of the classrooms, the cafeteria, and the library, or reading the newspaper while sharing a cigarette. They had formed the Democratic Union of Students, though they had not yet printed any leaflets; they were still arguing over which background color to use.

Then there was the Berber Student Alliance, which usually met outside the doors of the amphitheater. They had organized several successful conferences on Amazigh history and culture. Now they wanted to have a department of their own. The university already had departments of Arabic, French, English, Spanish, and German, so why, the Berber Student Alliance demanded, did it not have one for Tamazight? This was discrimination, they argued, part of a long-standing pattern in this country. After a sociology professor gave a lecture in which he said that the vast majority of Moroccans were racially mixed, the Berber pride students began to wear T-shirts emblazoned with Tifinagh characters.

The Saharawi students often gathered by the coffee machines. They had put up a banner in support of the independence of the Saharan territories, but other students savagely tore it down, called them "traitors to the national cause," and told them that if they did not like Morocco, they should go study at one of the Polisario Front's camps. The fights got physical; the police were called in. But they stood by while the students fought. Now the Saharawi students were talking about organizing a sit-in outside the administration building.

Then there were the three undercover cops, whom Youssef had mentally nicknamed the Three Basris. They often chatted with the uniformed police guards outside the lecture halls and had therefore blown their cover, but they did not appear to care. Perhaps that was the point: they *wanted* people to know they were there because it was easier to intimidate people this way. One of them was on his second bachelor's degree—he already had one in history—but the other two were much younger.

Every time Youssef tried to penetrate one of these cliques, he felt he was lacking some background, some essential element that would make it easier to know what to say, when to say it, and how to say it. He went inside the classroom and sat alone by the window.

DR. SABRI WALKED into class fifteen minutes late. He was young, in his late twenties maybe, and he casually leaned against the side of his desk when he spoke. "I'm sorry I'm late, guys," he said. He took his copy of *The Great Gatsby* out of his briefcase and, in an accent that, to Youssef's ears, sounded perfectly American, asked, "I assume you've all read the book, as I've requested?"

A few people nodded, while others looked studiously down at their notebooks, avoiding his gaze.

"Very well, then." He opened the book to the first page and read, his voice a deep baritone. "*In my younger and more vulnerable years my father gave me some advice that I've been turning over in my mind ever since. 'Whenever you feel like criticizing any one,' he told me, 'just remember that all the people in this world haven't had the advantages that you've had.'*" He looked up and smiled. "Ah, good old Nick!" Dr. Sabri spoke this way through-out the lecture, referring not just to the characters, but to the author as well, by their first names, as though he knew them.

Majoring in English had its advantages—homework con-sisted of reading novels (imagine that!)—so Youssef was pleased with the choice he had made. And *The Great Gatsby* afforded him a special treat: imagining himself in Robert Redford's role. He had seen the film adaptation at the Star Cinema, and when he had read the novel before class, he had found it impossible to picture a face for Jay Gatsby other than the one he already had in mind.

As the first hour drew to a close, Dr. Sabri asked, "And what of Daisy?" He looked around the room, waiting for opinions. The class was silent, united in its refusal to meet his eye. "Okay, so who is she?" he asked.

"A woman from the upper class," said a blond, curly-haired boy in the front row, his intonation rising, waiting for approval.

"Clearly, she is. But what else?" asked Dr. Sabri.

"Daisy is a lost woman," one of the bearded boys shot back.

"Hmm. I suppose it depends what you mean by 'lost.' What do you mean?"

"She spends time with another man, even though she is married."

"I hope you're not serious, man. If that were the definition of 'lost,' then half the women in this country would qualify."

The young man leaned forward on his desk, dropped his chin in his hand, and stared defiantly. "That's the problem."

Dr. Sabri looked away uncomfortably. "Okay, anyone else?"

Youssef raised his hand, and the professor looked at him encouragingly. "She is the dream — Gatsby's dream." A girl in the front row laughed out loud at his answer and turned to stare mockingly at him. Her skin was fair, her eyes playful, and her features delicate, like those of a miniature painting.

"That's a lovely answer, actually," Dr. Sabri said, looking appreciatively at him. "Let's see if we can figure out whether the book bears it out."

The girl pouted and turned around to face the blackboard.

AFTER THE LECTURE, Youssef came out into the corridor to find her waiting for him. She wore a green top that matched her jade earrings, and carried her mobile phone in her hand. "*Je suis désolée,*" she said. "I didn't think that Dr. Sabri was looking for that answer." She laughed easily, touching Youssef on the arm as she did so.

"Not a problem," he replied. He felt a surge of gratitude to his mother, because without her tutoring, his diction in French would not have been flawless. To listen to him, one would never have known he lived in Hay An Najat. The girl ran her fingers through her hair in a consciously flirtatious way. He was encouraged. "What's your name?"

"Alia," she said. "And you?"

"Youssef."

"*Salut,*" she said, flashing a smile that displayed perfectly aligned teeth.

"Have you seen the movie, the one based on the book?"

"Of course." She winked at him. "I haven't read the novel."

"Really?"

"What for? It's no different than the movie."

One of the Mercedes-and-Marlboros called her, and so, waving good-bye, she turned on her heel and walked away, leaving a trail of perfume behind her. Even though she had been rude, her apology made him feel he had judged her too quickly. He watched her as she caught up with the other Mercedes-and-Marlboros, all the while wondering if he would ever be able to be part of her group.

❖   ❖   ❖

The truth came out, Youssef would later recall, as a result of a simple football game. The Partisans had cleared a dirt lot of the trash that was regularly dumped in it, planted white poles and goal nets, and turned it into a football field for the young men of Hay An Najat. One Saturday afternoon, Maati bought a new ball at Derb Ghallef, and he, Youssef, and Amin went to try it out. When they arrived at the field, they found a group of boys already playing, using a torn ball stuffed with fabric. No one knew or recognized them.

"Should we come back later?" Youssef asked, looking around to his friends. Mounir, Rachid, and Simo had come along to play, too.

Without answering, Maati walked onto the lot, interrupting the game. "This is *our* football field," he said.

One of the intruders, a tall boy with a dirty white shirt and frighteningly thick eyebrows, walked up to Maati. "I don't see your father's name anywhere on it," he said. His teammates laughed, their ha-has overlapping. They came to stand behind their friend, arms akimbo.

Youssef spoke up. "We play here on Saturdays and Sundays, and we've never seen you before."

"So what?" Eyebrows opened his right palm, as though he were waiting for a better explanation. He seemed to be the leader.

"Let's all just play together," Amin said. "All of us against all of you."

Maati shook his head. "There are six of us and only five of them. It wouldn't be fair."

"What's the matter?" Eyebrows said. "You're afraid to lose?"

"Lose?" Youssef said, chuckling. "Who do you think you are? Mustapha Hadji? You're just a regular kid."

"Don't worry about the numbers, then. We can take you on." Maati twirled his soccer ball on his finger.

"So what are you boys going to do?" Eyebrows continued. "Play? Or stand around here whining, like a bunch of little girls?"

"Let's play," said Youssef. He was not nearly as good a player as Maati, but he felt a sudden, compelling urge to win. The two of them were on offense along with Amin, while Mounir and Rachid played defense. Simo was the goalkeeper. After only a few minutes of play, one of the intruders, a skinny boy who was playing barefoot, shot the ball into the right-hand corner of the goal posts. Simo dived for it but could not catch it. The intruders celebrated by giving one another high fives and big slaps on the back.

Maati immediately took the ball to resume the game, fighting heatedly with the other kids over every suspicious-looking move. Youssef goaded him; the idea that these boys would come play on this territory and score, even though they were out-numbered, was unbearable. Finally Maati managed to fool the intruders' defense and cross the midfield. He was on his way to the goal perimeter when Eyebrows caught up with him and kicked him. Maati pushed him to the ground.

"Faggot," Eyebrows said between his teeth. He shot to his feet and struck Maati in the face.

Maati seemed surprised by the attack; he was so rarely chal-lenged on his own turf. He punched Eyebrows back. The fistfight was almost comical: the tall, muscular Maati against the skeletal boy from no one knew where. Youssef and Amin rushed in to restrain Maati before he could do any harm. "You're an animal, you," he said, wiping his bloody forehead. "You can't play fair."

Eyebrows sent spit shooting out of the side of his mouth. "You outnumber us, and you complain about playing fair? That's a good one."

Maati raised his fist again, but Youssef stopped him. "We're done," he said, dragging him away. "Let's go, my friend." Blood dripped from Maati's forehead onto his white T-shirt. He touched the cut with his fingers, feeling for its depth. Someone suggested the Party's infirmary.

THE INFIRMARY TURNED OUT to be a small room with a cot along one wall and a glass-paneled medicine cabinet against another. A bearded man in a white lab coat sat at a desk reading a book. Youssef had heard from Maati that the nurse was a Senegalese man who had been a classmate of Hatim's in Egypt many years ago. They had moved back to Morocco together, and founded the Party with a group of friends. He stood up now.

"As-salaam, Moussa," Maati said.

"Wa 'alaykum as-salaam wa rahmatu llahi ta'ala wa barakatuh. What happened to you, my brother?" he asked.

"We were playing soccer and—"

"Sit, sit," Moussa said softly, pointing to the cot. "Let me take a look at you." He retrieved a first-aid kit from the cabinet. "In the name of God," he whispered before starting. He disinfected the cut. "You're going to need one or two stitches."

"It's just a cut," Maati said.

"It's too deep. Don't move," Moussa said. He sprayed an anesthetic and started to sew, working efficiently and in silence. Maati winced but didn't complain. "There," Moussa said. "It's done, my brother."

Hatim came in. "As-salamu 'alaykum," he said, a big smile on his face.

"Wa 'alaykum as-salaam," the three of them said mechanically.

"Wa rahmatu llahi ta'ala wa barakatuh," Moussa added.

It annoyed Youssef that the Partisans always used the unabbreviated, properly Islamic greeting, never once using any of the colloquial ones. He picked up the soccer ball from the floor and looked to the door.

"How are you boys?" Hatim asked.

"Praise be to God," Amin answered.

"What happened?"

"Just a little cut," Maati said. He stood up and dusted himself off.

"Take it easy, my son," Hatim said, smiling. "Have you kids started school?"

"Last month."

"And what are you studying?" he asked, his eyes full of sudden interest.

"Law," said Amin.

"English," Youssef said.

Maati looked around the room as though he wanted to be somewhere else.

"How wonderful. How wonderful. We could certainly use talented young men like you around here." He smiled again. "I was just coming here to show Brother Moussa this article in *Casablanca Magazine*." He held out a glossy magazine folded in half. "This journalist—Farid Benaboud—he'll print any trash he can find, so long as it serves his puppet masters."

Youssef and the others stared at him uncomprehendingly.

"Oh, you don't know Benaboud?" Hatim asked. "It's just as well, really. He's a disgrace. In this piece he praises one of the wines produced in Meknès. Can you believe the insolence? Qalt el-hya hadi! We are a Muslim country. We have no business having wineries here in the first place." Hatim had not raised his voice, but when he stopped speaking the room fell quiet, his words having drowned out the sound of everything else. "Take a look," he said, holding out the magazine.

Neither Amin nor Maati reached for it, so Youssef felt obliged to scan the article. He unfolded the magazine. On the opposite page was a color picture of a middle-aged man, under the headline NABIL AMRANI: 'OUR BUSINESSES ARE TREATED UNFAIRLY.' Youssef stared at the man in the picture, at his blue eyes and aquiline nose, his dark hair and wide forehead. The recognition was like a knife in the stomach—a kind of death. Yet instead of taking away life, it offered a new one, resurrected. Could this be his father? It was impossible. It was a mere coincidence, he told himself, a mere coincidence.

"You can keep the magazine, if you like," Hatim said. "You should read Benaboud's article in full to see what we're up against."

Youssef nodded, folded the magazine, and slipped it under his arm.

"Well, I won't keep you," Hatim said. "Good luck with the new school year." He held the door open, and the three of them filed out.

ONCE IN THE CORRIDOR, Amin turned to Maati. "I could have done without the lecture," he said angrily. "Next time, just go home and put Betadine on your cut, and save us all the talk."

Maati touched the dressing on his forehead. "But Moussa did such a good job."

They continued bickering, but all Youssef could think of was the photograph. He was afraid to open the magazine and draw attention to it. Taking deep breaths, he tried to quiet the beating of his heart in his chest. Amin and Maati stopped in the lobby to look at the list of programs pinned to the notice board. "Great. Another documentary on wild animals," Amin said. "And a Qur'an study class. Fantastic."

"What's wrong with a Qur'an class?" Maati said.

"I'm leaving," Youssef said. "Take care."

He walked away, leaving Amin and Maati outside the Party's headquarters. As soon as he turned the corner, he stopped and opened the magazine again. It was dusk, and in the diminishing light the picture did not look as frightening as it had in the infirmary. This was a blue-eyed man with the same name as his father. What did it mean? Nothing. The article was about a dispute between transportation companies and a government agency over the licensing of new bus lines. Nabil Amrani was quoted liberally throughout; it was clear that the journalist felt there was merit to his position. There was only one biographical detail Youssef could glean from the piece: that Amrani was a Fassi. But with a name like Amrani, of course, he would have to be from Fès. This did not mean much, either.

At home, Youssef slid the magazine under his mattress. He wondered what his mother would say if he showed her the picture. She would be able to confirm that this was just a man with the same name or, at worst, some distant relation of his father's. But receiving that reassurance meant having to talk to her.

"Youssef," she called from the yard. "Go get some water."

"I don't feel like going," he said. "And anyway, getting water is women's work." He expected her to reprimand him — he would have welcomed it, because then he could talk back — but she did not say anything. She finished preparing dinner and then went to get the water herself.

❖ ❖ ❖

The next week was hell. Youssef read and reread a sonnet for his poetry class, without being able to immerse himself in it.

During lectures, he stared out the window at the trees swaying in the fall winds, and when he returned to Hay An Najat he avoided his friends because he was afraid he might falter and tell them about the photograph, and about his mother's secret. He could not sleep at night. Was this man his father? Was his father alive? On Friday he skipped school altogether and stayed home, watching TV. Eventually he dozed off and dreamed that he was a bird, flying around and around, unable to find a resting spot. The creaking of the door when his mother arrived home from work awakened him. The lines around her eyes and mouth were not as pronounced as they usually were, and she had a big smile on her face. The unusualness of this made him do a double take. What was she so happy about?

"They gave me a promotion," she replied. She would manage the reception team now that her boss had retired, which meant a small raise. "Why are you in your pajamas?" she asked, her eyes full of disapproval and disappointment. "You didn't go to school today?"

"So what if I didn't?"

She dropped her purse on the divan and took off her jellaba. She seemed to be weighing what to say next. "You should think of the future," she said, her tone more conciliatory.

He chuckled. "The way you thought about the past?"

His mother slipped her shoes off and put on her slippers. "What are you talking about?"

He ran inside the bedroom to get the magazine and held it up to his mother's face.

"What is this?" she asked.

He corrected her: "*Who* is this?" For a brief moment, he felt like the hero of a courtroom drama, a prosecutor holding Exhibit A in front of a guilty defendant.

His mother gave him an icy glare. "Keep your voice down," she said. "The neighbors will hear you." She took her time getting her glasses out of her purse, put them on, and then finally took the magazine from him. Her eyes widened briefly, but otherwise she did not show any emotion. She is such a good actress, he thought, and a part of him admired her for her skill. But another part of him demanded answers and would not let go this time.

Finally she looked up. "What do you want from me?" she asked in a level voice.

"What do I want?" he croaked. "Don't you know?"

She shrugged.

"Is this . . . *him*?"

She nodded once and handed him back the magazine. He ran into the bedroom again, this time returning with the framed black-and-white photograph. "Then who is this?"

"Stop asking me these questions," she said. "They're not going to lead anywhere you want to go."

"Who is this?" he asked, his voice shaking even as he tried to keep himself from crying. The anger inside him threatened to consume him.

"Youssef Boualem."

"Who is he?"

"He worked as a driver for the Amranis. He helped me move to Casablanca and find a job."

"You named me after the driver?"

"He helped me. It seemed like the right thing."

With all his might, and without being aware that he was howling, Youssef threw the frame against the wall. Glass shards flew across the yard. "Why?" he asked. "Why didn't you tell me the truth? All of it?"

"And what else could I have done?" she asked. "You tell me. Your father was constantly away, attending political rallies or picketing factories. Your grandmother already had her eye on a wife for him, and I knew he would give in. I had no one, a-weldi. No home. No family. No place to go. And I didn't want you to grow up like me, in an orphanage, not knowing anyone, not knowing your parents. You already had a mother, but I wanted you to have a father, too. Someone who would be around every day. Was this a crime?" She paused and stared at him with such passion that he stepped back. "I should have killed myself," she said, without any apparent emotion, just a twinge of regret in her voice, as though she had suddenly decided, nineteen years later, that this would have been the better course of action. "Better to have killed myself than to suffer through this hell, to be punished for having taken care of you and protected you."

Youssef had not expected that she would force him from the pedestal he had constructed for himself and compel him to see that he was no more in a position to judge her than she him. "If you want to think about the past," she said, "then suit yourself. But as for me, I'm done with it."

She walked away, delivering him, once again, to the silence they had barricaded themselves in for the past few months.

❖ ❖ ❖

When Youssef woke up the next day, his first thought was that his father was alive, that he was somewhere in this city, so near, and yet as unreachable as if he had lived in New York or Beijing. What did Nabil Amrani look like in real life? What did his voice sound like? Was he tall and thin? Or short and stout? Was it true he loved to read, the way Youssef's mother had repeatedly told him, or did he hate it? Was he married? Did he have children? Did he remember the child he had left behind, or had he forgotten about the past?

Youssef thought of all the summer days he had spent in that musty bookstore storage room, reading. He had always felt a special kinship with the fatherless heroes of literature — from Inspector Ali to Tom Sawyer, from Batman to David Copperfield — but now he saw that all along he had been like everyone else; he had a father and a mother. Still, Nabil Amrani's existence was something he had to carry inside him; he could neither speak of it nor erase it. It was there whether he was alone or with his friends, whether he was at home or outside. Watching the different cliques at school, he wondered what it would be like to not have to play a part — to know, as easily as everyone else did, which group was his. After all, had he not been the bastard child of his mother, had he instead been the legitimate son of his father, his place in one of these cliques would be clear. The only thing worse than the hell of not knowing where he belonged, he thought, was the hell of knowing.

In class, Alia chatted happily with her friends, occasionally letting out a laugh that felt like a burst of warm sunshine in a cold, dark room. It lifted his spirits so much that he wished he could tape it and listen to it in a loop, all day long. She was talking about a family gathering that had taken place at her grandmother's house, with many uncles and aunts and cousins attending, and how utterly bored she had been by the musical band her grandmother had hired to entertain them. When the composition professor walked in and everyone turned away from her to face him, Youssef's eyes were still on Alia.

ON HIS WAY HOME that night, he stopped by the *téléboutique* to buy a fifty-minute card for his mobile phone. Amin was sitting on the stoop of the store, smoking a Favorite. Youssef leaned against the doorjamb, occasionally stepping aside to let a customer in or out. He listened to Amin talk about Soraya, who, it turned out, was studying law as well. "I saw her in the hallway today, and she was very friendly, if you know what I mean," he said, winking. "I'm telling you, she'll be going with me soon."

"Ah," Youssef said. "You'll win her with your gentle touch?"

Amin looked slightly miffed, but in truth he could not really counter the remark. Among his friends, Youssef was perhaps the most popular with girls, and today he could not resist showing off. He told Amin about Alia, her beautiful figure, her luminous skin, her perfect smile, her magical laugh, but Amin did not seem particularly impressed. "Sounds like she's rich," he said, shaking his head as though he knew her, or knew, without needing to be told, that she was.

"So what if she is?" asked Youssef.

"How can you say 'so what'? What planet do you live on? Everyone should know the size of his teapot."

Amin was starting to sound like an old man, Youssef

thought—already quoting proverbs. "She likes me," he bragged. "She'll come around."

Amin sucked on his teeth. "We'll see about that, O Antar."

There was a lull in the conversation. Youssef wondered if the moment was propitious, if he should tell his friend the truth about Nabil Amrani. He felt closer to Amin than to Maati, but it was such an enormous revelation—he would never be able to get the words out. Next time, he told himself. Maybe next time I will tell him.

Just then, Maati came up, wearing his usual navy blue sweats, the tank top that showed off his tanned arms, and a new, white skullcap on his head. He looked as if he were wearing two uniforms at once.

"I found a job," he announced.

Amin and Youssef were taken aback; neither of them had expected that Maati, the one who had flunked his high school exams, the one who always seemed a little on the slow side, would beat them to employment. "Mbarek u mess'ud," they said.

Youssef gave Maati a high five. "Hay hay! An employee!"

"Where will you work?" asked Amin.

"At the Party's headquarters. I'll be working in security."

"Security?" Youssef asked. "What do they need security for?"

"You know how it is," Maati said. "They have computers and documents and, you know, that sort of thing."

"They think someone might rob them?" Amin asked.

"It's not just that. I also have to keep an eye on who's coming and going. You know. *For security.*"

"How much do they pay you?" asked Youssef.

"Enough," Maati said, flashing his gap-toothed smile.

"Come on, Maati. Tell us."

"Fifteen hundred dirhams a month."

Youssef and Amin sighed in unison. "So that means you're paying," Youssef joked, taking Maati's pack of cigarettes from his hands. Maati immediately reached for the lighter in his pocket and held it up to the cigarette dangling from Youssef's mouth.

They walked back home together. These two were his best friends, his gang, his rba'a, the people with whom he spent all his free time. He had always been a part of this group at least, in spite of his terrible shame and his unspeakable secret.

A Place to Call Home

YOUSSEF WAS DRINKING his morning glass of tea when he heard the news on the radio: bus fares would be raised by forty centimes. Sitting next to him on the straw mat, his mother wrapped herself in her knitted shawl and clicked her tongue. "They raised them just two years ago!" But Youssef was too busy making mental calculations to answer. Forty centimes, four rides per day, five days a week, four weeks a month, three months per quarter: ninety-six dirhams. Having already spent most of his grant money on school materials, cybercafe fees, and minutes for his mobile phone, he would not be able to buy the pair of sneakers he wanted.

When he arrived on campus, his classmates were already de-bating the fare hike. Hicham, a stout man with the beard and white qamis favored by his friends in the Islamic Union of Stu-dents, had attracted a small crowd around him. "The increase in fares is a result of poor management," he said, his voice echo-ing off the high ceilings in the main hall. "If the government needs to raise money, why does it not impose higher taxes on bars—those places of filth and sin?" But Abdallah, who belonged to the Democratic Union of Students, interrupted his speech. "It's not that simple, my friend. Look, if the government hadn't misspent our money, they wouldn't need to raise prices in the first place. A general strike, that's what we need." Either proposal, it seemed to Youssef, was fine, so long as it led to the cancellation of the fare hike.

By lunchtime, students from the IUS and the DUS had come to agree: they would go on strike together. Standing outside the cast-iron doors of the main hall, Youssef watched the two groups congregate on the esplanade. They tried out some slogans—tentatively at first, and then with greater confidence. Dr. Sabri and two of his colleagues came out of the administration building and stood with their briefcases in hand, watching. Alia sat on the marble balustrade with a friend, smoking cigarettes, unaware of the gathering or unconcerned about it. One of the Three Basris spoke for a while on his mobile phone. The peanut, nougat, and chewing gum vendors packed up their wares and left.

Youssef jiggled the change in his pocket, counting it and recounting it by feeling the size of each coin. The crowd was getting larger and louder: chanting, whistling, clapping, and stomping in rhythm. Some of the men took off their sweaters or shirts and whirled them above their heads. Two women held between them a beige scarf on which the word ENOUGH was scrawled in black marker. The energy that drifted from the crowd was drawing Youssef in; still, he resisted. He did not want trouble.

Then the police trucks arrived. Dozens of officers in blue uniforms came out of rusty vehicles bearing the red and green stripes of National Security. The vague, festive energy that had hung over the crowd all morning turned purposeful and serious at once. Professors retreated into their offices inside the administration building. Alia and a friend drove away in a blue car. As the slogans grew louder, the officers formed one long line and took out their batons. Back home, Youssef remembered, the police had picked up Amin's father as he was walking home late one night. Even though he had his papers on him and had committed no crime—except, of course, for the crime of being poor—he was taken to the station for the night. He had been released the next day, barely able to walk on the feet the officers had savagely whipped with rubber hoses. Youssef looked at the students and at the police; and his allegiance came to him in a flash. He joined the protestors, letting the excitement of the moment course through him, giving him the intoxicating feeling that he belonged.

The slogans multiplied, going from complaints about the fare hike to angry heckling about the amount of state grants, the lack of proper cafeterias, the condition of classrooms, libraries, and roads. This seemed foolish to Youssef, because there was little chance that *everything* would change, but he still sang along with the others and threw his fists up in the air.

Then the police charged. Youssef saw the baton coming, but even as he tried to get out of its way, it landed on his ribs, knocking the air out of his lungs. He fell to the ground. The pain was so acute that for a few seconds he thought he might faint. A bitter taste invaded his mouth. In the melee above him, students used their shoes and schoolbags to hit back at the police. Youssef was trampled, punched, and kicked; he hit back blindly, gasping for air. There was a sudden opening to his right, and Youssef instinctively turned toward it. He saw the police dragging Abdallah away, his head bobbing with every step they took, blood streaming from his mouth. A surge of adrenaline shot through Youssef, numbing the pain in his ribs. He scrambled up, pushed his way out—and ran. The wind in his ears was like a whistle that urged him to go faster, away from the campus. When he got to the intersection, he crossed without waiting for the light to change.

He did not slow down until he got to a commercial street, several blocks down. He went into a bookstore. There was nowhere to sit, so he stood in front of the dictionary section. From his book bag he took out the rag he normally used to clean dust from his shoes and used it to wipe the sweat from his face. He straightened his shirt. He pulled up his pants. Now, finally, he allowed himself to take a deep breath—he nearly doubled over from the sharp pain. Something was broken. But of course he could not go to the hospital. What if the police were there, waiting to see who turned up? Besides, there was the matter of his mother. If she ever found out what he had done, he would never hear the end of it. "Keep your head down, and mind your own business," she told him, frequently and dogmatically. There was only one place for him to go.

❖   ❖   ❖

They sat in the empty café, at a table on which the waiter, a rotund man with puffy eyes, had laid several stacks of msemmen and harsha, bowls of nuts, and pots of coffee and mint tea.

Youssef contemplated the food without being able to summon any appetite. Moussa, in his white lab coat, sat next to him, balancing his chair on its hind legs, resting its back on the wall behind him. Hatim was across from Youssef, smoking a cigarette. Maati, too, had left his guard post to be with them. He picked up a piece of harsha and ate it in a few quick bites, leaving a trail of semolina crumbs on his blue shirt. He was growing a beard, but his facial hair wasn't cooperating. It grew here and there in tufts that curled in on themselves and stubbornly refused to connect.

"Drink, my son," Hatim said, pushing a tall glass of water toward Youssef.

Youssef reached for the glass, but the pain in his chest made him wince.

"You have to rest for a few days," Moussa said. He had examined Youssef in the infirmary, bandaged him, and told him he was lucky to have broken his eighth and ninth ribs. Had he been hit lower or higher, he would have risked a damaged organ, and then who knew what would have happened? "We thank God, in any case," Moussa added.

"You're safe now," Hatim said, smiling in a way that made Youssef uncomfortable. "And you will get better, insha'llah."

Youssef did not care if it hurt — he was simply relieved that he did not have to deal with the police or with his mother.

"How many students were there?" Hatim asked.

"About two hundred."

"And how many were taken into the police trucks?"

"I don't know. Ten or fifteen, maybe. I ran away, so I don't know how many others were arrested."

"Was there much blood?" Hatim asked.

What a strange question, Youssef thought, though he was willing to answer it for the sake of the article. The piece was Hatim's idea; it would be an eyewitness account of police brutality on student campuses, and it would run in the Party's newspaper, *At Tariq Al Mustaqim*. Youssef closed his eyes now and thought about those few minutes when the police charged. The memory had been preserved in jump cuts, and he played and replayed them in his head, hoping to see if he had missed any details. At length, he shook his head. "I don't know."

"There had to be," Hatim said. "They used their batons. In any case, we have the photos of you." Those, too, had been his idea. When Youssef had taken his shirt off in the infirmary, Hatim had immediately gone upstairs to his office and come back with a digital camera. "No!" Youssef cried, but Hatim waved his concerns away. "Don't worry, my son. I'll only take a picture of you from the neck down. No one will know it's you."

"Will you write the article yourself?" Youssef asked.

"No. I will leave that to the professionals at *At Tariq*. But they will tell *your* story, my son. You can be sure of that."

Amin came in. There had been a strike at the law faculty, too, but when Hatim asked him about it, Amin said he hadn't seen anything. "Well," Hatim said, taking his mobile phone out of his pocket. "I'll get to work with what we do have." He walked away, holding Moussa by the elbow and whispering to him.

Amin turned to Youssef. "Yak labas?" he asked.

"I'm fine," Youssef said.

Amin poured himself a glass of mint tea and blew on it to cool it off. "What were you thinking?"

"What do you mean?"

Maati and Amin glanced at each other. It was Maati who spoke. "Why did you get involved in the protest, my brother?"

"You're just going to bring trouble on yourself," Amin added.

Youssef shrugged. "They're my classmates. I had to do something."

"And what good did it do?" Amin asked.

Youssef did not reply. Behind the counter, the waiter turned up the volume on the radio in order to listen to an advertisement for lower prices on refrigerators and new ways to finance them. The TV mounted on the wall was set to a foreign satellite channel, and it broadcast a popular call-in show where a hijabed woman read people's fortunes in cards. Outside, children were playing tag, and in the distance a car screeched to a halt. Youssef did not want to think any longer about what had happened or what could have happened. The part of angry student activist wasn't for him; this much he now knew.

"And you?" Maati asked, looking at Amin. "Where were you, if you weren't in the strike?"

"With Soraya," Amin said with a wide smile. "Ah, that girl. Mmm-mmm." He moved his fingers in a circular motion, as if he were squeezing lemons.

Maati shook his head. "You'd better stop messing with her. I'm telling you, someday her brother will come find you."

"Stop? Are you kidding me?" Amin turned to look at Youssef as if to say, Can you believe this?

"She'll go all the way?" Youssef asked. He had never thought that Amin could get a girl like Soraya—or any girl at all.

"We're supposed to meet tonight." Amin winked.

"For real?" Youssef asked.

"Why would I lie about something like that?"

"Haraam," Maati said, shaking his head.

Amin leaned forward on the table. "What? What's going on?"

"Nothing. I'm just saying. It's not right."

"Since when is it not right? I never heard you complain when my brother took us to see that whore."

"It's not the same."

"Is that what your boss says?"

Maati tilted his head sideways. "But Soraya—"

"What about her?" Youssef asked.

"I just didn't think she was that easy."

"She's not easy, but she's not Rabia Al Adawiyya, either. She likes me. Here," Amin said, pushing the teapot toward Maati. "Go get a refill. Or do you have to ask permission from your boss for that, too?"

An unaccountable feeling of loneliness descended upon Youssef. He was used to such moments, but the events of the morning, his inability to share them with his mother, the pain in his chest—these made him more vulnerable today. The burden of his secret suddenly seemed to him far too heavy to bear. He glanced at Amin. If anyone could understand, it would be Amin, who was always angry with his father for spending his wages on drinking and gambling, and leaving the task of supporting the household to Amin's mother.

"Can you keep a secret?" Youssef asked.

"Of course," Amin said. "What is it?"

"My father's not dead."

Amin's mouth dropped open. The shocked expression on his face frightened Youssef. What imprudence, what foolishness, had overtaken him! What could he tell Amin, in the end? That his mother had had a child out of wedlock? He could not bear the shame of her actions, let alone the shame of describing them in words, out loud. And what would Amin think of him—the bastard child? No, this would not do. He had to play with the truth, create a version with which both he and Amin could live.

"He divorced my mother when I was still a baby, and then disappeared from our lives. She told me he was dead so I wouldn't ask her questions about him or ask to see him. And I believed her."

"How did you find out?"

"I could tell she was hiding something, so I asked her."

Amin looked confused. "But why is it a secret? You're not the only one around here whose parents have divorced."

Youssef had to think quickly. "I thought, well, everyone here thinks my father died, so there's no point in saying he's alive. It's not as if it makes any difference in my life."

"So where is he now?"

"He's here, in Casablanca. He has a business."

"Aw? Really? He's got money?"

Youssef shrugged. "I guess so."

"I can't believe . . ." Amin's voice trailed off. "And he never came to see you? Or paid his due?"

Even though he had divulged only a small part of the story, Youssef felt some relief already. "But please," he said, "don't tell anyone."

"Of course not. You're one of us."

There was comfort in those words, in hearing someone say that he belonged. "Don't tell anyone," Youssef repeated. "Not even Maati."

"Don't worry, I won't," Amin said. He popped another walnut into his mouth and then switched subjects, going back to Soraya and where he might be taking her in order to have some privacy. Youssef listened distractedly. He kept thinking of his foolish attempt to join the protestors. It was so hard to keep the loneliness at bay, but harder still to keep his mother's secret shuttered inside him.

❖ ❖ ❖

The smell of trash from the heap at the corner wafted through the air. Along the narrow street, many doors were ajar, letting out the sounds of TV sets, each one tuned to a different satellite channel, each blaring news in a language of its own. Youssef came to a bend in the road and then made his way up the hill, occasionally ducking under half-empty laundry lines. He stood aside to let pass a group of women bringing a bride from the hammam. The women let out their joy cries and clapped in rhythm to a bridal song. Life goes on, he thought, and no one cares what happens to anyone else. No sooner had he come through the door than his mother asked, "Were you in the strike?"

"No," he said, waving his hand as though the strike were none of his concern. He sat down on the divan and cautiously reclined against the cushions. "I left when it started."

His mother was sitting cross-legged on the floor, piling couscous into a mound on a large plate. "And you didn't see anything?"

"Not much."

She looked at him searchingly, but he held her gaze. Using a small spoon, she drew ribbons of sugar and cinnamon across the couscous mound. "We had several boys turn up at the hospital," she said. "I feel sorry for their mothers."

Youssef tried to think of a suitable response to this but came up with nothing. He did not know what it was like to be a mother, only what it was like to have one. Any sorrow he felt was for the other students, who, like him, had thought they were speaking up against unfair price hikes. His mother did not seem to have expected an answer from him; she was quietly pouring buttermilk into bowls. He got up to wash his hands before the meal.

"The police were there," she said, "asking those kids some questions."

Youssef felt a cold shiver travel down his spine. "Did they arrest anyone?"

"I don't know. One of the boys' fathers showed up and made a scene, threatening to call his brother in the Royal Armed Forces. So they backed down."

"That's good," he said. He spooned some couscous into his bowl of buttermilk.

"But they took down everyone's names and ID card numbers. Now, even though they weren't arrested, they'll be in the system."

Why was she telling him this? Was she warning him? Or was she just filling up the emptiness between them with idle chatter? He tasted the seffa. The buttermilk had coated the warm couscous and cooled it off. He let the combination linger in his mouth, tasting the sugar and cinnamon before swallowing. He was desperate to change the subject. "I saw Zohra, the teacher's daughter, on her way back from the hammam."

"Yes, she's getting married tomorrow, insha'llah."

"To whom?" he asked, though he knew the answer.

"A bus driver," she said, taking another mouthful of couscous. "That's what Maati's mother told me."

"You're not going to the henna ceremony tonight?"

"No."

She was trying not to show that she was upset by the snub, but perversely he persisted. "Why not?"

"They didn't invite me."

The neighbor women could be cruel, he thought, always making sure his mother knew her place inside their circle. He felt ashamed for having pressed her. "Those neighbors are cheap. They're not inviting anyone," he said, giving her this excuse the way he might put balm on a wound. "It's a small wedding, that's all." And as the words parted from his lips, he realized he was helping her save face as much as he was saving his own.

❖ ❖ ❖

The next day, a Saturday, Youssef went to the Oasis to meet Amin. They took a table in the back, directly across from the TV screen. The Widad was playing against the FAR, and although the local boys had started out strong, their striker fouled and two of their defenders did not seem to know how to communicate. By halftime, it was clear that they would lose.

"FAR will win," Amin said.

"Don't they always?" Youssef said dejectedly.

Hatim came in, a newspaper tucked under his arm. "The article on the strike is out," he said, a gummy smile broadening his face.

"So you're a celebrity now," Amin teased, nudging Youssef with his elbow.

"Careful," Youssef said. His ribs were still painful.

Hatim pulled out a chair and sat down. "Look." He laid *At Tariq* on the table, pushing aside the bottles of Coca-Cola, the sunflower seed shells, and Amin's ashtray. On the front page, in bloodred letters, a headline screamed: STATE BRUTALITY CONTINUES. Under it, in smaller type: DEMONSTRATORS BEATEN; FIFTY ARRESTED. Below the titles, two pictures of Youssef with a thin black strip masking his eyes.

"What's this?" Youssef said, sitting up. "You said my face wouldn't be in the photo."

"I took a lot of pictures," Hatim said, "and this is the one *At Tariq* used. Don't worry. Your eyes are completely covered. No one will know it's you. Go on, read the article."

Youssef swallowed. He gripped the paper and started reading the article, Amin looking over his shoulder:

The bus fare increase that was announced on Friday has already borne the fruits any casual analyst could have predicted. Student strikes took place on the campuses of Casablanca Aïn-Chok, Casablanca Ben-Msik, Rabat-Agdal, and Meknès, where hundreds of demonstrators marched to demand a repeal of the fare hike. Dozens of police officers in full riot gear came to quell the popular protests. They showed no mercy as they beat, brutalized, and in some cases tortured the students. One young man, a freshman in English (see photograph), suffered a concussion, two broken ribs, a back injury, and cuts and bruises to the rest of his body. "There was blood everywhere," he told *At Tariq Al Mustaqim* in an exclusive interview, "and we do not feel safe coming to campus anymore." Out-of-city students were chased back to their dorms, and reported that when the police were done searching their rooms, laptops, mobile phones, and other valuables had gone missing. The Party's chairman, Mr. Lahlou, declared, "We vigorously protest the involvement of the police in peaceful campus demonstrations. The Moroccan state continues to repress the will of its people, but we will continue to fight for the restoration of truth and justice in this country. By God. Through God. With God."

The rest of the piece was a description of the individual strikes on different campuses. "There's enough information here," Youssef said, "that they can identify me."

Amin sat back, having finished reading, but remained thoughtfully silent. He lit another cigarette.

"Impossible," Hatim said, shaking his head. "We didn't give your name, and we didn't say where you live or which campus you're from. Don't worry."

"Of course I'm going to worry."

"Don't worry," Hatim said, as though repeating the reassurance could make it come true. "I promise they can't find you, based on what's in here. Just consider what you've achieved for a moment. *Your story* is in the newspaper. Isn't this important?"

Youssef wanted to believe Hatim. After all, he was only one

of hundreds of demonstrators, and surely the police were not planning on tracking down every one of them? And they had already beaten him up. What else did they want?

"People need to know what the government does to the people whenever they speak up," Hatim said.

Amin shrugged. "Everyone knows. They don't need to read about it in the paper."

"What's this?" Hatim asked, his voice rising. "Are you on the state's side now?"

"Of course not," Amin said, raising his right palm up in defense. "Me, I'm just saying."

Hatim's voice suddenly softened. "I understand, my son. But it's important to document what's going on around us. How else will anything change? Have you seen Farid Benaboud's article in *Casablanca Magazine*?"

Youssef and Amin shook their heads.

Hatim clapped his hands. "Iwa, I can tell you: we did a much better job with these student demonstrations. Our newspaper is the mouthpiece of the people. *We* carry their stories and their concerns, not Benaboud. He didn't have a full report in his magazine. He didn't have original pictures. He didn't even have any direct quotes from demonstrators. But the worst of it was that he accused the Party of starting trouble on the Casablanca Aïn-Chok campus and of letting the other student organizations take the fall on the day of the strikes. What lies! Attacking us when all we are doing is trying to help. But what can you expect from that . . . that . . . that . . ." He seemed to be looking for the right word. "That Jew," he finally spat. "He wants to prevent the Party from making progress. But, by God, we will bring progress to this country whether Benaboud likes it or not."

Youssef could not understand why Hatim hated Benaboud so much, and he did not know what to say, not having read the other magazine's story anyhow. Someone called out to the waiter to bring two coffees and a plate of *mille-feuilles*. A jingle announced the end of the commercial break on TV. "The match is starting again," Youssef said. Amin folded the paper and handed it to Hatim, then moved his ashtray back to its spot and flicked the ashes from his cigarette in it. Hatim took the hint and got up. Now they turned their attention back to the match, but it was hard to stay interested, since the outcome was in little doubt. "What do you think of the article?" Youssef asked.

"Hatim goes on about changing things, but who's reading his paper? No one. And no one's reading Benaboud, either. The only articles that matter are those that make it into *Le Matin*. If you're not in *Le Matin*, you don't exist. And in any case, half the country is illiterate. It's what's on TV that counts."

Amin was right—none of the television channels had shown images of the strikes. It did not matter what anyone wrote.

4

THE AGREEMENTS

PROFESSOR HAMMOUCHE WANTED the class to discuss immigration, but no one was in the mood to debate. "In that case," she said, heaving a sigh, "we'll set up two camps, one for and one against." She randomly assigned people to each group and trudged through the hour-long debate, suggesting better adjectives, correcting subjunctive forms, or adjusting pronunciations. Youssef found himself in the group having to argue against emigration, even though he could not come up with any reasons why anyone should stay in the country. A life of dignity was in the realm of the imaginary: he was poor; there were few jobs and even fewer rights. Some people in Hay An Najat had tried hrig, and although hardly any of them had been heard from after leaving the country on a boat, he knew that if the chance arose, he, too, might be tempted to try his luck in Europe.

At the end of the class, Professor Hammouche passed around an assignment on family-law reforms. "You can work in groups of two or three," she said, "so long as you turn in a full list of your arguments." Youssef's eye immediately fell on Alia's back, on the cascades of soft brown hair he had wanted to run his fingers through from the first moment he saw her. He tapped her shoulder.

"We can work together," he said, "if you like."

Her eyes widened with surprise, but to his great relief, she smiled. "When do you want to do it?"

"How about next Friday?"

"*D'accord.* I'll give you my number and my address."

"You want me to come to your house?" Youssef asked, incredulous.

"Of course," she said, laughing. "Where else would we meet?"

What about your parents? he wanted to ask. What would they say if you brought a man to the house? In his neighbor-hood, no father would allow it because, as the hadith went, whenever a man is alone with a woman, Satan joins them as the third. But Alia did not seem to worry about such things. Using a pink feather pen, she wrote her address in large, loopy letters on a scrap of paper she handed to him. He gave her a confident smile, as though being asked to visit girls like Alia was something that happened to him every day.

❖ ❖ ❖

Waiting for Friday turned out to be excruciatingly difficult, so Youssef distracted himself by going to the Oasis. He had just sat down with Amin when Maati slid into the chair across from them. "Remember the idiot who hit me?" he asked. He set his keys and mobile phone on the table.

"The one with the thick eyebrows?" Youssef asked.

Maati nodded. "He's causing some trouble again. Up near Iqamat Al Hanan. Drinking beer at the street corner late at night, playing music on his boom box, being a nuisance. When Hatim described him to me, I knew exactly who he was talking about."

Youssef picked up Maati's new phone from the table. It was sturdy and slim, with a built-in camera and a colorful keypad — a nicer model than either Amin's or Youssef's mobiles, which they had bought secondhand at Derb Ghallef.

"What are you going to do?" Amin asked.

"Teach him a lesson."

"Why?" Youssef asked, setting the phone back on the table.

"What do you mean, why?" Maati said. "Don't you remember what he did to me?" He pointed to his forehead, to the scar that had begun to fade.

"But that was six months ago."

"And I haven't forgotten. Have you?"

Amin asked, "How are you going to find him?"

"I know exactly where he'll be. Hatim pointed the place out to me. Are you coming with me and Abdelmajid?"

Youssef scratched his head. "Now?"

"Yes, now," Maati said, grabbing his keys and phone. "What else are you doing?"

"I don't know," Youssef replied. "You're taking it a bit far."

Maati gave him a wounded look. "A-khouya, are you my friend or his?"

"Calm down," Amin said. "Of course, we're your friends."

Youssef and Amin followed Maati out of the café into the street, where Abdelmajid was waiting for them. They walked up the hill, crossed the tarred road, and went down the other side. At length they came to a cluster of new developments that the government had hastily built in the past few years. Eyebrows was standing by the hanout.

"Remember me?" Maati asked.

Eyebrows smiled. "One loss wasn't enough, you want a rematch?"

Maati punched him. Eyebrows tried to hit back, but Abdelmajid kicked him. They kept at it, both of them, until Youssef pulled at Maati's shirt. "He's had enough, Maati, come on." Amin, who had been keeping a lookout, said it was time to go, the boy had learned his lesson. Magnanimously Maati let Youssef pull him off, though he seemed unable to resist one last threat. "Don't ever come around Hay An Najat again, you hear me?"

❖ ❖ ❖

Friday came, at last. Youssef sat in the back of the bus, clutching the paper Alia had given him. On the loudspeaker an old song by Abdelhahim Hafed played, which put him in a romantic mood. Alia was unlike any other girl at school, so independent, so sophisticated. Thinking of her gave him an erection, which he covered with his notebook. As he was about to get off the bus, he heard the announcer say that "Ahibbik" had been performed by Abdou Cherif. That smooth voice could have fooled anyone, Youssef thought.

Outside, paved streets met at sharp angles, tracing a neighborhood that harbored none of the mystery of his side of town. Tree branches overflowed from behind garden walls—lemon and orange trees, red hibiscus, and purple bougainvillea. The street was quiet, except for the sound of water splashing in the distance and children laughing and calling out to one another to jump into the pool. When he arrived at Alia's house, a teenage maid in a faded blue housedress opened the gate for him.

He followed her up the slate path into a high-ceilinged vestibule. On the left-hand side was a formal living room, with damask-covered divans, a handwoven rug, and heavy velvet curtains. A painting of horsemen in full regalia, their rifles in the air, hung on one wall. On another was a framed family photograph: a patriarch and a matriarch, seated; around them, four handsome couples; and then children of all ages, among whom Alia. He tried not to stare, to act as though he entered homes like this every day.

Once he heard her bounding down the staircase in her heels, he quickly returned to his spot in the vestibule. "Youssef," she called out, and for a brief moment, standing in that room, with his name on her lips, he felt as though he had always known her, had always been a part of her life, had always belonged to her world. "Let's sit outside," she said, leading the way into the garden. "Do you want something to drink?" she asked. Without waiting for him to respond, she turned to call the maid. "Fatiha! Can you get me a Coca?" She turned toward Youssef to see if he wanted something.

"A Coca for me, too, please."

"So," she said, finally sitting down on one of the wrought-iron chairs. "The old Hammouche wants a paper on family-law reforms. Do you think she's trying to get rid of her husband?" She let her chin rest on her palm and smiled. She had not brought any books, papers, or pens, but Youssef took his notes out of his bag. He had read all the suggested articles, including the full text of the law, and he had painstakingly written ten pages of notes. It was all to impress her, of course. She glanced at his work. "You've done it all already! You like school, don't you?"

"You don't?"

"I don't know how long I'll be staying in university."

Before he could ask her what she meant, a middle-aged man in a white shirt and black pants came up the garden path toward them. "*Bonjour*," he said.

"*Bonjour*," Youssef replied, getting up and stretching out his hand.

"Papa, this is Youssef, a *copain de classe*," Alia said by way of introduction.

"Youssef *comment*?"

"El Mekki." Youssef knew well that such a name did not count in this man's eyes: it was not a chorfa's name; it did not have a pedigree. From the look in Mr. Alaoui's eyes, Youssef could see that he had been sized up and found wanting.

Mr. Alaoui said he was on his way downtown and asked whether Alia needed anything. "Nothing, thank you," she said, getting up to kiss him on the cheek. Youssef did not speak until after he heard the roar of her father's car outside.

"Your father doesn't mind you having me around?"

"Why?"

"Why?" he repeated, feeling foolish.

"He knows that nothing could happen between us, if that's what you're asking," she said. The casualness in her voice stung him. And why not? he thought.

"Besides," she said, "I'm already engaged."

"But how old are you?"

"Nineteen. I've been engaged since high school graduation," she said, waving her hand. A diamond solitaire shone on her ring finger. He had never noticed it before, or if he had, he hadn't thought of its significance. "We'll have the wedding in June, when my fiancé finishes school," she said. "Then I'll move to Agadir with him."

Why are you at school? Youssef wanted to ask. Why are you bothering to take a degree? And the most important, the most pressing question of all: Why am I here? The maid brought the drinks to the table, giving Youssef a half smile. Something in her expression made him wonder whether she had recognized him for who he was. He straightened his back and drank carefully, afraid to make one false move and reveal himself. Alia took her glass and chugged. She stretched her legs on the chair next to her. He could see part of her exposed thigh, all the way up to that soft, dark place he desired. He had to fight the urge to touch her.

"It's too hot out here," she said after a while. "Let's go up to my room."

He followed her docilely, dizzy with the possibilities that filled his mind. They sat on her sofa and she turned the TV on to a music channel. They watched pop singers, European, Middle Eastern, and American, taking turns gyrating for the camera. Soon he let his arm rest on her shoulders, then on her knee.

She turned to look at him. "What are you doing?"

"You don't want me to?"

She blinked.

He took this to mean yes, and before he knew it, his lips were on hers. He tasted her, the sweetness of the Coca-Cola still lingering on her tongue. Blood rushed to his head and his groin, leaving him nearly breathless. He put his hand on her waist; she drew him closer. He tried to ignore the pain in his chest, but it was too much.

"What is it?" she asked.

"I fell," he lied, "and my chest hurts."

"Oh," she said. "Lie down, then."

At that moment, everything around him receded into the background. The only sound he could hear was that of his own heart, beating in his ears. Fingers trembling, he unbuttoned her shirt and slipped it off her shoulders. When she reached for his pants, he felt he had been dropped right into one of the movies he had watched over the years, playing the part of the hero, the one who gets the popular girl. He slid into her, the warmth of her enveloping him so completely he had to take deep, long breaths in order to hold on. Over and over, he ran his hands on her hips and thighs, her breasts and her waist, wondering whether the moment was real. As he reached his climax, he felt like a warrior who had, at long last, conquered the country he coveted.

Afterward, as he lay on her bed, dreamily realizing what had happened, she gathered her shirt and skirt and went to her bathroom. He heard her wash herself, the water running for a long time. When she came back into the room, she was dressed again, a cigarette in her hand. She looked at her watch.

Reluctantly, he started to put his clothes back on. "When will I see you again?"

"I don't know," she said. "We'll have to wait and see."

Seeing him out, Alia spent nearly ten minutes at the door, talking about school. It was all a good show for the help, but Youssef knew that the maid would not say anything. Why would she?

He walked slowly up the street toward the bus station, wondering what it would be like to live here, in Anfa, with people like the Alaouis, the Filalis, the El Fassis — and the Amranis. He could be one of them. At home, he would sit and have breakfast with his father, listen to the back-and-forth between his young brothers, smile at their altercations. At school, he would casually mention that he had to tutor his sister in math or chauffeur his little brother to school. He would have Alia for a girlfriend.

He was so lost in his dreams that he missed his stop and had to sneak back on the returning bus. He found Amin at his usual spot in the Oasis, smoking a cigarette. Youssef could not resist bragging about Alia.

"Forget about her," Amin said yet again. "She's not for you."

"She's crazy about me," Youssef said.

"She's not from your world, man," Amin said. "You're wasting your time."

"What do you know about girls, anyway?"

"I know about rich people. My father spent his life working for them."

Youssef fell silent. The mention of anyone's father usually had that effect on him.

❖ ❖ ❖

At school the next day, Youssef stood by the main doors with his friends, but his eyes scoured the crowd for Alia. When she failed to appear at the first class, he began to worry. Was she in trouble? He walked out of class and spent the next two hours waiting outside the main entrance, calling her mobile phone, and watching for her car. It was almost eleven when he saw her pull into the parking lot. He ran to meet her as she climbed out of the car in a green shirt and a worn-out pair of jeans. Her eyes were puffy.

"Alia," Youssef said, reaching for her arm. "I was worried." When his fingers touched her skin, he felt an electric jolt of recognition, and the memory of their afternoon together flooded his mind. He could still feel the weight of her breasts in his hands, the shape of her hip, the way she moved when he thrust himself into her. He wanted her again, and he felt himself harden.

"What's going on?" she said, frowning.

"You weren't in literature class. I thought something was wrong."

She groaned. "Nothing is wrong. I just overslept."

"Ah." He put his arm around her shoulders.

She set herself free from his arm. "What are you doing?" She turned to look around her, worried that someone might have noticed the gesture.

"Nothing, I was just walking you inside."

"I don't need to be walked inside. Listen, just because we had a good time yesterday doesn't mean you're my boyfriend."

"I just . . ." Youssef stumbled.

Alia shook her head in disbelief, or maybe it was irritation; Youssef didn't know. She turned around and went to find her friends. He had made some mistake, but he didn't know what it was or how to fix it. For the rest of the day, he stayed away from her, even though he could not help watching her from the corner of his eye. She certainly didn't seem to act any differently: she stood with her friends, bought coffee from the espresso machine, giggled in class. Meanwhile, he couldn't concentrate on anything.

At night he called her mobile phone, hoping to apologize for whatever it was he had said that had upset her and to finally get an explanation for her strange behavior, but she sighed audibly when she heard his voice. "Don't be such a bore," she said. "We had fun. But now it's time to move on."

He hung up and lay on his bed, listening to pigeons walking on the tin roof of the house. He had been nothing but a distraction for her. If he had been a Filali, though, would she have dismissed him so casually? Always, and especially on days like this, he thought of what could have been. If he had grown up in a normal family, with a father, would he and his mother be struggling so much? This question usually made him feel melancholy, but now that he knew his father had been alive all along, he felt angry and bitter instead. Why should he and his mother be struggling so much? Perhaps that was why his mother had lied to him all these years: she had traded the anger of what should have been and given him instead the sadness of what could have been. She had tried to be patient, to be good, to be wise. But Youssef was not so willing to make the same bargain.

He took out a pen and, in the margin of his notebook, wrote down his real name, the name he had been denied. The 'alif in the middle of his new last name added balance and majesty. It stood like a guard, ready to defend itself; like a witness, ready to speak up. There was a heft to the syllables when they were spoken. They left his lips without pause or hesitation, making him feel that they had always belonged together. On the left-hand page he wrote his name in Latin characters: Youssef Amrani. The first letter of his last name looked like a house in which his first name might finally find a home, and the dot on the last letter had the finality of a judge's hammer.

He stared at the name for a long while, wondering what kind of a person Youssef Amrani was. His existence until that moment had been nothing more than a role—he had played the part of Youssef El Mekki, lived in his house, eaten his food, slept in his bed, and gone out with his friends, but all along he had been Youssef Amrani. *That* was who he really was. If he could be Youssef Amrani, he would not have to play any part at all. He could be, at long last, himself.

PART II

5

Lost and Found

At the precise moment Nabil Amrani picked up the phone to call his wife, his secretary buzzed him. All morning he had been undecided about whether to return Malika's call, because he knew their conversation would inevitably end in a bitter argument. This was how it had been since they had returned home from their trip to Paris two weeks earlier. It was supposed to be their first vacation alone, as a couple, since Amal had left home to study at UCLA, and for days they talked about how a return to the city where they had spent their honeymoon was the best twentieth-anniversary gift they could give themselves. It was all ruined, though, by a single phone call.

They had been walking in the Luxembourg Gardens when Malika pointed out the little children sailing their boats on the pond. "Do you remember," she asked as she linked arms with him, "when Amal insisted on having a red sailboat? The rental man said he only had blue ones left, but she said no, and she waited for an hour until a red one was returned. She was five, I think."

Nabil smiled and pressed his hand upon his wife's. How the years go by in a blink, he thought. "She was a stubborn child. Always sure of what she wanted."

"Let's call her right now," Malika said, stopping.

"But it will be late in Los Angeles," Nabil protested. Looking at his watch, he said, "It's one in the morning over there."

Ah, if only she had listened to him. They would still be blissfully ignorant, and happy. But as usual, Malika had not listened. She dialed the number on her mobile phone. The line rang for a while but Amal did not pick up.

"She's sleeping," Nabil said, leading Malika by the arm. He smiled again when he saw a little boy trying to pick a daisy from one of the flower beds; his mother caught him in time. In the distance, a violinist was playing a sonata by Bach. A cool May breeze blew; Nabil buttoned his jacket. Malika kept dialing the number until finally someone picked up. It was not Amal—it was her roommate Lindsay. Malika did not speak English well enough, so she immediately placed the mobile phone to his ear, forcing him to take over. Thus it fell upon Nabil to ask to speak to his daughter, only to be told that Amal was in San Francisco for the weekend with her boyfriend. "What boyfriend?" he asked, stopping.

The worst of it, of course, was that when they finally managed to reach Amal, she did not show any remorse, nor did she have the wisdom to deny the relationship. Nabil could have said he believed her, even though he didn't, and the matter would have been closed. But his daughter had never been the deceiving type. She readily admitted that she was dating an American, a photography student. Naturally, Nabil had to do what any sane father in his position would have done: He fumed, he yelled, he threatened. Then he hung up.

Malika wanted to get on a flight to Los Angeles immediately, to talk some sense into Amal, but Nabil forbade her categorically. It was up to Amal to apologize. The days wore on, their stay in Paris ended, and still she did not call. When they returned to Casablanca, Nabil told his bank to stop automatic transfers to Amal's account in Los Angeles. His reasoning was simple. Amal claimed that she was old enough to make her own decisions, and if she was old enough for that, then surely she was old enough to pay for her own studies. Malika, of course, was furious. She called him morning and evening to argue that he should "stop the nonsense," that he needed to "get on with the times."

Nabil knew better, though. If he let Amal get away with this, then what next? She might get the idea that she could marry an American. Whom had he been working for all this time? And to whom would he leave his share of the business? Some foreigner who would take her away to his country, away from her family, her home, her homeland? A few lean weeks would convince Amal of her mistake, and she would fly back home and ask for his forgiveness.

But Malika did not—or refused to—understand. She said that their nephews, Tahar's son and Othman's son, were dating American girls while studying in New York, without the slightest risk of being cut off. But it is not the same, Nabil wanted to scream. They are young men, and that is what young men do. Of course, none of this would be an issue if Amal had been a boy. Things would have been so much easier for him if she had. When Malika was pregnant with Amal, he had not been concerned about the baby's sex at all. They had their whole lives ahead of them. Even during Malika's second pregnancy, he had not cared whether the baby was a boy or a girl. But after four miscarriages, after the doctors said that he and Malika needed to stop trying, that her uterus would not carry another baby to term, he had caught himself wishing that Amal had been a boy. By then she was already six years old, still just a baby, but the realization that she would be his only child had changed everything. He had pushed her, yes, but she always did well under pressure. She outscored her cousins on all the standardized tests, loved to read, spoke fluent Spanish, played a mean game of tennis, shared his love of Laabi's poetry and his passion for Andalusian music. She was his prize. He would not lose her to some American.

Nabil's secretary Fadila buzzed him again. A young man downstairs was refusing to leave, she said, even though he had been told that Mr. Amrani was too busy to see him. "What's his name?"

"Youssef El Mekki."

Nabil thought for a moment, running the name through his memory. "I don't know him."

"Sir, he says that you know his mother."

Nabil sighed; he knew where this was going. These days, young people were getting pushier, coming up with all sorts of strategies to find a job, even if they had to shame you into offering them one. On his last trip to Rabat, he had seen the famous sit-ins in front of Parliament. Every day, a couple of hundred young men and women stood under the palm trees across the street, waiting for the representatives to come out so they could hassle them for a solution to their "situation." Nabil's leftist days were not that many years behind him, and he still prided himself on having a liberal fiber, but when he saw those young people in front of Parliament, he could not help but wonder: Did they seriously expect that jobs would be handed to them? And how effective was it, anyhow, pestering MPs like that? How different this generation was from his — thirty years ago, opportunity was to be taken, not asked for like a favor or demanded like a right.

And now, this Youssef fulan. Nabil figured he had to be one of the desperate ones, the kind that staged showy stunts to get attention. Just the other day, Nabil had heard a young man on the radio turn a request for a pop song into a plea for a job, hastily giving out his mobile number before the DJ cut him off. Nabil felt terrible for these young people, but he could not talk to just anyone who stalked him in the lobby. Imagine how many would follow. "Have security escort him out," he ordered.

Now he dialed his home number. Before he could hear one ring at the other end of the line, Malika had picked up. "What are you going to do?" she asked.

This was how their arguments always started. She wanted him to *do* things, she simply could not stand by and let things *be*. She had no patience — and why should she, when she always got what she wanted? Nabil deferred to her on most decisions, but when his honor was at stake, she had no *voix au chapitre*. "Nothing," he said. "Just give her some time to think about what she's done."

"I already spoke to her this morning."

"What?" He felt like smashing the receiver against the desk. A set of silver-framed family photographs stared back at him. Suddenly they seemed to him testaments of a historical era, a bygone time when his wife and daughter still had love and respect for him, rather than the contempt they seemed bent on showing him now. He had fallen into disgrace: a man whose wife disobeyed him and whose daughter made a fool of him. He had to exercise all his self-control not to scream—the two secretaries might hear him. "I *told* you that I would deal with her," he said between clenched teeth.

"She's my daughter."

"So what? This is for her own good."

"Do you want me to tell you what she said or not?"

"What could she say?" Nabil said, raising his voice despite himself. "What could she have to say for herself?"

There was a long silence on the other end of the line. "You two are so alike," Malika said with a sigh.

"What do you mean?"

"You're both so stubborn. She said if you weren't going to send her money, she'd do it on her own."

Nabil chuckled. "This I'd like to see, Malika. How is she going to pay for college?"

"I don't know. But if you don't call her, she might do something drastic."

"Like what?"

"I don't know. Use your imagination. She could marry the boyfriend. Have you thought about that?"

"Of course I've thought about it. Don't worry; it won't come down to that. I have a plan," he said. But he did not, simply because he had not expected Amal to call his bluff. He muttered something about having to get back to work and hung up. He dropped his head in his hands. How dare she? And for whom? For some useless boyfriend? Because that's what it was—he was sure of it. He was sure it was nothing but defiance. If she had really cared for the young man, she would have called and tried to work something out, apologized, asked that they meet him. Or if she had not cared for the young man at all, she would have prevented her father from finding out. Other girls would have been more discreet about their relations, then gotten a doctor to sew them back up. But his daughter had made a declaration. It was his turn to respond, and at least he had responded in the proper way.

He scratched his chin, even though he had shaved in the morning and his skin was smooth. Maybe Malika was right. The only reasonable thing to do was to book a flight to Los Angeles and sort it out himself. He would have to invent some excuse for why he was visiting Amal in the middle of May, out of the blue. But it wouldn't do any good, because she could still go back to seeing the young man after he left. On the other hand, if he brought her back home to Casablanca, something might transpire. People would ask why she had returned home before finishing her degree. And if anyone found out about what she had done, *he* would be the one shamed. He would have cried

had he not thought it unseemly for a man to let himself go. The
loud, hostile buzz of the interoffice phone startled him. "What
now?" he barked.

"I'm really sorry, sir. It's about that young man. He said to
tell you that he is the son of Rachida Ouchak."

Nabil's eyes watered, despite his efforts. It's just the shock,
he told himself, the high emotion of this morning. He blinked
forcefully and cleared his throat. He had not heard that name
in so many years. A lifetime. Rachida Ouchak. She had been
the young nurse, hired to care for Malika during her delicate
pregnancy. Rachida was one of his egregious mistakes, he was
sure; he should not have looked at the help at all. Most of his
escapades (if you could call them that) had been with other
students at the university in the late seventies—girls who, in
the liberal wave that was sweeping the nation, did not care
about what people thought of them, or at least could afford not
to care—but never with someone in Rachida's position, and
certainly not with someone who worked in the house. But she
was different from the other girls his mother hired from the
countryside; she spoke French fluently and had the manners
of one of his station. He remembered her long brown hair, her
green eyes, her freckled skin, how he had enjoyed teasing her
every time he saw her, just to watch her face turn pink. After a
while, she had started to run into him on purpose. It had been
a bit of a victory to get her to give in to him.

"What should I do, sir?"

The worried tone in his secretary's voice unlocked another
memory. His mother had fired Rachida, saying that she had

stolen something, though he knew it was because his mother had found out about the afternoon trysts in the pool house. He stood up, looked around the room, as though the answer could be found hidden somewhere on the leather armchairs, the red Berber rug, or the ugly glass sculpture in the shape of a treble clef that his wife had bought for him.

"Give me a minute," he said.

He turned around and, facing the window, looked out at the street below. He could see the parking lot of his building, filled with cars, and the attendant directing someone out of a spot. This boy downstairs, what did he want? A favor, probably. His mother must have sent him here to ask for one. Nabil's father always warned him that one should not be too kind to the help, the workers, the common people, lest they lose respect for you. When Nabil had started out in business, he had dismissed his father as just another conservative, a member of the old guard, someone who did not understand the new Morocco that was being shaped by the children of independence, people like Nabil. But over the years, bit by bit, he had come to see that there was some wisdom in his father's view of the world.

Still, this was a different case. The least he could do for Rachida was help this son of hers. He buzzed his secretary and told her to send him up and have him wait. Cracking open a side window, he lit a Dunhill, savoring it slowly. He considered calling his old friend Rafael Levy and asking him what he thought of the situation with Amal, but he was too embarrassed to admit what had happened; and in any case, Rafael didn't have any children, so perhaps he wouldn't understand.

He looked at his watch; it was almost lunchtime. Maybe he should go home early to see if he could talk some sense into Malika. He called his secretary. "What's his name again?" he asked.

"Youssef El Mekki, sir."

"Send him in." The argument with Malika had made him break into a sweat, so he loosened his tie and undid the top button of his shirt. The door swung open, and Nabil stood up to face the young man. The blue eyes, almost as bright as his own, caught him by surprise. How could it be?

They shook hands. "How are you?" Nabil asked, more out of habit than out of concern.

"*Je vais très bien, merci.*"

Good elocution, Nabil noticed. "What can I do for you?"

Youssef cleared his throat. "I am not here to ask for a favor." He wore a white button-down shirt and a pair of beige pants that, on someone else, would have given the impression of respectable poverty, but on him somehow came across as casual chic.

"Then what are you here for?"

"I think you know."

Nabil stared. It could not be. Again the tears came, unbidden. He blinked furiously and cursed himself. If he did not watch it, he might soon turn into one of those effeminate men whose wives boss them around. In his shock, he reserved a moment of wonder for the work that memory could do, and for the fact that it could preserve as well as erase details of the past. When he had heard that Rachida Ouchak's son was downstairs, he had simply assumed that she had married and had had children by this El Mekki whose name Youssef bore. He simply did not think about her pregnancy or about the abortion she was supposed to have had.

In truth, even back then, he had not thought about it very much. By the time Rachida had gotten pregnant, he had already tired of her and moved on, and anyway he was preoccupied with his political work, with the petitions he and Rafael were drafting, the cases they wanted to bring to court, the articles on workers' rights that they were trying to publish. He had given Rachida the money for the abortion, and she had disappeared from the house almost overnight. Of course, he had never asked his mother about it — it was not something you talked about — and Malika had no idea; she was on bed rest. In this way, Nabil had willed himself to forget about this pregnancy, relegating it to a deep, dark corner of his mind that would have remained unexplored had this young man not come today to point the light of his existence in its direction.

❖ ❖ ❖

They sat at a corner table at La Mouette, with a view of the Atlantic. La Mouette was one of the few places he went to on his own or with friends, but never with his wife — it was a refuge from the world over which Malika presided. He looked at his menu in silence, reading and rereading the seafood specials without being able to parse the phrases. What was happening in the world? One minute he was bemoaning the fact that he had an only daughter, and the next this young man walked in.

If he were a religious man, he might have called it a miracle, but he liked to think of himself as a rational man: it was a coincidence.

The waiter came, and Nabil ordered the first item on the list. Now, with the menus out of the way, there was nothing to do but look at Youssef. There was so much he wanted to ask: where he had grown up, where he lived now, what he studied, what he liked to do, whether his mother had married—so much to find out about this young man, his son. (The words forced themselves on his brain like intruders breaking open a door: *My son.*) Yet, selfishly, the most pressing question on his mind was the most prosaic. "How did you find me?" he asked. "Did your mother send you?"

"The phone book," Youssef said with a contented smile. "And no, she didn't send me. She doesn't even know about this."

The reassurance filled Nabil with relief. Whatever it was that this boy wanted, it would be more easily handled if Rachida was out of the picture. For a moment he reveled in the thought that they were the only two people who knew about their filial bond. He began to relax.

"How old are you?"

"Nineteen."

Nineteen years. And all this time—

"What about you?" Youssef asked.

How impertinent. Asking an older man like him about his age. He answered nonetheless. "Forty-nine."

"So you were thirty when . . ." Youssef's voice trailed off.

Nabil looked away. He did not know what to say.

The waiter arrived with their drinks. Youssef took the straw out of his glass of Coca-Cola and set it aside, while Nabil rattled the ice cubes in his scotch and soda. "How do I know you're who you say you are?" he asked, still unable to use the words that banged around in his head. *My son. My son.*

Youssef frowned. "Are you calling my mother a whore?"

"No, no, no," Nabil said, raising his hands and leaning forward, as though to signal to Youssef to keep his voice down. "I am just asking."

"When did my mother leave your employ?"

This boy liked to use complicated expressions. Why couldn't he say "her job," like everyone else? Nabil rubbed his chin, making a show of thinking. In truth, he had no idea. He remembered Rachida well enough, but he was fuzzy on the details.

"It was in November," Youssef said.

"Okay," Nabil said, ready to accept this date as easily as any other.

"And I was born June 25."

Six months younger than Amal, Nabil thought. Good Lord.

"What do you do?" he asked. "Do you go to school?"

Youssef nodded. "I'm about to finish my first year in college, going into my second."

"And what are you studying?"

"English."

"Oh," Nabil said. Almost by instinct, he wanted to boast about Amal's studies in America. Then he restrained himself. He was not sure how much he wanted to tell the boy yet.

"I've been top of my class so far," Youssef added in a casual tone, though his eyes fixed Nabil's.

Nabil could not suppress a smile; at least the boy wasn't an imbecile, like so many young people these days. The door of the restaurant swung open and a woman entered, her tight-fitting black dress showcasing generous breasts and round hips. She went to sit at a table with a friend. Nabil turned his attention back to Youssef and found him staring at the woman with the same expression of lust he knew must have been on his own face only seconds before. There was nothing unusual about a young man of Youssef's age looking at a pretty girl, and yet Nabil could not help seeing something of himself in that lust for the fairer sex, which, despite his being a husband and father, had consumed him for many years. It did not have to be the result of heredity; it could just as easily be a coincidence, but now Nabil was starting to believe he could not dismiss every detail as happenstance. In a whisper, he asked, "How is your mother?"

"She's fine," Youssef said. Thinking about it for a moment, he added, "She's not very happy with me."

"And why is that?" Nabil spoke with benevolent concern, when in truth he was terrified of what the existence of Youssef meant, for him as well as for his family. Yet from the moment he had cast his eyes on this younger version of himself, he had been unable to look away.

Youssef shrugged. "She has certain ambitions for me."

"There's nothing wrong with that," Nabil said, somewhat defensively.

"She wants me to be . . . like her dreams of me," Youssef said. There was a calm conviction in his voice, and it made Nabil feel sorry for Youssef's mother, for what she must be going through with her boy.

Their orders arrived. Youssef picked up his fork. On the back of his right wrist was a large scar in the shape of a paper clip—a testament to events Nabil knew nothing about.

"So who do you want to be?" Nabil asked.

"Myself."

Nabil wanted to ask, And who are you? But he knew the answer would take years to unfold. And all this time, he had been living across town, going about his life, working at his business, watching his nephews grow, lamenting the lack of a male heir—unaware that he had had one all along, someone he could have groomed, someone with whom he could have shared what only fathers and sons can share, someone he could have cherished alongside Amal.

Youssef cut a small piece of crayfish and examined it carefully before placing it in his mouth.

"Do you like seafood?"

"I'm not sure," Youssef said, looking up, his eyebrows knitted in a quizzical frown.

Nabil's thoughts wandered helplessly to Amal. She adored seafood. When they went to the south of France on vacation, she ate *moules frites* every night until she got sick. She had spent one evening bent over the toilet bowl in their hotel room, Nabil holding her forehead as she threw up. And the next day she had ordered something else from the seafood menu. How much had he missed about this boy's life? The things that a father knows about his son—the kind of food he likes, the soccer team he cheers for, the girl whose photo he keeps tucked in a book—all this he had missed.

"It's an acquired taste," Nabil conceded, lifting his fork and

spearing a piece of *sole meunière*. "It takes some getting used to."
He had many questions for Youssef, but each one he had posed
so far had been met with a broad reply. He tried something
else. "You said your mother didn't know you were coming to
visit me."

Youssef nodded.

"Are you going to tell her when you get back home?"

"Probably."

"You're not sure?"

"What do you think? Should I tell her I found you?" His
tone was halfway between calm authority and veiled threat.

Nabil was not used to being addressed this way by anyone,
much less by someone of Youssef's age or station, and yet instead of being annoyed, he was completely helpless. It was as
though the boy could see through him, could see how much
he had always wanted to have a son. "I don't think you should
yet," he said, his voice throaty.

"Then I won't."

Nabil took another sip of scotch.

"What about you?" Youssef asked, chin raised. "Will you tell
your wife?"

"No." Nabil was too embarrassed to explain that he could
not face his wife if such a revelation were to come out.

"What about your daughter?"

Nabil sat up. "How do you know I have a daughter?"

"The photo on your desk."

"I see. What about her?"

"Will you tell her?"

Youssef stared so intently that Nabil felt forced to explain, "We're not speaking right now."

The waiter came to clear their plates. Nabil noticed Youssef looking at his watch, but he ordered a cup of espresso anyway. "What does your mother do?" he asked. "Does she work?"

Youssef blinked. For the first time, his self-assured manner seemed to vanish. "Of course she works," he said. "She's a clerk at the hospital." A pause, and then that defiance returned. "What else could she have done after what happened to her?"

Nabil tilted his head, not knowing whether he should agree or disagree with the boy. In reality he did not feel a sense of responsibility over what had happened because he was still engulfed in the feeling of surprise — he had not known. Suddenly he wondered what he would have done had Rachida not disappeared. He would probably have found her a job somewhere after the abortion, given her some money to get started again. He could not have imagined, back then, that he would spend his life yearning for a son. He finished his espresso and paid the bill.

THEY WALKED OUT of the restaurant. Nabil offered Youssef a ride, but he declined, saying he would just walk his lunch off, and he turned around and walked away. Nabil felt a pinch in his heart, a disappointment that their time together had already come to an end. He ran after Youssef. "Wait. Where do you live?" he asked, realizing that he had not thought of asking this most basic question during the meal.

"Hay An Najat."

Good Lord. In a slum. Nabil was revolted at the thought that his offspring, his flesh and blood, an Amrani whose ancestors had fought battles and won wars, conquered land and ruled clans, been part of the power structure of this country for as long as anyone could remember, lived in a place like Hay An Najat. It made his blood rise to his cheeks. "That's very far from here," he said, keeping his voice as neutral as he could manage. "Are you sure you don't need a ride?"

"I'm sure. Thanks." He smiled and, with a little wave of the hand, turned around and walked off.

Nabil stood, keys in hand, watching Youssef walk away, gripped with a sudden fear that this son who had magically appeared in his life would just as magically disappear from it; that he would do what Amal had done and turn his back on his father. It was not coincidence that had brought him. What happened today was a sign. Nabil had been given another chance, and he resolved then not to make the mistake of letting his son slip through his hands the way he had his daughter.

6

THE OTHER SIDE

THE FIRST TIME YOUSSEF walked into the lobby of the AmraCo building and asked to see Nabil Amrani, he was told that Monsieur le Directeur was in Paris. The second time, Monsieur le Directeur was at the bus depot in Aïn Sebaa. The third and fourth times, he was taking part in a business conference downtown. The fifth time, he was in a meeting whose duration could not be predicted; it was not until 6 p.m., when the night watchman arrived, that Youssef had gone home, only to return early the next day. His persistence annoyed Mr. Amrani's assistant: he could hear her screaming as the front-desk clerk held the receiver away from his ear. He was nearly depleted of courage and energy when, on the seventh day, he was told he could have five minutes with Mr. Amrani.

He took the elevator up to the eighth floor. With barely a glance in his direction, Nabil Amrani's assistant pointed to a leather sofa across from her desk. He sat down quietly. On the wall to his right was a poster of a pristine beach, with a handsome European couple frolicking in the surf. A large caption read: MOROCCO: DISCOVER THE MAGIC. Keeping her eyes on her

computer screen, the assistant typed without pause. He waited
for more than half an hour, alternately shifting his gaze from
the sandy beach to the assistant. Suddenly, Nabil Amrani spoke
through the loudspeaker on her desk. "Send him in, Fadila."

Youssef didn't move. A part of him wanted to run in; the
other, to run out.

"Are you deaf?" Fadila asked irritably. "Go in now. He's ready
to see you." She walked to the inner door and opened it wide.

The moment had come. To stand in front of the father he
had never known, hear the timbre of his voice for the first
time, watch his face for signs of resemblance—all this made it
difficult to speak. Nabil had the same complexion, blue eyes,
and wavy hair as Youssef, but he also had the yellow teeth and
purple lips of a heavy smoker, a potbelly that indicated a love
of beer or food, or both, and a disorderly appearance, as if he
had been interrupted in the middle of a private moment. Along
with the inevitable disappointment that results when reality
collides with dreams, Youssef noticed something unexpected:
the complete despair in his father's eyes. It made Youssef want
to reach out and touch him. But as he took a few steps inside
the room, his father's expression of despair gradually changed,
replaced by barely contained impatience. He felt so out of place
in this well-appointed office, and so disconcerted by that look,
that he couldn't help being distant. As he extended his hand,
he gazed at his father coolly.

"How are you?" Nabil said mechanically.

"*Je vais très bien, merci.*"

A fleeting expression of surprise passed on his father's face.

This was exactly what he had feared—his father had already judged him without knowing anything about him.

"What can I do for you?"

"I am not here to ask for a favor." On the desk between them were several silver-framed photographs. One showed a middle-aged woman, presumably Nabil's wife, wearing a burgundy caftan and a wide gold belt, but all the others showed a girl at various ages: as a young child in a blue gingham dress, smiling widely to display missing milk teeth; as a teenager, looking moodily at the camera, over a book she was reading; as a young woman, wearing a black dress and holding her father by the arm at a reception. It surprised Youssef how pleased he was that the girl (his sister? Yes, of course, it had to be his sister) looked more like her mother, while he resembled his father.

"Then what are you here for?" Nabil said, his voice barely above a whisper.

A sudden sense of propriety descended on Youssef. He was too embarrassed to explain who he was: the forgotten bastard child. The words refused to come out. "I think you know," he said at last. That did not seem to help. Nabil raised quizzical eyebrows but did not speak. Youssef whispered, "I am your son."

Nabil's face lit with genuine surprise.

He doesn't know? Youssef thought. That was impossible. How could he *not* know?

"I think we should talk about this outside."

Even in his disappointment, Youssef could not help noticing how similar his father's reaction was to his mother's, and to his own. She had kept the secret of his birth for almost his entire life. He himself had disguised the truth once he had learned it. Now that the time had come for his father to confront it, his first reaction was to get out of the office, to take Youssef away from the eyes of others.

The sight of Nabil before him, so comfortable, so confident, so clearly used to having the world go his way, unlocked something deep in Youssef, and when it opened, it demanded that he do something—anything. So when his father turned around to get his suit jacket, Youssef grabbed a star-shaped silver paperweight from the desk and slipped it into his pocket. He had never stolen anything, and immediately regretted it. He would have to put it back, but his father now looked directly at him, gesturing toward the door. The paperweight felt heavy in Youssef's pocket, weighing him down as he went with his father down the hallway, down the elevator, down the street.

❖ ❖ ❖

Youssef was used to the neighborhood stalls where young men like him gathered to eat fried sardines or roasted chickpeas, and to the cafés where they drank tea and played cards, but he had never been inside a place where the waiters' jackets were not threadbare, where the food trays were not cracked, and where music did not blare out of the loudspeakers. At La Mouette, even the air was different. This could have been my life, he thought. This *should* have been my life. As soon as they were seated, his father leaned in and asked, "How did you find me?"

Youssef peered at him over his menu, unsurprised that this

was the first question on Nabil Amrani's mind. His father knew all about him; his earlier expression of surprise had been nothing more than an act. "The phone book," he said. He went back to reading the seafood specials. Those prices—did people really pay this much for a meal?

The waiter came to take their orders, bending obsequiously as he wrote down what Nabil Amrani wanted. He kept saying "N'am a-sidi" every time he had a chance. When his turn came, Youssef ordered the most expensive item on the menu. Because Nabil asked him how old he was, Youssef felt it appropriate to ask a few questions of his own. "How old are *you*?"

"Forty-nine."

His father had been thirty when he had gotten his mother pregnant. Could he not have acted like the grown man he was and taken responsibility for his actions?

"The picture on your desk—that's your daughter?"

Nabil nodded. "Amal."

"And how old is she?"

"Twenty."

"Twenty?" he repeated, incredulously. His mother had told him that she and his father had planned on getting married; she had never mentioned that he was already married—or that he had a child.

"And a half. She turned twenty in January."

They were only six months apart in age. Her mother had been pregnant with her when his own mother had gotten pregnant. Why had his mother not told him this? Hers was not some youthful, careless love affair; it was an affair *tout court*. Did her lies ever end? What else was she hiding?

His father drummed his fingers on the table. "I thought your mother had an abortion. I didn't know she hadn't."

Youssef felt the hair on the back of his neck stand. Could it really be true? Did his father not know, or had he not bothered finding out? How could he have been so careless? Youssef was trying to think of what to say, but he came up with nothing. When his plate of crayfish arrived, he stared at it, unsure where to start. He managed to slice off an edible piece; he made a mess of it.

"Do you like seafood?" Nabil asked.

Perhaps I cut the crayfish the wrong way, Youssef thought. He felt his cheeks redden with embarrassment. "I'm not sure," he said, frowning.

"Does your mother know you've come to visit me?"

"No."

"Are you going to tell her when you get back home?" Nabil asked.

"I don't know," Youssef said. Was he worried she might go tell his wife? "Should I?"

"I don't think you should," Nabil said, looking down.

"Then I won't," Youssef promised. At least not for now. We haven't put anything yet in the tagine, so it can't burn, he told himself to justify his silence.

Nabil was pensive for a while. When he spoke again, his voice was warmer, tinged with a kindness that had not been there before. He asked Youssef about his life, where he went to school, what he wanted to do after graduation, listening intently to the answers. His father's curiosity pleased Youssef, though he also felt a sudden desire to protect his privacy, to keep Nabil from finding out everything about him at once.

Youssef made a great show of looking at his watch, but Nabil insisted on finishing his cigarette. It was nearly two o'clock when they left the restaurant. Outside, the sun shone in a cloudless sky. Lunchtime traffic had subsided, and the parking lot itself was empty. Nabil offered Youssef a ride in his black BMW, but Youssef turned him down. What was the point? Besides, he did not want his father to know where he lived, in case his father decided to pay his mother a visit unannounced. Youssef needed some time to think about what had just happened. He waved Nabil off and told him he had to go someplace else first.

❖   ◆   ❖

By the time Youssef returned to Hay An Najat, some of the stores were closed and would not reopen until midafternoon, after the 'asr prayer. But Amin was at the street corner with Maati. He was complaining that Soraya, whom he now called his girlfriend, was being harassed.

"Not me," Maati said, his hands raised in defense.

"But it's those Party goons," Amin countered. "They tell her to cover herself or to wear different clothes."

"Can't you tell them to leave her alone?" Youssef offered. "You work with these people."

"It's not me," Maati said. "But I can talk to them."

"Hmm," Amin said, sounding doubtful.

Maati looked at his watch and said it was time for him to go back on duty, to his watch post.

"More like a doghouse," Amin quipped, but only after Maati was safely out of earshot.

They were alone at last. Breathlessly, Youssef recounted the meeting with his father, whispering in such a low voice that Amin had to lean in to be able to hear. The longer Youssef spoke, the more incredulous Amin looked. He asked Youssef to repeat the part about how Nabil stood up from his desk and took him to lunch as soon as he had heard the truth.

"Let me see it," Amin said.

Youssef surrendered the paperweight, and Amin held it up to the light to get a better look. "How much do you think we can get for it?" he asked.

Youssef shrugged.

"Fifty, I think," Amin said.

Youssef sucked his teeth. He did not want to sell the paperweight, and he regretted now having mentioned it to Amin at all, but there was no taking it back.

Amin turned the paperweight around and around in his hand. "What is it for, anyway?"

"For keeping thick files closed. But I think it's mostly just for decoration."

"Get up, my brother. Let's see if Tarek wants it. I'm dying for a cigarette."

"Okay," Youssef said reluctantly.

"Are you going to tell Maati?"

"No."

"Don't worry, I won't tell him."

At Tarek's bric-a-brac store, Amin made up a story about how one of his relatives had given him the paperweight as a gift but he didn't have any use for it. Tarek looked skeptical but said nothing; half his store was filled with stolen merchandise. "Thirty," he said.

Amin shrieked, "What? Who do you think you're talking to? Give it here."

Tarek relinquished the paperweight, watching with mild amusement as Amin began a tirade. The price was an insult. Who did Tarek think he was dealing with? Surely he would not treat someone from the neighborhood the way he would an outsider. And look at this—this was real silver! Any jeweler would want it, either for resale or for melting.

Tarek held up his palm. "Thirty. Take it or leave it."

"We'll take it," Amin said. "You thief. Shame on you for taking advantage of one of your own."

Tarek handed over the coins and went back to fixing a radio.

Amin and Youssef bought themselves a whole pack of cigarettes from the grocer's. It was a luxury; ordinarily they could only afford to buy single cigarettes from the boy at the corner. "So what are you going to do next?" Amin asked. "Are you going back to see him?"

"I don't know yet."

"Maybe you can get some money from him."

"You think?"

"Sure. If he's as rich as you say he is, he'll want to pay up to keep this from his wife, won't he?"

"I'm not going to blackmail him, if that's what you're asking."

"There you go again, using complicated words. Who said anything about blackmail? I'm just saying, you could get something more than a paperweight."

"I don't want anything from him."

An uneasy silence fell between them. The recycling man passed them, pushing his cart and calling out "Bali al-bi'!"

A Peugeot 103 motorcycle came up the street, honking as it neared the intersection.

"You're right," Amin said. "Rich people like Amrani, they'd find a way to cheat you out of the money anyway."

"Exactly," Youssef said, relieved that Amin's ruminations had taken another turn.

❖ ❖ ❖

One of the Mercedes-and-Marlboros was bragging about having received a private tour of the 2M studios. Youssef felt compelled to outdo her, so he told the anecdote—a lie, but he had told it often enough, and with enough detail, that it no longer felt like a lie but like a good story—about how he had once met Tayeb Saddiki right outside the theater where one of his plays was being staged. Youssef hunched his shoulders and cleared his throat to imitate the build of the playwright and his baritone voice; he pretended to be pestered by a girl for an autograph and a role.

"Are you Youssef?"

Youssef turned around to find a young man in a pressed shirt and black pants staring at him.

"Who's asking?"

The young man pointed to a black car parked on the street. "Mr. Amrani."

The window in the back was lowered and Nabil waved and smiled. Youssef felt his knees go weak from the shock.

"Who is that?" one of his classmates asked, suddenly interested.

It was an occasion that might not arise again, so Youssef couldn't resist bragging. For once, for just this once, it would not be a lie. "My father," he said with a half smile.

He waved good-bye to the other students, followed the driver out to the curb, and let him open the door. Youssef slid onto the leather seat next to his father, who put his hand on his shoulder, in a gesture that was halfway between a warm embrace and a friendly pat on the back.

"What are you doing here?"

"I came to see you. You said you studied here."

"I do."

Nabil glanced out the window. "It didn't look like you were doing much studying," he said. "Let's go, Omar." The driver started the engine, easing the car out of the parking space and onto the main street.

"What do you mean?"

"Aren't classes in session right now?"

"Did you come here just to check on my schedule?"

"No, of course not. I was just teasing you. I thought you had a good sense of humor."

"Glad to see I amuse you."

Nabil seemed taken aback. He looked straight ahead of him, at the prayer beads that hung from the rearview mirror. "Would you like to go for a ride?" he asked. "I want to show you something."

"Okay," Youssef said, sitting back. The radio was set to Medi 1, the air-conditioning was on, the leather seats were comfortable, but his palms were clammy and he could not stop the nervous tapping of his foot. He looked out at the university buildings as they passed by. So this was what it was like, being driven home from school instead of having to take two buses and then walk another half a kilometer on the red-dust road that led to Hay An Najat. Nabil was humming along to the overture of "Bent Bladi," and when Abdessadeq Cheqara began singing, he sang along. He seemed to know all the lyrics, including the complicated lines Youssef could never remember.

The driver turned onto a quiet side street and parked in front of an eight-story apartment building with a white facade and windows made of mahogany-colored wood. The doorman got up when the car stopped in front, and did not sit back down until Nabil and Youssef had entered the elevator. They got off on the tenth floor and went into apartment 27. "Come in, come in," Nabil said.

Youssef took a quick glance at the horseshoe-shaped mirror at the entrance. He was in a white T-shirt, while his father wore a polo shirt with an appliquéd lion's head, the insignia of the Royal Golf Dar Es Salam. "What's this?" he asked.

"It's my apartment," his father said with a smile. "And now it's yours."

"What do you mean?"

"You said you lived in . . ."

"And?"

"And . . ." Nabil opened his arms as if they could take in the entire apartment. "Wouldn't you rather live here? Take a look around before you say anything." He took out his pack of cigarettes and went to the dining room balcony to smoke.

Youssef stood in the large, sunny living room, with its painted wood ceiling, marble floors, and overstuffed sofas. A breeze blew through the white gauze curtains on the open window. He walked through the corridor to the first bedroom. There was a comfortable-looking bed, a vanity, a mirrored wardrobe, and an oil painting of a Qasbah at sunset. The second bedroom was almost identical to the first, as though the decorator had suddenly run out of inspiration. The only difference was that the painting was of a felucca on the Bou Regreg at sunset. Youssef went to the balcony that gave out onto the park and took in the view. Back in the living room, he noticed a big stack of DVDs on the entertainment center. *Wall Street, Apocalypse Now*—movies he had seen, but there were also many others he had not seen, like *The Battle of Algiers*. In the kitchen, he found dishes in the cabinets but almost no food in the refrigerator.

Nabil's voice came from behind, startling Youssef. "I don't spend that much time here," he said. "I come occasionally, when I want to get away from the office or when I don't have time to go home." His voice had the hollowness of an empty box. "So what do you think?"

"I can't live here," Youssef said. He assumed that this was what he was supposed to say; he had to show some pride and turn down the offer. But of course he *could* live here; he would love it. He felt suddenly ashamed of his mother's house, and he tried to think of something else, lest his expression betray his temptation.

Nabil pried one key out of his set. "You don't have to make up your mind right now," he said. "Just take a key."

"But why?"

"Because you're my son."

Though Youssef had fantasized about this acknowledgment for a long while, he was unprepared for the way the words were spoken—so calmly, so matter-of-factly—and for what they could mean. His resistance melted when Nabil embraced him. His eyes pricked him, but he held back the tears because he did not want to appear emotional in front of his father, a stranger he had yet to know.

❖ ❖ ❖

On only a few occasions in the past had Youssef been reluctant to go home to the tin-roofed house he shared with his mother. When he was thirteen, he had mashed pods of mkhinza under the teacher's desk so that the class had to be canceled because of the smell. He had been suspended and told to bring his mother in to see the principal. Then there was the time when he had been caught, with Maati and Amin, sneaking into the Star Cinema. The volunteer usher had dragged him by the shirt all the way home to confront his mother.

But neither time compared to how he felt tonight. When he walked through the door, he found her bent over a large piece of red fabric, cutting it in half. "Look at this," she said. "I bought it for fifteen dirhams a meter. Can you believe it?" She smiled; her eyes sparkled with happiness at the bargain she had managed for herself. "Are you hungry? There's still some harsha left."

"No, I'm not." He sat down on the divan next to her, watching as she worked on the fabric laid out on the table.

"I'm going to make a tablecloth out of it. Maybe even napkins."

"Great."

"What's wrong?"

She always knew when he was hiding something, even when she could not get it out of him. Unable to meet her gaze, he looked down at his shoes. "I need to talk to you," he said. The words came out uneasily, strung together by guilt and regret.

When he looked up again, his mother had dropped the fabric and the scissors. She was glaring at him as though he had just confessed that he planned to kill someone. She slapped him. "Please," he said, holding her arm away from him. "Don't hit me."

"Why?" she screamed. "What do you think you're going to get out of him?"

"Didn't you hear what I just said?" Youssef took out the shiny apartment key and showed it to her. "He's already given us an apartment. We can move out. We don't have to live here anymore."

His mother let herself fall on the divan now, her head between her hands, tears running down her face. "My God, my God."

"What's wrong?"

"You don't know who you're dealing with," she said, shaking her head.

"Then why don't you tell me?"

"These people—they'd never do anything for you. They didn't want you when you were a baby. And now you think it's going to change?"

"What people are you talking about? My father—"

At the word, his mother blinked.

"My father gave me the apartment," Youssef said. "Look at the key, right here. It's ours. We can go there tomorrow and I'll show it to you if you don't believe me."

"It's not that I don't believe you, my son," she said defeatedly. "It's that I don't believe them."

"What is that supposed to mean? Are you saying you don't want to move?"

"Move? Of course not. We have a house, it's ours, and I'm not about to give it up."

"You call this a house?"

She took the insult in silence. She put the fabric, thread, and thimble in her basket and went to lie down in the bedroom, facing the wall.

Youssef followed her. "Tell me," he pleaded.

"What is there to say? You obviously want to go."

"Of course I want to go. My father wants to take care of me—of us. Don't we deserve it, after everything we've been through?"

"Life doesn't work that way. It's not about what you deserve or what you don't deserve."

"Then what is it about?" he asked, folding his arms.

She turned around to face him. "It's about doing what you think is right without expecting a reward for it. These people never wanted to do the right thing. Your grandmother threw me out on the street when I told her I was pregnant. She called me a whore. She threatened to call the police if I didn't leave. I swear to God, she would have killed me if she thought she

could get away with it. And where was your father? He was attending some rally or other. Not once in the past twenty years
did he come looking for me or for you. And now that you're
a young man, now that you're a college student with a bright
future ahead of you, all of a sudden he wants to help you. And
you believe him."

"Why shouldn't I? What his mother did wasn't his fault."

"Have you asked yourself what his wife will say when she
finds out about you? What his brothers will do? Do you think
they will welcome a son into their midst? Someone who has a
claim to the inheritance? Wake up, my son. Wake up."

Youssef shook his head. "Let's not get ahead of ourselves. We
have the apartment — that's already something."

She screamed out of frustration. "I don't want his cursed
apartment. You can have it if you want. But I'm not moving."

"Why are you so stubborn?" he asked. She did not answer,
and her silence infuriated him. Before he knew it, the accusa-
tion flew out of his mouth: "Why him? He was already married! And his wife was pregnant!"

In her eyes was a shame he had not seen in their previous arguments. It was this detail she was embarrassed by, nothing else.

"Come with me," he said more softly.

"No. I'm not going anywhere. You're embarrassed to live here
with me. Iwa, now is your chance to find out what life's really
like. Go ahead and go."

Until now, Youssef had not known how to feel about his
father's gift, much less about his intentions, but his mother's
outburst had gotten the better of him. Now he had no choice

but to leave. He walked out, slamming the door behind him. It was all her fault, he thought. All of it. Why didn't she have an abortion? Why did she have to bring him into this world, to live like this? Was this the kind of life she wanted for him? Or for herself? He shoved his right hand into his pocket. His fingers touched the key, turning it around and around.

SON AND LOVER

YOUSSEF STOOD UNDER the shower until the water turned cold. Wrapping himself in the thick blue towels he had found neatly stacked in a cabinet, he sat on the side of the bathtub, staring at the bidet. His mother had told him about these fixtures, but he had never seen one before. When he felt warm enough to cast aside the towels, he dressed in yesterday's clothes; he had stormed out of the house without packing anything. Perhaps he would go back today, when his mother was at work. If he came and went unseen, then his mother could tell whichever story suited her best to justify his absence. He wanted to make his departure from her life as easy as his entrance into it had been difficult.

There was no food in the kitchen, but he found some coffee. He carried a hot mug to the balcony and lit a cigarette. The street below was quiet: no bicycle bells or car horns, no piercing cries of children playing football. A brown falcon with a twig in its beak flew to the roof of a building on the right. For over an hour, Youssef watched the bird's comings and goings, fascinated by its color and shape. Back home, he only saw pigeons and sparrows, which spent as much time on the ground as in the air. The falcon was graceful and precise, swooping down and pulling back up at great speed. When it finally settled down, Youssef went back inside the apartment.

Out of boredom, he went to the larger bedroom, which faced his own across the corridor. The armoire contained a few button-down shirts, trousers, and ties. On the nightstand was a week-old newspaper, folded to the business section, and two books of poetry. Nothing exciting. He opened the drawer; there, nestled between hand towels, was a pack of condoms. The old dog, Youssef thought—he is using this apartment for meeting women. Women like my mother. What am I doing here? What am I doing with this man who is still cheating on his wife after all these years?

He put on his shoes and left the apartment. On the third floor, he nearly ran into a middle-aged woman carrying three baguettes. He flattened himself against the wall to let her pass. "Good morning," she said, walking past him and sizing him up quickly as she did so. When he got to the ground floor, the doorman jumped to his feet to greet him, but, afraid of being asked what he was doing in the building, Youssef ran out without saying a word. Who did he think he was fooling? Anyone here would know that he was an outsider.

He walked down the wide street and turned right, away from the gurgling water fountain at the roundabout. Doormen were sweeping the tiled sidewalks outside their apartment buildings or washing the cars parked in front. There were no hanouts, but there was a giant supermarket with a garish blue and yellow sign. Stores were everywhere, selling everything from toys to furniture, from electronics to lingerie. It surprised him that there were no young men his age standing around at street corners. Where were they all?

Hunger made him stop in front of a fancy patisserie called L'Abeille au Bois Dormant. A little boy dressed in a sailor suit kept tugging at his father's shirtsleeve and pointing at a *mille-feuilles* in the display case. The mother patted his head and said something to him, and he grinned. Youssef stared at the family until his eyes glazed and he saw his own reflection in the windowpane instead. Slowly, the urge to go back home began to dull. He did not miss the smell of garbage or the sight of cows grazing on trash. Nor did he miss collecting water at the fountain. What he did miss: having a father. Nabil had not chosen the name Youssef when he was born, or danced at his circumcision ceremony, or taken him to the hammam when he was old enough, or taught him how to ride a bicycle.

Now there was a chance that the emptiness that had been the hallmark of his life could be filled. The future was uncertain, but at least he could see the glimmer of a future — except that he had run away from this new beginning, and all because of a pack of condoms. So what if his father brought women to the apartment? No one was forcing them to come. Youssef felt around in his pocket for his last remaining twenty-dirham bill, and then he walked inside the patisserie and asked for a croissant.

"YOU SHOULD HAVE CALLED," Nabil said, his voice rising with excitement. "I didn't know you were here, or I would have come earlier."

"I wasn't sure . . ." Youssef said, rising from his seat. He did not know what he had been unsure about. His father did not ask.

"Have you eaten?"

"I had breakfast."

"Oh," Nabil said, consulting his watch. "I don't normally eat here, that's why the maid doesn't cook. I will talk to her about it. Why don't we order you something for lunch?" He took out restaurant menus from a drawer in the kitchen, picking a place called Dina's Diner. He unfolded the menu and held it up between them. The questions pressed themselves against Youssef's lips, begging to come out: Where do you live? Why didn't you have other children besides Amal—and me? What about your wife? Does she know about my mother? What do you want with me? And, most important, this: Do you think, maybe, someday, you might love me?

Instead, the first question that tumbled out of Youssef's mouth was, "Do you like hamburgers?"

"I'm not very hungry," Nabil said. "I just thought you might like this restaurant. It's popular with young people," he said. "But yes, I do like hamburgers." He tapped one line on the menu with his finger. "Try this one," he said. "My daughter always orders it when we go there for lunch."

"Amal?"

Nabil's eyes looked darker, as though a cloud had moved in to block the light. "Yes."

"Does she go to school around here?"

"No. She studies business in the U.S." Here, Nabil seemed unable to suppress a smile. "At UCLA."

All morning, as he had sat alone in the apartment, thinking about his father, Youssef had told himself that he should try not to look back on the past and should focus on the future instead. Yet already he could not help feeling a touch of envy upon hearing about his sister's studies at UCLA. This was what people like the Amranis did: they studied in private schools, went to university in France or Canada or the United States, and then came back to run the country, while the rest of the people got by on fifteen hundred dirhams a month. Youssef had heard a rumor that one of the government ministers smoked Cuban cigars that each cost that much — and he was never seen on TV without one.

"You said you were not speaking to her?" he asked.

"It's a long story," Nabil said. He cleared his throat. Then, in a low voice, he explained, "She disrespected me."

What exactly did this mean? Youssef could guess, though, that it had something to do with a boyfriend. What a foolish girl, he thought. Why had she not been more discreet? Suddenly he felt a surge of affection for her, for the outcast she had turned out to be. "Is she coming home this summer?" he asked.

"No."

The expression on Nabil's face made it clear that Youssef would not have gotten to meet her even if she was. Give it time, Youssef told himself, give it time. If she did not come to Casablanca for this summer vacation, she would be here for the New Year, and he would ask to meet her then.

"Shall we order?" Nabil asked, picking up the phone.

Youssef chose the hamburger his father had suggested.

When the food arrived, they sat across from each other in the dining room. Youssef bit into the hamburger and discovered that it was smothered in blue cheese. The mere sight of the mold disgusted him. Still, he forced himself to eat it.

"How does your mother feel about your moving into the apartment?" Nabil asked.

Youssef told him what had happened.

Nabil let his chin rest on his hand and then drew a long breath. "I have to tell you, I'm not surprised. Your mother does things her own way."

"What do you mean?"

"She's just . . . one of a kind."

In his wallet, Youssef had a silver khamsa his mother had made him carry for years, hoping, in an uncharacteristically superstitious way, that the talisman would protect him from the evil eye. It was the only memento he had of her.

"You need to be patient," Nabil continued. "Your mother will come around eventually."

Youssef could not imagine what it would take for his mother to accept that he wanted to be with his father *and* with her. She was so sure she was right. Time alone would not be enough to make her see she was wrong.

Nabil got up to leave, saying he would be back tomorrow at lunchtime and maybe then they could spend the afternoon together. He handed Youssef some money and told him he would make all the arrangements. Youssef was not sure what arrangements were meant, but he was afraid to ask. He closed the door behind his father, feeling nauseous. By the time he walked back to his bedroom, he had to rush to the bathroom to throw up.

❖   ❖   ❖

In the Introduction to Linguistics class, Dr. Rafik was explaining the difference between phonemes and allophones ("think of allophones as speech sounds that belong, together, to a single phoneme"), but all Youssef could think of was his father. He felt trapped inside the classroom, while life — as unpredictable and frightening as it was — was happening outside, in the city. In his African literature class, he would normally have participated in the discussion of *Season of Migration to the North,* but he couldn't help checking his watch. At last it was time for a break. He stepped out to smoke a cigarette and found Amin waiting for him in the inner courtyard.

"How are you, my friend?" Amin asked, getting up to shake hands. "I stopped by the house twice, but you weren't there."

"I was at my father's apartment."

Amin whistled. "Really? What's it like?"

They sat down together on a bench, under competing banners, one promoting an upcoming conference about the work of Mohamed Choukri (OUR NATIONAL TREASURE), and the other calling for a boycott (*AL KHUBZ AL HAFI* HAS NO PLACE IN OUR MUSLIM SOCIETY). On the ground were strips of eucalyptus bark and shriveled hibiscus flowers. Youssef drew his breath, wondering whether he should describe the more obvious comforts of the place or the details that made it seem like a personal refuge for his father — the antique cigar cabinet, the dog-eared copies of *Souffles,* the collection of commedia dell'arte masks that lined the hallway. "It's very nice," he said, opening his hands. "I don't know."

"Are we going to see it sometime?"

He picked up a strip of bark and twirled it in his hand. "Of course. We can go there now, if you like."

THE MAID, A MIDDLE-AGED woman who quickly averted her eyes whenever Youssef looked at her, was sorting through several bags of groceries when they walked in. "What would you like me to cook, Sidi Youssef?" she asked. Just like that. Not "Youssef," not "son," not "you," but "Sidi Youssef." No one had ever spoken to him this way before; he was not sure what to say. He glanced at Amin and then shrugged and said she could make whatever she preferred.

"You have a maid?" Amin asked, once they were in the living room.

"I didn't know she'd be here." Youssef heard her opening and closing drawers as she prepared the meal. He did not even know her name.

"So he gave this to you?"

"He gave me a key."

"Is your mother going to move in?"

"No."

Amin didn't seem to have heard the answer. He was rummaging through the DVD collection. "There's at least five thousand Dirhams' worth here," he said. "Maybe more."

"Do you want to watch something?" Youssef offered.

They sat on the sofa, feet tucked under them, and watched an action film together. The maid brought a tea tray without Youssef's having asked for it. Amin drank three glasses in a row, making loud sipping noises. "You know," he said, "I could bring Soraya here."

"She's letting you . . . ?"

Amin nodded.

Youssef whistled. "Just be careful," he said, unable to explain why he worried about the girl, about what would happen to her if she were to get pregnant. Surely, Amin was smart enough to use protection.

Sometime after noon, the key turned in the lock, and Nabil came in. Youssef gave his father a quick hug and turned to introduce Amin.

"Amin *comment*?" Nabil asked as they shook hands.

"Chebana."

"Are you in the same class as Youssef?"

"No. I'm majoring in law."

"Oh. What year?"

"*Douzième*," Amin said, when of course he meant *deuxième;* he spoke in a thick accent.

Nabil put his briefcase on the table. Slowly, almost deliberately, he took off his jacket, then began to roll up his sleeves.

Amin got up. "Iwa, I leave you in peace."

"You can't leave now — it's past twelve," Youssef said. "Stay for lunch."

"No, I have to get going. Take care of yourself."

AFTER YOUSSEF WALKED Amin out, he found Nabil on the balcony. He pulled out a cigarette from his pack of Favorites, while his father patted his pocket for his Dunhills.

"Did you have a good morning?" Nabil asked.

Youssef shrugged. They were quiet for a while, watching the city, its rooftops dotted with satellite dishes. The maid had already cleared the tea tray and was setting the lunch table. "Messaouda," Nabil called out. (Ah, so that was her name!) "Bring a bottle of red wine."

"Yes, sir."

Nabil slid open the glass door and entered the dining room from the balcony. "You don't seem to like school very much," he said. "We'll have to think of something for you to do. A degree in English isn't going to lead anywhere."

Youssef wanted to say something in his own defense, but he could not think what.

Nabil quickly added, "It's not your fault. It's the university's. It churns out graduates who have no marketable skills. And with the new reforms, they're even awarding degrees in three years instead of four. But we'll think of something." He uncorked the bottle of wine and poured himself a glass. "And we should also go get you some clothes," he added, glancing at Youssef's shirt.

They sat down across from each other at the dining table. Youssef stared at the tablecloth, black stripes on a white background. "How was *your* morning?" he asked.

"Very busy. But in the next few weeks, I'm going to focus on our hotel business and let my brother handle the transportation company. That should help ease things up a bit for me."

Youssef was suddenly reminded of the strike at school. "Why did your company raise bus fares?"

Nabil looked up in surprise. "Why?" he repeated, as though

he could not believe that someone would ask such a simple question. "For the same reason the other companies did. Because of profit margins," he said, taking a sip of his wine. "The government raised the price of fuel, which decreased our profits. And we wanted to expand our fleet, so we needed higher revenues. All the other companies did it, too."

His matter-of-factness sent a chill down Youssef's spine. At the university, the students had demonstrated, endured the punches and batons, but they had never stood a chance. This was about business, about making as much money as possible; it had nothing to do with what was fair, much less what was right. From outside the front door came the sound of a barking dog. Back home, he thought, no one owned dogs. They roamed about in the street, looking for food. Sometimes people would put out a bit of bread or some milk, and other times little children would chase them down alleys. "Do you have a dog?"

"We used to, but he passed away a few years ago." He seemed on the verge of saying something else, but thought better of it.

His mobile phone rang, and when he saw the incoming number, he looked annoyed; he let it ring until it went to voice mail. Within minutes, though, it rang again. "Hello," Nabil said. "No, I didn't hear it the first time . . . Why? . . . I don't think she can do it, Malika . . . Well, maybe she can, so at least she will have learned something . . . It's too late, anyway . . . Oh, good . . . Around eight . . . No, the blue tie . . . Okay, 'bye."

"Your wife?" Youssef asked.

"Yes."

"Was she wondering why you're not home for lunch?"

"I rarely go home for lunch. I usually have meetings, or sometimes I just come here. It's too long of a drive, especially with all the traffic these days." He put his fork and knife side by side on his plate. "This friend of yours, do you see him a lot?"

"Every day. Well, almost every day. He's on a different campus and we're on different schedules."

"Well, maybe that's not such a bad thing. Better to make a clean break. Start fresh. Don't you think?"

Youssef stared at his father in disbelief. He did not want to make a "clean break" from his friends at all; they were a part of his life, part of who he was. Yet he was tempted by the promise inherent in his father's words: a new beginning with his father, a chance to rewrite his life. Perhaps he could see Amin at school or in a café and avoid bringing him to the apartment.

❖ ❖ ❖

Youssef went to see his mother at work because the chance of her making a scene there was slim. Men and women, some carrying baskets of food or bags of linens, were waiting outside the hospital for visiting hours, but the guard waved him inside the compound. A nurse in a white uniform sat on a bench smoking a cigarette, next to two cats sleeping in a patch of sunlight. Youssef saw his mother as soon as he entered the lobby, and once again he was impressed by her self-control. She stood up calmly, greeting him as though nothing had happened, and took him through the ether-smelling corridors to the back office.

"How are you?" he asked even before she had closed the door.

"Fine, by the grace of God."

"You look a bit tired."

"It's nothing. How about you?"

"I am fine, by the grace of God."

He wanted desperately to say something that would make the choice he had made more bearable, for both of them. She adjusted the shirt of her uniform and ran her fingers over her forehead. "Amin came to ask about you," she said.

"Yes, I know."

"He asked why you haven't called him."

"Wait, when did he come by?"

"Just yesterday."

"What did you say?"

"I said that you must have lost your mobile phone, or that it was stolen."

"Did he believe you?"

"I don't know."

Youssef was too embarrassed to tell her that he hadn't called Amin since his visit to the apartment a week ago. He wanted to bring Soraya, but Youssef didn't have a good excuse for telling him he couldn't.

"In any case, you shouldn't worry about Amin," his mother said.

"Why not?"

"Because the only thing that should be on your mind right now is your studies. Amin is not a good influence. I always see him at the street corner. He's going to flunk his exams."

"He'll pass, insha'llah," Youssef said, rather optimistically, since Amin had never been a good student.

"Have you been preparing for your exams?"

"Yes, I have. We sit for them next week."

"May God grant you success."

"Amen."

"How is your father?" she asked, and then her face flushed pink.

"He's fine," Youssef said, smiling. He was not sure how much more she wanted to hear.

"Have you met his daughter?"

"Not yet," he said. "She's out of the country."

She pursed her lips, but he detected some relief in the loosening of her shoulders, as though she were pleased to hear he had had no contact with Nabil's family. Turning to look at the door, she said she had to go. She stood on her toes and kissed his cheeks.

❖ ❖ ❖

For weeks and weeks, Youssef watched his father. Nabil used his knife to cut his meat, but switched the fork back to his right hand before placing it in his mouth. He held his glass of Bordeaux by the stem and swirled the wine inside before taking a sip. He never took a nap after lunch. The cigarettes he smoked were red Dunhills. Whenever he commented on an article in the newspaper, which was often, he used words like *déontologiquement*. He loved the films of Martin Scorsese, a name he pronounced Scor-say-zee, which was news to Youssef—he had been saying Scor-sayz, the way it was spelled. Nabil spoke to his driver and to the maid in brief, utilitarian sentences, and he never said please or thank you. Sometimes government ministers would call to ask him for advice or favors; he always said yes. He always stared at beautiful women, even college girls he would have been far too old to pursue, but maybe he did *that* for a reason. He loved listening to Umm Kulthum, and when he didn't know he was being watched, he would sing along with her, rolling the words of Ahmed Rami in his mouth as he looked out the window of his car. He couldn't stand men with long hair, or girls who smoked, but he hated the Ikhwan with long beards and the women with headscarves even more. He never went to mosque, but he let Messaouda take a long break on Fridays so she could go to prayers. He gave her so much alms money to distribute among the beggars that Youssef began to wonder if his father had a guilty conscience. Nabil drank far too much—or at least Youssef, who was not used to alcohol, thought it was too much. Nabil never talked about Amal. He never talked about his wife. He never talked about his brothers. He was worried about gaining weight and always asked Messaouda to cook with less fat. When he saw a band of children selling single sticks of chewing gum on the Corniche, he complained that they were ruining the neighborhood. At the store where they had gone to buy some clothes for Youssef, he offered expert advice: If you get this Lacoste shirt, it will go well with your pair of dark-rinse jeans; don't buy this wide-lapelled shirt, it's out of style; and what are you thinking? You can't wear yellow with that complexion. His French was exquisite, of course, but his English was so good that he was able to answer an American reporter's questions. He complained about the African migrants who had started to appear all over town—don't

we have enough problems finding jobs for our own people?
He called them all ʿazziyin, and he said they should all be sent
home. In traffic he yelled at other cars even though he did
not drive. He never went anywhere without his two mobile
phones. Once, as they were smoking cigarettes on the balcony,
he quoted a verse from Laabi (*Ô comme les pays se ressemblent /
Et se ressemblent les exils*) — Youssef did not know it was Laabi;
it was Nabil who had said so. He cracked his knuckles. He
was allergic to avocado. On two separate occasions, he showed
up at the apartment without his wedding ring. He stubbornly
insisted that England had a written constitution, until Youssef
pulled out one of the encyclopedias that lined the bookshelf in
the hallway and showed him he was wrong. He loved to tell
stories, and often he would start to laugh before the punch line
of a joke had been delivered. Youssef watched his father. And
he learned.

Heir to the Past

Ramadan came, with its slow days and busy nights. Because most bars were closed for the entire month, Nabil brought a friend of his to the apartment for drinks, introducing him as Farid Benaboud of *Casablanca Magazine*. Youssef recognized the name; this was the man Hatim complained about incessantly. Nabil presented Youssef as his cousin's nephew, who had come to visit from Moulay Driss Zerhoun, near Meknès. The journalist seemed not to suspect anything—didn't everyone have lost relatives, aunts and uncles and cousins from a small town, people whom one hardly thought of except on those occasions, every few years, when they visited?

Benaboud was doing a piece on the economy. The government had launched yet another campaign to promote Morocco to wintering Europeans looking for sun and sand and the obligatory bit of the exotic, and Benaboud wanted to know whether Nabil Amrani thought this campaign might work. When Nabil spoke, his voice had a different cadence, as though he were reading from a prepared text. "We do have the capacity, of course," he said, "to attract more tourists, from around the world. The Ministry of Tourism was right to call Morocco 'the most beautiful country in the world.' We do have a beautiful country. That is not the issue at all. The issue, frankly, is that the Islamists are giving us an image problem. You have Jean-Pierre or Marie-Louise sitting at home in Paris, they see people like those imbeciles from the Party on the TV news, screaming about how everything in this country should be done 'by God,' or 'with God,' or 'through God,' so of course Jean-Pierre and Marie-Louise get scared, and they decide to go to Marbella instead of Marrakech for their Christmas holidays." He paused, allowing Benaboud enough time to write down what he had said.

"But aren't you giving the Party more credit than they deserve?" Benaboud asked. "There are plenty of tourists around. They don't seem to pay attention to the Party."

"No. These people—they don't want what's best for the country. We do. We're creating jobs; we're offering training; we're providing services. But what are they doing? Preaching!" He had spoken so fast that flakes of peanut appeared around the edges of his mouth.

"They are popular for a reason," Benaboud said. "Maybe they have serious concerns about how the country is being run, just like everyone else."

"The country is doing fine, if they will just let it be."

At this, Benaboud sat back in his chair. "But are the jobs you're creating really helping? If you're creating a hundred jobs at fifteen hundred dirhams a month, how are people supposed to live on that? They're still going to live below the poverty line and they won't be able to send their children to school."

"Rome wasn't built in a day," Nabil said, putting a second peanut into his mouth. "Do you want another beer?"

"Yes, please," Benaboud said.

"I'll get it," Youssef said, jumping to his feet. He was grateful for the break in the conversation. Even though he had not said anything, he felt as if he had been gossiping about someone he loved, and en-namima haram. It made him feel guilty. He took his time fetching a beer from the refrigerator and then returned to the living room.

"The government really needs to help our sector," Nabil was saying. "One problem, for example, is the false guides. It's impossible for a foreign tourist to have a good time if he's going to be hounded by guides at every corner. And sometimes, even in the resorts, the tour guides pester them. So we need a more"—he chewed while trying to come up with the right word—"a more *muscular* approach to this problem. We need state help in ensuring that our tourists can have a good time in peace." As he spoke, his eyes bulged in indignation, as if it had been he who had been bothered by guides on his way around town. He got up to use the bathroom, leaving Youssef alone with Benaboud. On the stereo, Jacques Brel was singing, and the journalist drummed his fingers along with the rhythm of the guitar.

For lack of anything else to do, Youssef cleared his throat. Benaboud turned to look at him. "What do you think? Do you agree with your uncle?" he asked.

"I never noticed the tourist guides."

"I guess there wouldn't be any, in a small village."

In Youssef's village, there were no tourist guides, perhaps, but there were plenty of peddlers and smugglers, hustlers and hawkers, brokers and fixers, vendors and dealers, beggars and drifters—all the people who, in the end, made up the other, the greater half of the country. And when he thought of them, something stirred inside him, compelling him to answer. "What's their crime, anyway?" he asked. He took a sip of his soda, trying to sound as confident as his father had. "The government has outlawed so many things; soon they'll outlaw making a living."

Benaboud looked up. "Good line," he said, carefully writing it down.

"Don't mind my cousin's nephew," Nabil said, returning to his seat. "You know what they say: if you're not an idealist at twenty, you have no heart, and if you're an idealist at thirty, you have no brains."

Youssef was the first to laugh, because he knew it would please his father, and he always delighted in seeing his father's pleasure. The conversation quickly turned to where it was supposed to lead: an article or a column that would shift the discussion of the government's latest marketing campaign to a debate over tax breaks and incentives for hotel owners. They continued talking late into the evening, eventually moving away from business matters to personal. "And how old is your daughter now? Ayah, is it?" Nabil asked.

"Ayah, yes. She's eleven. About to go into the sixth grade."

"At Lycée Lyautey, I take it."

"No, we couldn't get her in. They put us on the waiting list."

"I know the director. I can talk to him."

"Really? We were told that we would not make it in this year because there were too many people ahead of us already."

"Of course you can make it," Nabil said, with the confidence of a man to whom rules did not apply. "I'll talk to him. It's nothing at all. You can't take chances with your daughter's education."

It was already late by the time Farid Benaboud got up to leave, and he seemed to have forgotten Youssef's name when he tried to shake his hand. Nabil reminded him, "Youssef, my cousin's nephew." So went the lie. They became good at it, both of them, Nabil doing the introductions most of the time, but Youssef chipping in when someone asked him who he was, with the exact role that his father had picked for him.

❖ ❖ ❖

Youssef no longer avoided the doorman, the maid, or the cleaning lady. He began to exchange *bonjours* and smiles with his neighbors. He spent his days at the university, though his interest in his studies began to wane, his father's remarks on public schools having turned him into a skeptic.

He was returning home one night when he saw one of his neighbors, the Filali son, from the eighth floor, go into the café across the street. Hoping to strike up a conversation, Youssef followed him.

Filali was seated at a table near the window, talking on his mobile phone. In what seemed like a nervous tic, he was repeatedly tucking a strand of hair behind his ear. Youssef took a seat at the next table; a waiter in a tight black shirt brought him a menu. Twenty different varieties of tea, and none looked good. He ordered an espresso and a slice of chocolate cake. He had been eating so many sweet things lately that his father had warned him against cavities, but he could not resist. He had put on two kilos; his mother said the extra weight suited him.

Filali was talking about getting his laptop fixed, complaining about the service at the computer repair shop. If only he would get off the phone, Youssef could start a conversation. He ate slowly, keeping watch on Filali out of the corner of his eye. When Filali hung up, Youssef turned to him: "Try taking it to the repair shop on Boulevard Zerktouni."

"*Pardon?*" Filali said.

"I overheard you talking about your problems with your laptop. I took mine to the repair shop on Zerktouni, and they were able to fix it in two days."

"Oh, really? Thanks."

"I'm Youssef. I think we live in the same building, across the street."

"Ziyad," Filali said, offering his hand. "Thanks for the tip." He texted something on his mobile phone, his thumb working quickly over the keypad, then turned to look at the door.

"You go to school around here?" Youssef asked.

But Filali did not answer. He smiled at a pretty girl who had just walked in. "Sorry I'm late," she said, and sat down across from him, leaning over to kiss him on the cheeks. Youssef looked around the café, at the patrons absorbed in their own conversations. There was nothing to do but go home.

❖ ❖ ❖

In June he sat for his second-year exams, which he barely passed. Still, he received a gift of five thousand dirhams from his father. Most of the money was spent on designer clothes, patent leather shoes, belts that came in felt bags, a mobile phone everyone coveted. He spent his summer days at the movies: when he saw everything at the Megarama, he went to the Dawliz, and when he had seen the shows there, he went to the Eden Club. He crisscrossed the city looking for films, and the ushers got used to his arrival, with his soda and his bars of chocolate.

And there were the girls—ah, the girls! How much easier it was to get their attention now. The first one he had met at a café, a brunette with heavy eyeliner and too-dark lipstick. He had taken her to a movie, and when he had opened his wallet to pay for the tickets, she had grinned like a child in front of a candy display. Later she nodded quickly when he asked if she wanted to have a drink in his apartment. And it was true what his friends said: if a girl goes home with you, she will sleep with you. He had barely tried to kiss her when she reached for his belt. They ended up on his bed, and when the moment came, he used one of the condoms he had taken from his father's drawer. She would be the first of many, the combination of his looks and his new money working like magic.

And yet at night, when he lay down in the dark, in the terrible silence of that empty apartment, he thought of his mother, alone in her little house in Hay An Najat. She would be watching TV, knitting a sweater or folding laundry or shelling sunflower seeds or mending a sock or peeling the skins off boiled chickpeas— she could never stay still. Although he saw her every week at the hospital, he missed her presence at home, the sound of her breathing across the bedroom at night. He thought of Maati, strutting around the neighborhood, in his un-Islamic tank top, showing off his biceps. He thought of Amin, too. By this time of year, the three of them would have started going to the beach, playing volleyball, and smoking hashish whenever they could get any; they would buy bowlfuls of snails in spicy sauce from a vendor by the side of the road, or go home for plates of fried sardines. He wondered whether they were still doing all these things without him. And then his thoughts would circle back to his father. Youssef was ashamed to see he was more like a mistress than a son: he spent hours waiting for a man to show up and was happy only when they were together. What was becoming of him?

❖   ❖   ❖

August came, and with it an unaccountable sense of gloom. At the Tahiti Beach Club, where he spent idle moments, Youssef could not see the seagulls in the blue sky or hear the breaking of the ocean's waves without reflecting on the rootlessness of his new life. He usually sat alone at one of the tables, but even when he was with a girl, or with one of the young people who haunted the place, he never felt that he was one of the regulars. Most of the time, he was reduced to being an unwilling eavesdropper. He heard three socialites discuss vaginal reconstruction ("A cosmetic surgeon in Rabat is the person you should go to—I'll give you his number"); two recently returned NYU students say how much they had missed home ("For me, Morocco is like the Shire in Tolkien's novels—it's so beautiful and quaint"); a professional cadre complain about his boss ("She has a degree from here and she thinks she knows better than I — I who went to Ponts et Chaussées").

He played H-Kayne on the stereo every morning, as if the music could somehow conjure up his mother, his friends, his old neighborhood. One day his father complained. "Don't you have anything else to listen to?" he asked, loosening his tie. Youssef snapped, "*This* is the music I like," and he raised the volume on "Malna." His father didn't say anything but stared thoughtfully at Youssef, as if trying to think of a way to negotiate a difficult but crucial turn whose time had come.

"How would you like to work at the Grand Hotel?" Nabil asked. He owned a large stake in it, he said, and would be happy to arrange for a job if Youssef thought he might be interested.

"I'm still in college," Youssef said, without much conviction.

"I know. But you would work only part-time. Think of it as a job-training course. And if you like it, you can continue there after you graduate."

Youssef lit a Dunhill. Unlike almost everyone else he knew at university, he had not thought or worried about employment; his mind had been on other things. Even now, with this offer, he could not really think about the job itself. What he really wanted was to meet his father's family — the wife, the daughter, the new puppy that Nabil had mentioned last week. If this job meant a few more hours with his father, it might be worth it. "Do you work at the hotel, too?"

Nabil chuckled. "No, of course not. I work at my office at AmraCo."

Youssef felt stupid for asking such a silly question, and then resentful toward his father for making him feel this way. He stamped out his cigarette. "I really don't know. I'm still in school."

His father looked at him, his face full of an unusual weariness. "It's for your own good," he said at last. "You know as well as I do that your university degree alone won't lead anywhere in this country."

Again there was that needless reminder that, despite all the effort he might put into it, his schooling would amount to nothing. Real jobs were for people who went to higher institutes, or engineering school, or medical school—or anywhere abroad. For Youssef, there was only the prospect of a degree and maybe a third-rate job, if he was lucky.

"Getting into the hotel business will be good for you," Nabil continued. "It will give you some experience."

Youssef had never thought about "getting into the hotel business" or any kind of business at all, but the phrase suggested something grand, something that had potential. And there was, too, in the way his father had suggested he join the family business, a faint promise that Youssef might follow in his footsteps and be acknowledged as his son.

"But," Nabil added, "if you're going to learn the trade, you can't tell the other employees you're my son. Because you can't learn anything if they're afraid of you. If they think you can get them fired, they cannot teach you anything. You need to learn exactly how things are done at that level, if you really want to see the big picture in the hotel business."

His eyes looked sincere; his explanation made sense; his tone was calm. But Youssef was afraid to believe. "You're just afraid they're going to find out you have an illegitimate son."

Nabil blinked, surprised by the bluntness. "Why do you react this way?" he asked. "Can't you see that I have a plan?"

"What plan?"

"By this time next summer," he said, counting on his fingers, "you will have work experience. You will have a degree. You will get your driver's license. You will go to London for an internship. And I will get you a position at AmraCo. Then I will speak to my wife."

Youssef felt helpless before this image his father had drawn. He was his father's creature, waiting to be trained before it could be shown to the world. Yet he was ready to put up with all of it if, in the end, his father kept his word. There was no reason not to believe him.

THE GRAND HOTEL

YOUSSEF RUBBED HIS BARE CHIN, the skin smooth from the close shave earlier in the morning. That had been one of the conditions of employment at the Grand Hotel in Casablanca: no facial hair. Also: no skullcaps, no tribal tattoos, no police record, no qualms about the presence of alcohol. The bellhops wore white jellabas and red fezzes, but all the other employees in the hotel had to wear a suit. Bareheaded women could work anywhere, but those who wore headscarves had to work in the back office. The restaurant was called Al Minzah, but the menus were printed in French. Welcome to Morocco, Youssef thought, no need to experience the real country if a sanitized version can be had instead.

Besides the clothing and grooming rules, the manager, Ahmed Mezzari, explained that certain behaviors were not allowed in front of tourists. "You can say hello and smile," he said. "But never stare, no matter how they behave or how they are dressed. I'm sure your parents taught you the proverb: *Shuf we skut*. So look, and keep quiet. If the customers attempt to speak Darija Arabic, never correct their pronunciation. And never, ever, under any circumstances, try to befriend them. Being friendly does not mean being friends." Now Mr. Mezzari walked Youssef over to introduce him to his supervisor.

Amina Benjelloun sat in her corner office surrounded by piles of dossiers and papers. Framed diplomas and certificates of excellence were displayed on one wall, like a prized stamp collection. In the corner, a blooming white orchid leaned to the right, as if trying to get close to her. She pushed her tortoiseshell glasses up her nose. "Oh, right. Youssef El Mekki," she said. "Please have a seat." She waited for Mr. Mezzari to leave before she herself sat down.

"So you're here for the assistant position?"

"Yes."

"And do you have any experience in events management?"

"No," Youssef said, already feeling uncomfortable.

"A degree from a tourism school?"

"No."

"That's what I thought." She shook her head slowly. It was clear she did not want him for this job, any more than he wanted it for himself, but here they both were, accomplishing the will of Nabil Amrani; after a minute or two, Amina Benjelloun rose to the occasion. She described the Grand Hotel's events program. "We have eight meeting rooms for professional events, such as conferences and seminars, and for personal ones, like weddings or birth celebrations. I want us to move away from the personal events and focus more on professional ones, which last longer and bring us more income." She spoke quickly and precisely, moving her hands to emphasize her points. There were no rings on her fingers, he noticed, and she wore a dark pin-striped suit over an immaculate white shirt. Not a single strand of hair was out of place in her chignon. Youssef pretended to understand everything she said.

She took him on a tour of the premises before giving him his assignments for the day, speaking in a tone of careful indifference. He had to prepare signage for the annual meeting of the Moroccan Association of Dentists, check that Meeting Room C had been restocked with bottled water and soda, set up the projector for the African Photographers' Conference, and call the florist to order white roses for next Saturday. And when all that was done, he had to alphabetize her client files. Could he handle this by lunchtime?

❖ ❖ ❖

During the first few weeks, Youssef worked diligently, taking every opportunity to show Amina Benjelloun that although he had gotten this job through connections, he was smart and capable. How could she resent him for being connected? Wasn't that how most jobs were meted out in this country? Even when she made him redo all the name cards for a meeting between French investors and Moroccan ministers, just because she did not like the typeface, Youssef did not complain. "You're right," he said with feigned enthusiasm. "It looks much better like this."

The Grand Hotel hosted a nearly uninterrupted series of such meetings. Foreigners were buying up utility companies, sugar plants, textile firms, banks and hotels, telecommunications start-ups, and even fertilizer factories. Local supermarkets were becoming outposts of international chains. Three-hundred-year-old riads in the medina were being converted into bed-and-breakfasts. Gated communities were being built for European retirees. At every turn, Youssef watched his compatriots sing the praises of the most beautiful country in the world and then sell it to the highest bidder.

Toward the end of the fall, when the weather had begun to cool, a film crew stayed at the hotel for fourteen days to shoot scenes for a thriller set in New York, Tehran, and Peshawar. Morocco was substituting for Iran; or maybe for Pakistan, Youssef was not sure. He dared not come near the male lead because Ahmed Mezzari had warned that anyone bothering the international actors would be fired. Then Youssef saw Mohamed Majd having coffee with the film's director in the patio café. Majd was probably playing the wise older man; he was too old for a terrorist part. Youssef could not resist asking for an autograph, which Majd granted with an amused smile. Somehow Amina Benjelloun found out and lectured him. "You are an employee here," she told him, "not a client. Behave accordingly."

Once, while he was having tea at the hotel café, he spotted a woman who looked familiar. It took him a few minutes to place her in his memory: she had sat behind him in Spanish class during his first year at university. A history major. What was her name? Loubna fulan, a sweet girl who loved to repeat the sentences the professor wrote on the board. *Me llamo Loubna y tengo diecinueve años.* Youssef was about to get up and surprise her with a hello, when he saw a middle-aged man with white hair that fell weakly on either side of his balding head slide his expansive body onto the divan next to her. The man called

out to the waiter to bring a bottle of wine. He had a Gulf accent—Kuwait or the Emirates. Youssef's national pride was
stung; this was a rare emotion, usually reserved for that day,
every four years, when Morocco's football team was defeated at
the World Cup. What was Loubna doing sleeping with this old
man? It wasn't as if she didn't have admirers at school. These
girls, he thought bitterly, they act all shy with us and then they
do it with rich foreigners. He shot her a reproachful look as
he walked past her table to leave. His disapproval did not last,
though, because there were too many women like Loubna or-
biting around the hotel. Soon they just became part of the de-
cor, like the silver samovar and tea set displayed in a corner of
the foyer or the Berber rugs hanging on the walls of the salon.

❖ ❖ ❖

Payday arrived. Youssef lined up with the other employees at
the cashier's window. He took his time counting the money,
snapping the bills between his thumb and forefinger the way he
had seen it done so often at the market. The sum was much less
than what his father routinely gave him, but there was a special
pleasure in receiving it. For the rest of the day, he attended to
his duties at the office with a smile on his face and a lightness
to his step. After his shift, he went straight to the hospital to see
his mother. He was told she was working upstairs. "Some tea,
my son?" one of the receptionists asked.

"No, thank you, Auntie. Don't trouble yourself."

"No trouble at all." She took him to a back office and went
to get the tea.

Youssef had barely taken a sip when he heard his mother's familiar step, a bit heavier on one foot than the other. He rose in preparation to greet her. When she appeared, he noticed at once that her brow was furrowed. They normally met on Tuesdays, not Fridays, so perhaps she feared he had come here with bad news.

"Mother," he said, bending slightly to hug her.

"What are you doing here?" she asked. "You don't have class?"

"I came to see you. No, I don't have class. Dr. Akharfi is away at a conference."

"Really?"

He reached in his pocket for his wallet. "Yes. I wanted to give you this."

"I don't need money," she said, biting her lip.

"Here," he said quickly. "It's my money. It's not from him." He knew she would not have taken Nabil Amrani's money if he had offered it, but now that he was working and earning his own living, surely she would let him take care of a few things at home. Maybe she could buy a decent stove, or repaint the house, or install proper lighting.

"It's not his money?"

"I have a job now."

Her eyes opened wide. "A job? Where?"

"I work at the Grand Hotel."

She sat down. "But what about your studies?" she asked. "You didn't give up school, did you?"

"No," he said. "It's a part-time job. I'm still going to school."

"But how will you keep up?" She stared at him with such concern and worry that Youssef grew uncomfortable.

"I'll be fine," he said, handing her a wad of bills.

"I can't take this."

"Why not?"

"You need it more than I do. Just focus on your studies. Don't get distracted by your job."

"Will you please stop worrying about me?" he asked, his voice at a higher pitch than he intended. Already he was getting irritated, even though he had spent no more than a few minutes with her. He softened his voice to ask, "Will you please let me help you?"

"But I don't need the money."

"Of course you do. Why don't you take it and buy something nice for yourself?"

"I can't."

"Please," he said. Now, on his third try, she took the money and slipped it in the pocket of her lab coat.

With this out of the way, Youssef had nothing else to say. For so long he had wanted to prove to her that she had been wrong about him, that he could find his way with his father. Now that he had a job, he derived no pleasure from having been right. Instead, he wished he could rekindle their memories of happier times, before his father's existence had opened this abyss between them.

❖   ❖   ❖

One Friday night, Youssef was catching up on episodes of one of his favorite TV shows when he heard the key turn in the lock. He jumped to his feet and went to the front door. It was his father. "What are you doing here?" Youssef asked. His father always came to the apartment at lunchtime, never in the evening.

Nabil sighed. "Don't you want to start with a 'good evening'?"

"Good evening," he said, irked at having been so impolite.

His father took off his jacket and sat down on the sofa. "How are you?"

"I'm fine. What are you doing here?" Youssef asked.

Nabil shrugged. "Benaboud wanted to meet in a quiet place."

"What about?"

"He wants some advice. The police have been bothering him lately."

"You have friends in the police?"

"No one is friends with the police," Nabil said wearily.

"So why does he want to talk to you?"

"We'll find out." He loosened his tie and went to the liquor cabinet.

Nearly an hour went by before Benaboud buzzed the apartment to be let in. Dark circles underscored his deep-set eyes, and he seemed to have lost weight. Nabil poured a drink for Benaboud, who started to talk, without preamble and at a quick pace. "Did you hear about the blind item we ran two weeks ago? Two hundred words. Amusing. Anodyne. Dull, even. I mean, we run these guessing games from time to time, and we've never had any trouble. Anyway, in this case, it was about a government minister who was seen at a casino in the north, gambling five thousand dirhams at a time. And we said it must pay well to work for the state, just ask employees at his ministry. That's it. We didn't say his name or which ministry he oversees, and we didn't pass judgment on his gambling habit. But now he's come forward to say he's been libeled, his reputation has suffered a blow, et cetera. What I don't understand is why they choose to give us trouble over something so silly. Last month we did a story on the ridiculous bonuses and tax breaks government ministers get; six weeks ago we had something on prostitution; before that we had an interview with an imprisoned Salafist. I would never have thought they'd come after us for a blind item like this one. It's so arbitrary." He looked at Nabil expectantly.

"Yes," Nabil said. "I didn't read the item, but I heard about the scandal from my brother. It's terrible."

There was a pause in the conversation. To fill up the silence, Youssef went to the kitchen to look for something to serve with the wine. When he returned with a tray of cheese and crackers, he found Benaboud sitting at the very edge of the sofa, leaning forward. "The dossier is already with the prosecutor," he said, "and one of my contacts is telling me they'll ask for five hundred thousand dirhams in fines. I can't pay, obviously. I'm going to have to shut down the magazine."

"Unbelievable."

"My coeditor suggested we put together an open letter to the government, and that we have our supporters — academics, intellectuals, human rights activists — sign it."

Nabil sat back. He looked like a man who had bitten into a

date only to find it infested with pest. "Farid, you're asking for too much," he said, looking away toward the bay windows.

"I wouldn't ask if I didn't think it was important, Si Nabil. Crucial, even. If we can pull off having important names like yours on our petition, it will send a strong message."

Nabil took out a cigarette, tapped it against his pack, and lit it. "I can help pay for legal costs."

"It's not a question of money. We can always ask for donations, we've done that in the past, and they've served their purpose. What we're trying to do now is different. We're trying to show that the elite of this country, our academics, our activists, our business leaders, support freedom of expression and that they stand with us."

"I can't put my name on this petition, Farid."

Benaboud wiped his palms on his pants. "Journalists in my generation, we all grew up looking up to people like Nabil Amrani, like Rafael Levy, like Fatima Bourqia, like Hamid Senhaji—all those who dared to speak up during the Years of Lead. You wrote so many articles for opposition newspapers when you were my age. And to have your support now would make all the difference."

"Look," Nabil said quickly, "you have to understand. I have thousands of employees who depend on me. I can't afford to do politics."

"But it's not a question of politics," Benaboud said, "it's a question of principles."

"I can't take the risk."

An awkward minute passed. "Well, thank you all the same,"

Benaboud said as he got up. He walked, slouching toward the front door with Nabil by his side.

THE SPRING SEMESTER STARTED, but Youssef did not attend the first week of classes. He was in his final semester now, but, he reasoned, little happened in the first few days, anyway; people were still returning from vacation, still buying the books they needed. When he next went to visit his mother at the hospital, the first question she asked was, "How is school?"

Of course there was only one answer that would keep her happy. "It's great," he said. "I have Dr. Hammouche again this year. You know how much I like her. And Haddad is teaching fiction. Everyone says he's fantastic."

His mother smiled, sitting down across from him.

"You're still working for your . . . at the Grand Hotel?"

"Only a couple of afternoons a week and on Saturdays." It was so easy to lie; all he had to do was divine her thoughts, and speak them.

"And you—how are you?" Youssef asked.

"Fine, by the grace of God."

"Here," he said, handing her some money.

She took the bills and slipped them into the pocket of her lab coat. "I will save this for you."

"No, no, don't save it. Use it for yourself."

"We shall see."

Somewhere in the hospital, someone howled in pain. Youssef stood up, startled. A shuffle of footsteps down the hallway, and the howling stopped. "How is Amin?" he asked, sitting down again.

"I saw him a few days ago. I wonder if that boy does anything but stand at street corners. He asked me again about you, and I told him that you had gone to Marrakech, to stay with one of my cousins."

"But you don't have any cousins."

"How would he know? Did you tell him?" She had taught Youssef never to speak of her being an orphan. She was ashamed of her own birth.

"No, no."

"I've never liked him, you know."

"He's a good man," Youssef said. "What about Maati?"

"I don't know. He's still working for the Party. I never see him. Maybe you could come to the house and visit me. That way you can see Maati for yourself."

"I can't. I have to finish reading a novel for Dr. Hammouche's class."

"You said it was Haddad who was teaching fiction." Youssef's mother's face was impassive, her voice level.

"I did? I meant it the other way around."

"You're lying to me," she said with a sigh. "You're still not in school. You have given up on college."

"Look, I'm sorry. I promise I'll go back next week. I've just been having a good time at work, and really, the beginning of the semester is always so slow." His chair squeaked as he got up. "I should get going." He kissed the back of her hand. "I'll go back next week," he repeated, but from the look in her eyes he knew he had no more convinced her than he had convinced himself.

❖ ❖ ❖

Bottom line, business outcomes, event marketing, event legacy—
Youssef began to imitate the terminology that Benjelloun frequently used. The words filled his mouth, satiating any need he
may have had for an education. One afternoon, when he should
have been preparing for his finals, he sat with his laptop in
the living room, trying to learn how to use a project-planning
software. His father came home, looking weary.

"What's wrong?" Youssef asked.

"It's nothing," Nabil said. He kept jiggling his keys in his
pocket.

"I was about to have a cigarette," Youssef said. "Do you want
one?"

They stepped out onto the dining room balcony. Even after
all this time, Youssef had not tired of the view from his tenth-
floor apartment. Nabil took a long pull from his cigarette. "I'm
traveling to the U.S. in a couple of days."

"*Ah bon*? To see Amal?"

A quick nod.

"You never told me you were getting ready for the trip."

"Something came up. An emergency. It's very last-minute."

His father would not say anything more, Youssef knew. "Is
she coming back?"

"Yes. I think so."

"So will I finally get to meet her?"

"We'll see," he said, head tilted.

Youssef could not decide whether it would be better to press
his father now, or if he should be patient for just a little while
longer, since everything else seemed to unfold exactly as Nabil
had promised it would.

"When do you get back?"

"In three weeks."

"*Bon voyage, alors.*"

Youssef's father gave him a hug. And then he was gone.

PART III

Perhaps home is not a place but simply
an irrevocable condition.

JAMES BALDWIN, *Giovanni's Room*

10

An End, a Beginning

Amal awoke to the sound of a camera clicking; Fernando was sitting at the edge of the bed, taking pictures. He was an early riser, always cheerful in the morning, whereas she loved to sleep late and was irritable for a while after waking. When she spent the night at his apartment, he listened to music on his headphones, edited his work, or lifted weights while he waited for her to get up. When he spent the night at hers, he usually rummaged through her books for something to read. Sometimes, if she stirred and seemed about to wake, he would slide in next to her, the coolness of his skin against hers giving her goose bumps. He would brush her hair away from her face and cajole her into getting up. They would talk endlessly about nothing and everything. Or they would read the *Los Angeles Times*, Fernando commenting sarcastically on the headlines. Or they would make love.

Amal gathered the sheets over her, turning to face the other side. "Don't," she said, her voice still hoarse from sleep. She heard the shutter click again. It felt like a tiny hammer hitting her skull. She groaned. Another click. She drew her breath and, pushing the covers off, sat up, feeling tired. She stretched her arms above her head. Behind her, she heard Fernando taking another picture of her back. "The light was too good to pass up," he said, finally capping the lens and putting the camera on the nightstand. He came around the bed and dropped on his knees before her, slipping his arms around her waist. He was still in his boxers and a T-shirt with the logo of Amnesty International — he had interned for them two years before and had a stack of these shirts at her apartment for the times when he spent the night.

"Yeah?" She ran her hand over his shaved head. She felt the spiky growth of hair under her fingertips. "You want a picture of me looking grumpy?"

He laughed and kissed her. He tasted of coffee, and she thought how a cup might be just the thing, but before she could ask whether there was any left, he bent down to look underneath the bed. He pulled out what looked like a picture, covered with brown paper and tied with blue raffia ribbon. "This is for you," he said.

"What's the occasion?" she asked.

"Graduation, of course."

"It's not for another ten days."

"I know," he said. "I just wanted it to be a surprise, especially since I won't be able to make it to the ceremony."

Amal pulled the ribbon off and tore the paper to find a photograph of her, transformed into a Warholesque silkscreen, her hair shaded green, her eyes a light blue, her lips a dark pink. On the back of the picture was a receipt for a printmaking course she had seen advertised some weeks ago in the Santa

Monica College catalog and had wanted to take. "I love it," she said. "Thank you." He smiled, clearly taking pleasure in her happiness.

She reached for her T-shirt and a pair of shorts from the other side of the bed. "God, I'm so tired." The night before, they had gone dancing at a club in Los Feliz and stayed up until 3 a.m.

"Want some coffee?" he asked.

"Sure." Amal followed him out of the bedroom. She put the silkscreen photograph on the mantelpiece in the living room, pushing aside three votive candles and a pack of cigarettes and sweeping the dust off with her hand. This class would be a nice release after work. She was doing an internship for a market research company, running polls and statistical analyses. She went to the kitchen, where she sat across from Fernando at the Formica-topped table by the window. The book he had been reading lay open, the inside facing down. He poured her a cup of coffee and pushed a plate of already-prepared toast in front of her. Then he let his chin rest on his hand as he watched her.

"How does it feel?"

"How does what feel?" she asked, looking up.

"Graduating, of course."

"Good, I guess," she said. "You've done it, too." Since finishing school at UCLA the year before, Fernando had kept up his part-time job as a photographer and freelance music reviewer for a weekly magazine while trying to decide what he wanted to do next. He still had not figured it out; he had been talking about going to graduate school.

"Yeah," he said, "but . . ." His voiced trailed off.

Outside, cars passed by on Franklin Avenue, their pace slower on this Saturday morning. A woman was pushing a cart full of recycled cans down the sidewalk. At the diner across the street, a line was already forming even though it was only a little after ten in the morning. "Do you want to go look at the apartment?" she asked.

"It's a bit expensive."

"We can manage it," she said. "I'll be working soon."

The doorbell rang.

"I'll get it," Fernando said, getting up.

"If it's the neighbor, tell him we don't know who steals his newspaper, and he should stop bothering us," she said as she carried her plate to the sink.

There were indistinct voices; the rising tone of questions, the falling one of answers. Amal walked out of the kitchen into the corridor. Her father was on her doorstep, his tall frame filling the doorway. She gasped. At once she noticed the extra strands of gray in his hair, the new wrinkles, the leaner waist, made more apparent by the black leather belt. He wore a polo shirt and beige slacks, and he jiggled his keys in his pocket—a sign, she remembered suddenly, that he was angry. A shiver went down her spine. Behind him, nearly hidden from view, stood her mother, looking at once exhausted, happy, and surprised. Malika was in a white skirt suit with a diamond brooch pinned to the lapel. Her hair was styled in a bob, her lips meticulously rouged.

"*Mais qu'est-ce que vous faites içi?*" Amal croaked.

"*Eh bien, on est là pour ton diplôme!*" Nabil replied, and then, in a heavily accented English, he added, "You did not think we would miss it!" After what seemed like an interminable pause, he pulled her to him, hugging her tightly against his chest, nearly taking the breath out of her lungs. On his shirt she smelled cigarettes and Dior Homme, reminding her of all those times she had sat next to him on the terrace of their home in Casablanca, where she would keep him company while he smoked his after-lunch Dunhill. When he let go, she stepped gingerly aside, unsure her legs could carry her. "Come in," she said.

It was her mother's turn to embrace her. Had it been two years already? Amal remembered a time when she, too, would wear Givenchy or carry Hermès because she wanted so much to look like her mother. She already had the same long hair, the same brown eyes, the light complexion, but she had wanted the elegance, too, the soft touch, and, above all, the strength. Where would Amal be if not for her mother? The words from Malika's first letter after the argument were still imprinted in her memory: *You will find this out soon enough on your own, dear child, but a man's honor is easily bruised. What you might not know is that he'll be the last one to admit it to other men. So when I pointed out to your father that your sudden return home in the middle of the term would surely make his brothers ask questions, that they'd want to know what had happened, he suddenly wasn't so eager to go and get you.* Now Amal noticed that Malika looked shorter, or perhaps it was Amal who had grown taller since the last time they had seen each other. "*Qu'est ce que tu as grandi!*" Malika said.

"It's only been a couple of years, Maman."

"Still, you look so different," Malika said, scrutinizing her daughter's face. "And your hair is so much longer." She stroked the ends of it on Amal's shoulders.

A stunned Fernando was still standing by the door. Realizing this, Amal opened her hands wide and, switching back to English, said, "Fernando Stewart, this is my father, Nabil Amrani."

"We have already met," Nabil said, looking up and down at Fernando, who stood barefoot, hand extended. The print on his boxers — red cherries on a blue background — seemed suddenly ridiculous and out of place. Amal wished he had taken the trouble to put his jeans on before opening the door. Nabil continued staring but did not offer his hand.

"Yes," Fernando said, regaining his composure. A familiar twinkle of defiance lit up his eyes. "Yes, we did. Please come in," he said, stepping aside.

"And this is my mother," Amal added.

"How do you do?" Malika said, extending her hand and smiling stiffly.

Everyone walked in. For the first time since she had moved in, Amal felt ashamed of the faded curtains, the coffee table with two pens stuck under one leg to keep it steady, the dusty miniature TV in the corner. There were no crystal vases, no silver-framed portraits, no souvenirs from faraway vacation places, none of the things that might have been there had her father still been a part of her life, had he still made all the decisions — had he still paid for everything. (He had helped her move into her first apartment in Westwood and had decorated it himself. Amal had sold most of those knickknacks at a garage sale to pay her utility bills.) Now, instead, there was a Berber rug she had not been willing to part with, stacks of books by the window, running shoes under the coffee table. There was also that silkscreen on the mantelpiece, which her father examined closely before sitting down.

Amal headed back into the bedroom, Fernando following her. He picked up his jeans from the floor. "What is he doing here?" he whispered.

"I don't know," she replied. "I think they're here for graduation." She slipped on a black top and a pair of jeans, checking her reflection in the closet mirror. The color had gone from her face, and her brown eyes seemed bigger against her pale skin. She stood, staring at herself, then quickly rummaged through her drawer for a pair of earrings to wear. She went back to the living room.

"Mr. and Mrs. Amrani, would you like some coffee?" Fernando asked evenly.

"Yes, thank you," Nabil said, barely glancing at him. "Aji tgelsi," he told Amal, patting the space on the sofa between him and Malika. Ordinarily, Amal's parents spoke French to each other and to her, using Darija Arabic only with the maid or the driver. ("Sounds like Russia in 1916," Fernando had joked when Amal had told him about the language use.) But it was clear now that they did not want to risk being understood, in case Fernando spoke some French. Instead of sitting next to her father, she dropped into the armchair to the right, her arms hugging her knees.

"I know your mother's been paying for your school," Nabil began.

Malika crossed her long legs and shot him an angry look. "It's my money, I can do with it whatever I want."

Amal raised a surprised eyebrow at her mother's tone.

"What I mean is," Nabil said conciliatorily, "I knew Amal wouldn't have lasted two years on her own if you hadn't paid her tuition."

The comment was directed at her mother, but it stung Amal more than she expected. "Is this why you're here? To talk about money?"

Fernando walked in with the coffee tray. Malika did not touch her cup, but Nabil took a sip from his. "Hmm, this is very good," he said in English, sounding surprised. "What kind of coffee is it?"

"Brazilian," Fernando replied, sitting down on the second armchair, across from Amal.

"Oh," Nabil said, staring at Fernando for a while, as though he had just realized some important fact. Again he spoke in Arabic. "And this is your . . . friend," he said. "He is very dark."

Amal knew a remark like this would come sooner or later, and yet she did not know what to say in response.

Malika jumped in. "His mother is from Brazil."

"I thought you said he was American," Nabil said to his wife.

"He is," Amal replied. She glanced at Fernando. His eyes questioned her, wanting to know what was going on, but she could not begin to translate for him. What was there to report?

Nabil stared at his wife for a few seconds and then turned his attention back to Amal. "Anyway, look, I'm not here to talk about money or about *him*. I just meant that I know a lot more than you think. You think you can fool your father, but you can't."

"I've never pretended to fool you," Amal said. "You're the one who stopped talking to me."

"We're not here for this," Malika said impatiently. "Lli 'ta llah 'tah."

"You're right," Nabil said. "The past is dead. We're here about the future."

"My graduation is the future?"

"Of course," Nabil said. And then, almost as an afterthought, he added, "We're very proud."

Sure, Amal thought, there are still appearances to keep up back home, brothers to convince that all was right with the world, cousins to brag to about the graduation of an only daughter, friends to invite to the biggest homecoming party anyone had ever seen, employees to tell about a new executive at AmraCo. In the Amrani family, this was how things worked. What would his friends say if, instead of the official line, they learned that she was getting ready to move in with this young man, who was too dark for her father's taste?

"But there's also something important that we have to discuss," Nabil said.

Malika glanced at Fernando. "We can't talk here."

"Right," Nabil said. "Why don't we meet for dinner tonight? Do you remember where the Beverly Hilton is?"

Amal nodded. She had stayed there with her parents when they had come to help her move into her dorm room her freshman year. "What do you want to talk about?" she asked. Now she, too, glanced at Fernando, who surveyed the scene with a calmness that belied the feelings he must have had at being surrounded by people who talked about him but not to him.

Her father's expression turned grave. "Something very important. Something about our family." He took a card out of his wallet and handed it to her. "This is the hotel's address and phone number, just in case."

He stood up, and everyone else followed.

"Come at eight o'clock," he said, starting to walk out. He turned around suddenly. "Where's your car? I didn't see it in the parking lot."

"I sold it a long time ago."

"I see. Then we'll pick you up."

"There's no need," Amal said. "Fernando can take me."

"Come to dinner alone," Malika said. "This is a family matter."

"We'll send a cab for you," Nabil said.

"Fine," Amal said. She opened the door for them, forgetting that Moroccans do not open doors for departing guests for fear of giving the impression that the guests are unwelcome. Months later, she would remember this moment and wonder whether this was the first sign of her having become a different person, or the last.

Nabil walked down the stairs to the street, but Malika lingered at the doorstep. She put her hand on her daughter's cheek. "You look so grown-up now." Her eyes watered; she blinked a few times. "It seems like only yesterday you were waving a stubby finger at me and telling me you wouldn't come out from under the table."

Amal chuckled. "I'm not a baby, Maman."

They hugged. Nabil honked. He was behind the wheel of a rented black BMW, just like the one he had bought for her when she started school. It had gone to pay her rent for a few months, before she found her first job — teaching aerobics at the student center. That was followed by stints as a copy-shop clerk, a math tutor, a receptionist, and an intern at a medical research company.

Amal walked back inside the apartment, closed the door, and leaned against it.

"What was all that about?" Fernando asked.

Amal told him the little she knew.

"It must be some big news, then," Fernando said, chewing his lip, "for them to have flown six thousand miles just to tell you. I wonder what it could be."

She shrugged. "I've no idea. But it can't be any good."

Fernando put his arm around her shoulders. "Don't worry. It's not like he can take his money away *twice*."

They showered and got dressed and went to see the apartment — all at Amal's insistence. She wanted to go on with her day as if her parents had not shown up, but it was no use. Although the property manager left them alone for fifteen minutes while they walked through the rooms, opened closets and windows, and checked water taps, Amal wandered around the apartment without seeing it.

"So?" Fernando asked, after they stepped out.

"It's nice," she said.

"The south-facing bedroom doesn't get enough light."

"I guess so."

"We wouldn't be using it as a bedroom, anyway. So maybe it doesn't matter."

"I guess you're right."

"You don't like it?"

"It's fine."

"Did you change your mind?"

"Of course not," Amal said, slipping her hand in his and walking back toward the car. "We just have to keep looking. Let's look again tomorrow. Maybe something better will come along."

❖ ❖ ❖

The sight of the red overstuffed chairs and the elaborate flower arrangements in the hotel lobby brought Amal memories of a life of comfort she had nearly forgotten. She went to sit on the circular sofa. A causeuse. From the French *causer*, meaning "to chat." Only, she thought, this was the worst sort of chair for chatting, since you could not really face your interlocutors on it. The elevator doors opened, and her mother came out, wearing a tailored black dress and a row of pearls. Her father followed, looking even more aged than he had earlier that morning. Amal stood up, said hello to her father, and kissed her mother on the cheeks. Her parents did not address or make eye contact with each other. It's already awkward, she thought, and we haven't even sat down for dinner. She followed them into the hotel restaurant. The waiter, a young man in a long-sleeved white shirt that did not quite cover the tattoos on his arms, came by for their orders. Amal asked for a green salad and a glass of water.

"Is that all you're having?" Nabil asked, eyebrows raised.

"I'm not hungry."

"You should get something."

Amal put her hand on her stomach. "I'm not really hungry."

"But a salad?" he persisted. "That's not enough. Get something."

She gave the waiter an apologetic look and quickly scanned the menu. "Could I have the scallops, please?" she asked.

She looked around the dining room. A group of Hispanic businessmen seemed to be concluding a deal; two couples were enjoying the flambéed dessert their waiter had just brought them. Their apparent ease made Amal feel disconnected from the place. Her father had ordered a bottle of champagne, and it arrived now, along with two fluted glasses. "Could I have a glass as well, please?" Amal asked the waiter, already fetching her identification from her purse. Her father looked at her and seemed on the verge of saying something but held it back.

"Let's have a toast," Malika said. "For Amal, congratulations on finishing your degree."

Amal took a sip, delighting in the cool, sparkly taste. "I changed my major from business to math," she said to her father.

"Even though a business degree is more useful," he said, shrugging. Then, casting a glance at his wife, he added, "But of course, we're very proud." He took out a blue velvet case from Azuelos Jewelers. "This is for you," he said.

Amal opened it to find an exquisite ruby-encrusted platinum khamsa. "Thank you. It's beautiful." She did not get up to kiss him—it felt odd to be affectionate with him now. She had dreamed about the moment when they would see each other again, hoping that somehow things between them would return to normal, that they could talk the way they had before, that he would love her again the way he had before. But one look at him that morning, and she had known, in her heart, that things had changed. A part of him—the part that for years had made Amal the very center of his universe—was gone. And if it was gone, then why was he here? Why was she here?

The food arrived. Still, neither of Amal's parents broached the topic. "So what's the big news?" she prodded.

Malika sat back in her chair and turned to look at her husband, an expression of disgust on her face. Nabil cleared his throat. "Amal, my child," he said, his voice unusually low. "Many years ago," he continued, "I made a mistake." He refilled his glass of champagne. He cleared his throat. He pushed his fork to the side of his plate.

An exasperated Malika finally turned to Amal and said, "What your father is trying to say is that he seduced one of the maids and got her pregnant. He has a son. Younger than you."

"What?" Amal dropped her fork and turned to look at her father.

Nabil clicked his tongue. "There's no need for that tone, Malika. I didn't even know about his existence."

"So you say."

"Are you calling me a liar?" His voice rose, making a couple of heads turn at the next table.

"Wait," Amal said. Both her parents turned to look at her, and she had the strange feeling of being the referee at a match between two teenagers. "Just wait a second. You have a son? I have a brother?"

Nabil nodded. "His name is Youssef. His mother used to work for your grandmother Lalla Fatema, up in Fès. And I swear to you I didn't know she had kept the baby. She was working in the house one day, and the next she was gone. Your grandmother said she'd fired her, and I never heard from her again," he said. "I still haven't," he added as an afterthought.

"*Il ne manquerai plus que ça,*" Malika said. "We have enough problems with the son. We don't need the mother."

Amal was still trying to comprehend what was going on. She had a brother! And all these years of thinking she was an only child—at times loving the attention it granted, and at others resenting it deeply, but always wondering: What if? What if I had a brother or a sister? Would my father have kept up all the comparisons with Uncle Othman's children and Uncle Tahar's children? Would he have gotten so upset over Fernando? Maybe he would have turned a blind eye, maybe he would have been too busy with another child to worry so much about controlling everything in her life.

"How old is he?" she asked

"Twenty-one," Nabil said. "Six months younger than you."

"Six months?" Amal repeated. Her father was cheating on her mother while she was pregnant with her.

Malika poured herself another glass of champagne.

"What does he look like?" Amal asked.

"He looks like me," Nabil said, suppressing a smile. "Dark hair. Blue eyes."

He looks more like my father than I do, Amal thought, surprised by her sudden jealousy of someone she had not even met. "What does he do?"

"Right now he's working for me, learning the hotel business. He's finishing an English degree, so with some training, the hotel trade might be a good fit for him. He seems to enjoy it."

Enjoy it? When it came to her career choices, he had never seemed to care whether she enjoyed what she did. "But how did you find him?"

"He found me," Nabil said, looking suddenly delighted. "Can you believe it?"

Amal nodded, looked down at her plate. The sauce around the scallops was already turning thick. She took another sip of champagne. She had eaten very little and now the alcohol was starting to go to her head. "And when did he find you?" she asked.

"Let's see. We're in May. So just about two years ago."

So this was why he had remained silent for so long. He finally had the son he'd always wanted. She was the first draft of his book of love, and when it had not turned out the way he wanted, he had started over with Youssef. She would never compare to this son, who would listen to him, who would live up to his expectations.

"Why are you telling me about this now?" she asked.

Malika turned to her and said, "Amal, I just found out a little while ago myself. Your father was keeping this from me."

Nabil heaved a sigh, turned the stem of his glass around in his fingers. "I was waiting for the right moment. I wanted to get to know him."

"I take it you must have hit it off," Amal said. She put her napkin on the table and looked at her watch.

Malika reached for her daughter's hand across the table. "Wait, don't go."

"I told Fernando to pick me up at ten. I should be going."

"You didn't eat," Nabil said, raising an eyebrow.

"Didn't you hear me the first time, Papa? I said I wasn't hungry." She stood up.

Malika turned to her husband and said between her teeth, "See what you're doing to your family?"

Nabil took out his pack of Dunhills and lit a cigarette. Almost immediately the waiter rushed up to the table. "There's no smoking in the restaurant, sir." Nabil put his cigarette out on his filet mignon. The diners around them had stopped speaking, all of them far too interested in the scene unfolding before them.

"Wait for me," Malika called. In the lobby, she put her arm around her daughter's shoulders and walked with her to the causeuse, where they sat, sharing one seat. "I know it's a shock, my daughter. It was the same for me when I found out. At least you heard about it from us. Me, I found out because of rumors at the beach club. He's making a fool of me."

Amal stared straight ahead. "I hate him."

"No, no," Malika said, shaking her head. "You don't. All of this will pass, I promise."

Amal chuckled. "You promise?"

"We're a family. We have to endure the good and the bad together."

"That's a good one. And where was he the past two years?"

"*I* was there for you."

Amal nodded.

"You have to come home to Casablanca with me."

"He has the son he's always wanted. What does he need me for?"

"*I* need you, child. I can't handle this by myself. I need you there."

"But I can't just drop everything and go."

Malika stared at her daughter. "You love him." It was a statement that needed no confirmation. She seemed disappointed with Amal and shook her head slowly. "You have to break it off with him before it gets serious."

"What?" Amal said. In their correspondence and weekly phone calls, Malika had never said that she disapproved of Fernando. Perhaps she had assumed that it would not last.

"This relationship," Malika said, sighing, "it has no future." She said it in a tone that suggested her daughter should have realized this long ago.

"How would you know?" Amal asked, her voice raised. She got up and walked through the lobby to the street. She craned her neck, trying to spot Fernando's car.

"Look," Malika said, catching up with her. "Don't be so upset. Just think about what I said. Think about your family. Think about your future."

Amal remained quiet. Long minutes passed, and still the words cut through her as though they had just been spoken. What was she supposed to do? Give up Fernando and go back home? Was she to pretend they had never met?

Looking down, Amal noticed a few stubborn blades of grass growing between the curb and the sidewalk. When she was a little girl, her father had pointed out a beautiful daisy that had grown between two slabs of marble stone on the terrace. He had marveled at how even the most fragile of creatures can move a crushing object by the sheer force of its will to live. She had looked up at him, squinting at the light that surrounded him as he spoke, and he had patted her shoulder, the way he usually did when he told her a story. The memory made her miss her father.

Amal spotted Fernando's car up the street and stepped off the curb to wave. He parked his old Honda and climbed out. "Hi there," he said to Malika. "Nice to see you again."

He slipped his arm around Amal's shoulder and kissed her temple.

The display of affection seemed to irritate Malika. "I will call you tomorrow, OK?" She started walking back toward the hotel.

"Good night," Fernando called out to her back. Then, turning to Amal, he asked, "How'd it go?" He released her hair from its bun, and the weight of it on her shoulders made her feel at once like her usual self.

"Let's see," she said. "My father cheated on my mother while she was pregnant with me. And it turns out I have a younger brother."

Fernando's eyes opened wide. "That's bigger news than I thought! I thought they were going to ask you to go back."

"That, too."

"Oh."

They got into the car. On the radio, Dave Gahan was singing an old Depeche Mode song, reminding Amal of the night she and Fernando had met up at a club in Hollywood to go dancing, their first time together. A ball formed in her throat. "Let's go somewhere," she said.

They ended up at a coffee shop not far from the apartment, a little place they often went to late at night. Amal recounted her dinner with her parents. It was the kind of moment, she told him, when one knows that nothing will be the same again, when life suddenly splits into Before and After. She had long suspected that her father had been unfaithful (she had heard her parents fighting when she was twelve or thirteen) but she did not know his infidelities were as old as her—older, in fact.

"What did your mother say?"

"Not much, I don't think. I've never seen her so broken." Amal was angrier on her mother's behalf than on her own. She wished there was something she could do. She wanted, of course, to go back home and be with her mother, but the finality of what her mother was asking was a sacrifice she was not prepared to make. Giving up one love for the sake of another—who made bargains like this? Then it dawned on her that her father was precisely the sort of person to do that. She drew her breath, suddenly remembering a particular moment at dinner. "You should have seen the look on my father's face when he was talking about Youssef—like he was the best thing that ever happened to him." She rubbed her eyes.

"But your brother—can you imagine?" Fernando said. "Growing up all this time, never knowing his father, or his sister. Poor guy."

"I don't want to talk about him," Amal said. She was far too wrapped up in her own pain to think of the pain of others. "What about you? What were you doing while I was with my parents?"

"Working on my résumé," he said. He finished his coffee and, noticing that she had finished her tea, asked, "Ready to go home?"

Amal smiled at the word he used, and put her hand on his arm. Whenever she was with him, she found it hard not to touch him, as though she were making up for hours of not being with him. They arrived at Amal's apartment to find three messages on the answering machine, all from her mother, a woman who clearly took special pleasure in using the redial button. "Amal, *c'est Maman*," she said in a singsong voice. She asked Amal to call back immediately. They were still listening to the third message when the phone rang again. Fernando looked at Amal. "Do you want to pick it up?" he asked. She shook her head and unplugged the cord. Then she put her arms around him and asked if he was feeling sleepy.

THE PHONE RANG almost immediately after Fernando plugged the cord back in on Sunday morning. Amal was brushing her hair when he handed her the receiver. Malika, sounding disturbingly cheerful, asked if Amal would like to go to the county museum. Amal said she had to study for her last final, but her mother sighed and complained about having to come halfway around the world just to be turned down by one's only daughter. Amal felt a mixture of guilt and irritation, and guilt won out. (Is it not always so with mothers?)

She turned off the phone. "I have to go meet my mother."

"All right," Fernando said. "I guess I'll go look at the apartments alone, then."

"I'm sorry," Amal said. "Maybe we can go when I get back? Or do you want to come with me to the museum?"

"I don't think so, sweets. Your mother can barely stand to look at me."

"I'm sorry."

Fernando shook his head. "Not your fault. I'll call or e-mail if the apartments are any good."

When Amal arrived at LACMA, the esplanade was packed with tourists. Her mother waved at her from outside the box office. "How did you get here?" her mother asked as she kissed her cheeks.

"By bus."

"I thought Fernando would drop you off."

"I didn't ask him."

"You should have told me. I could have picked you up or sent a cab for you."

"Where's Papa?" Amal asked, wanting to change the subject.

"He didn't come."

"Why not?"

"I just didn't feel like spending such a beautiful morning with him. It's just us two," Malika said. Amal smiled; she felt a touch of their lost complicity returning. Her mother linked arms with her, and they walked through the double doors of the museum. As they strolled through the galleries, stopping occa-

sionally in front of one or another painting, Malika shared all
the gossip from back home: her driver's son had managed to get
into engineering school; the maid had decided to wear a hijab
and refused to serve alcohol when there were guests; there was a
journalist who kept hounding Uncle Othman for an interview;
Aunt Khadija had taken a secret trip to Paris to get a face-lift;
Cousin Jaafar had been caught with drugs at the airport and
his father had to call in favors to prevent his arrest.

They stopped in front of a small Delacroix, an 1833 water-
color of Moroccan street musicians. *Strolling Players* was the
kind of Orientalist painting that must have been in high demand in the salons of Europe at the time. It looked nothing
like Amal's memories of home, and yet it made her miss it. Her
mother squeezed her hand. "You have to come back with us."

Amal did not reply, as if silence could make the demand go
away.

Malika drew her breath. "I know you love each other," she
said. "But someday you will learn that love is not enough. People in America are not like us. They are different. They live
together without being married, they don't think about what
families they're getting into, they break off relationships as easily as they start them. That's not how we are."

Amal pulled her hand away and turned to look at her mother.
"Are you saying that Fernando's going to break up with me?"

"Amal, you don't understand. A relationship is difficult
enough without all the other complications you're adding to
it. I only want what is best for you. And this young man may
be nice, and you've had fun with him, but now you've finished

your degree and it's time to think about the future, to think about what you'll do next. You belong in your own country, with your people, with us, your family."

"I can't go back for good. Not after what Papa did."

"Your father loves you. He is just too proud to admit he made a mistake. But look what happened to him. He's learned his lesson, I think, and I know he wants you back, too. Otherwise he wouldn't be here."

"I can't go back, Maman."

"Of course you can. You can come back with us after graduation. We'll spend a couple of weeks in Spain, and when fall comes, you can start work. You don't have to work with your father; you can find work anywhere you like."

Amal shook her head.

"If you won't do it for yourself, do it for me. Do you know what I've gone through? Everyone is talking about how crazy your father has been acting, and your uncles are upset about the appearance of this boy—this Youssef. They're worried what your father will do with his share of the company, whether he'll give him something. They told me they won't let it happen. I need you back home. If you come home with me, I'm sure your father will come to his senses, and everything can go back to the way it was before. Please, Amal."

Amal looked at her mother's pleading face, at the despair so clearly painted upon it. Amal had made a tacit promise of love, and she had been happy, but now she was being asked to be loyal to another bond, one that did not ask just for love; it demanded duty as well, and it rewarded with approval, with ridat el-walidin. A part of her crumbled right then, and as they walked through the galleries, she became aware of an emptiness inside her that widened slowly and steadily.

They went to lunch at a restaurant nearby, and as they waited for their orders, Nabil appeared and pulled up a chair. "How was the museum?" he asked.

Amal looked at her mother, who hid behind her menu. How carefully they had planned the meeting; Amal had not suspected anything.

"Fine," Amal replied.

"It was *wonderful,*" Malika said. "We had a good time." She started to talk about what she wanted to do during her stay in Los Angeles, and complained that there was not enough time to go to San Francisco for a few days. "We were supposed to get here on Thursday night, but we missed our connecting flight from New York," Malika said. "We had to wait for an early morning flight on Friday."

"It took us three hours to go through immigration," Nabil explained. "It was bad enough that they fingerprinted me, like a common criminal, but then they took me to another room for a full search, and then after that, we still had to wait an hour and answer more questions."

"Every time we come to this country," Malika said, "we see it getting worse."

"Your mother told me you wanted to stay here," Nabil said. "Why? They hate us."

"It's not like that," Amal said.

"How quickly you forget, my daughter. Do you remember your first year here, when you called me, crying, because someone taped a photo of Osama bin Laden on your dorm room door?"

"It was Halloween. Some idiot thought he was making a joke," she said.

"And?"

"And nothing," she said. "You're right. I was very upset."

When she went home that night, she huddled under the covers in bed and tried to quiet the pull of allegiances inside her. She closed her eyes, hoping for sleep, for escape.

IN THE WEEK leading up to graduation, Malika called every day. She asked Amal to go out, and each time they met, she chipped away at Amal's resolve. Amal was so busy with her that she barely saw Fernando, instead staying out late with her mother, driving her around town, from Olvera Street to the Santa Monica Pier, from the Getty Center to Griffith Park, though what her mother really loved was Rodeo Drive. They often brought back shopping bags full of clothes to the apartment, and Malika would try on the new outfits, admiring herself in the mirror, while Amal lay across the bed watching her and offering comments.

Her father often joined them. He sat quietly in the backseat, and once, when Amal took a shortcut and Malika protested that they would get lost, he simply said, "Let her be. She knows what she's doing." They ordered pizza one night and stayed in, and when it arrived, Malika complained about the grease while Nabil got up and looked through the kitchen for napkins. He sat on the old sofa, balancing a paper plate with a pizza slice on his lap. How easily they fell into their old patterns, Amal noticed, Malika chatting away while smoking a cigarette, Nabil periodically contradicting her, and Amal sitting between them, alternately agreeing with one or the other, trying to keep them both happy.

WHEN GRADUATION DAY ARRIVED, Amal was too worried about lunch — to which she had insisted that Fernando come — to follow the commencement speakers, with their talk of new beginnings and their words of admiration for the grandness of youth. She was the first to get into the car when they headed for the restaurant. By the time Fernando walked in, five minutes late as was his habit, Amal and her parents were already seated at their table. He was wearing a green shirt that brought out the color of his eyes, and a dark-rinse pair of jeans that were a nice change from the frayed ones he usually wore. Malika stood up to welcome him and smiled at him with the practiced ease of a woman who could turn the charm on or off at will. "How are you?" she said in her accented English as she signaled to him to take a seat next to Amal. "Did you have trouble finding the restaurant?"

"I found it okay, it's just that I couldn't find parking," he said, also smiling. He glanced at Amal with a look that seemed to say, Can you believe she's actually making conversation with me?

"Oh," Malika said, turning to look at the valet station outside the window.

Fernando leaned in to kiss Amal, but she offered him her cheek. He let his arm rest on the back of her chair. In halting French, he asked Nabil whether he liked the city so far. "It's not the first time I've been here," Nabil responded in English. "I have visited three times before."

"Of course," Fernando said.

The waiter came by and Fernando scanned his menu quickly. When his turn came, he asked, "I was wondering, what exactly is the *consom*?"

"*Consommé,*" Nabil corrected him. "It's a light soup. Like a broth," he explained with a half smile. "Do you serve it hot or cold?" he asked the waiter.

"We serve it cold, sir."

"Oh, good," Nabil said.

"I'll have that, please," Fernando said, handing his menu to the waiter. "And the grilled fish as well, please."

They toasted Amal with white wine. Then Malika asked Fernando what he did for a living. Amal looked at her, surprised. Why was she asking a question whose answer she already knew?

"I'm a photographer."

"A photographer? How interesting. And where do you work?"

"I freelance for a weekly paper in Santa Monica."

"Freelance," Nabil repeated, as if he were learning a new word.

Then he asked about Fernando's family, whether they lived close by, and Fernando had to explain that his parents were divorced when he was very young and that his father lived in the Bay Area, while his mother lived in New York with his younger sister. Malika asked him how his parents had met, and he said they had both been students at Berkeley in the early 1980s, married in graduate school, and divorced by the time they started working. Her parents were carefully picking Fernando apart, Amal knew, demonstrating to each other and to her that he did not fit in their world.

"THAT WASN'T SO BAD," Fernando said as he parked his car outside Amal's apartment after lunch.

Amal gave him a dark look. "You think?"

"What's wrong?"

"Nothing."

He sighed. "Why do you say 'nothing' when you don't mean it?"

Amal opened the passenger-side door. "I should get going."

"Wait," he said, reaching over her and pulling the door shut. "Tell me what's wrong."

She stared at her shoes for a while, then in a soft voice said, "They want me to go back."

"I know. How long will you be gone?"

"I don't know."

"What do you mean, you don't know? Are you telling me you're leaving for good?" His voice rose an octave.

"It's all a mess," Amal said, shaking her head, her own voice rising. "A huge mess, with my brother and everything. I'm going to meet him when I get there, and then, I don't know, my mother wants my father to rework his will. It's a mess."

"So when are you coming back?"

"In the fall, maybe."

"Maybe?"

"Please," Amal said angrily. "Don't be like this. Don't ask me to give you answers. Right now, I have no answers." She opened her door again. "Look, maybe you can visit me there."

"Yeah, like you say, maybe."

"What's that supposed to mean?"

"Nothing." And then he chuckled at the word he'd used. He

had his hands on the steering wheel, and now he let his head rest upon it.

Amal felt yearning for him light inside her. She touched his arm, but he didn't look up. She was afraid to say something that would break her resolve. Now there was the task of saying good-bye, the task of being part of a family. "I'll call you tomorrow," she said softly. Then she stepped out of the car and walked up the steps to her building. She did not hear his engine start until after she had already gone inside her apartment and dropped, fully clothed, on her bed.

11

THE RETURN

"It took a while to make all two hundred copies," Youssef said as he entered Amina Benjelloun's office. He had spent the past hour at the copy shop, where each machine the clerk used seemed to be afflicted with a different problem — low toner or malfunctioning feeder — so that the job had to be done manually. He placed the conference programs on her desk and was about to leave when she stood up. "I'm sorry to have to do this," she said, "but I have to let you go."

Was this a joke? He was only about thirty minutes late on this task, and in any case it wasn't his fault. Perhaps the secretary was in on it, waiting behind the door, ready to open it and start laughing with Benjelloun at the prank they had pulled. He was already forcing himself to smile, to show that he could be a good sport, when Benjelloun picked up a sealed envelope from the desk and handed it to him. "Your pay for this month."

"Wait," he said. "You can't be serious. Why are you firing me?"

"We just don't need you anymore."

Everything around him — the paper-covered desk, the diplomas on the wall, the potted plants — seemed to recede into the

background. Her face suddenly appeared magnified. Mesmerized, he stared at her broad forehead, the scratch along the top
of her tortoiseshell glasses, the beauty mark at the base of her
neck, which he had never noticed before. It took a moment for
words to form in his mind and to string together into a sentence. "I didn't do anything wrong."

"Maybe not. But unfortunately we no longer need you. Don't
forget to turn in your badge on your way out." He detected no
satisfaction in the way she said this, even though she had never
liked him and had not wanted him on her team. But this was
unfair; he had worked with dedication, neglecting his studies to
focus on his job, and now she was firing him. Without realizing
it, he stepped forward and gripped the back of the chair before
him. Had he looked down he would have seen his knuckles
turn white from the effort.

"I am sorry," she said.

"I didn't do anything wrong. I think you should reconsider."

"Are we going to have a problem?"

"Your boss will find out."

"If you don't leave, I will have to call security."

Maybe it was a mistake, Youssef thought. She was told to cut
down on her staff, and forgot that Nabil Amrani himself had
asked her to give Youssef a job. It had been a long while after
all, and she had hired two other people since she took him on.
"Do you have any idea who you're talking to?" he asked.

She gave him a half smile. "I know exactly who I'm talking to."

Youssef looked at her uncomprehendingly. When it was clear
he was not going to move, Benjelloun picked up the phone

and pressed a button, whispering into the receiver. A moment later, the door flew open and two security guards rushed in. Youssef turned around to face them. "A-'ibad allah!" he said, finally raising his voice. The guards took him out of the office and into the hallway. "What is this hogra?" he yelled. "She fired me for no reason!" He turned to look at the men who held him, but each one avoided his eyes, as if they had known all along that he was getting fired. They took off his badge and pushed him out into the street. He fell on the pavement, one knee under him, the other twisted in a painful arc. He limped across the street, feeling as though he were trapped in a film in which he was unable to deliver his own lines and was forced to say another character's dialogue instead. Something was wrong.

❖ ❖ ❖

The look on the doorman's face when Youssef arrived home told him that what had happened at the hotel was not a mistake. The doorman stood up quickly, his red prayer mat sliding from the back of his chair to the ground. He picked it up with one hand and held the other up to stop Youssef from going in. "What is it?" Youssef said as firmly as he could. He walked past the old man into the lobby and pressed the button for the elevator. "I'm in a rush."

"There's no need to go up there, my son," the doorman said, his voice tinged with weariness. "The locks have been changed."

Youssef whipped around to face him, his worn beige suit

hanging loosely on his thin body, his mouth nearly toothless, his eyes disappearing under the folds of his lids, his forehead marked by a round spot of piety. Even though Youssef knew that this poor, devout man would never have dared touch the locks without an order from his father, he could not help yelling. "Are you mad? How dare you change my locks?"

"It was the owner who did it," the doorman said.

"Who are you talking about?"

"Madame Amrani called me from abroad. She told me a locksmith would come."

So she was the one behind all this. Madame Amrani, his mother's rival, and now his, too. "Does my father know about this?"

The doorman remained silent.

"He's my father."

The old man looked away.

"Do you know that? Do you know he's my father?"

"Whatever you say, my son."

It was useless. "What about my things?" Youssef asked. "Where are they?"

"I have them." The doorman went inside his ground-floor office and fetched a large pillowcase filled with clothes. "Here."

"This is it?" Youssef asked. "What about my books? My movies? All my shoes?"

"I only took what I could while the locksmith was waiting, my son. Don't get angry with me. Take it up with her when she returns. And if you think I took anything from you, you're welcome to check inside the office."

Youssef felt like shaking this man, who had been nothing

but kind to him, this helpless man, who was like so many other people in the country, completely disabused of the notion that there was much use fighting against injustice. The only thing that stopped Youssef was the look in the man's eyes, a look that made it clear he would accept this indignity as he had accepted all the others life had dealt him.

YOUSSEF CARRIED HIS BAG to the nearest café and sat there all afternoon, his chin resting on his palm. He took out his mobile phone to call his father's secretary. "Who is calling, please?" she asked in the nasal voice he remembered.

"This is . . . Driss Ayyadi," Youssef said. "I'm a journalist."

"I'm sorry, sir. He is out of the office."

"Do you know when he'll be back?"

"I'm not sure."

It annoyed Youssef that Fadila was so protective of her boss as to keep the date of his return a secret—unless, he thought suddenly, she had been *told* to remain quiet. "That's too bad," he said, trying to hit the right note of professional rather than personal disappointment. "I wanted to talk to him about a piece I've been commissioned to do for *Le Monde.*"

The mention of the French newspaper got her attention. She spoke quickly now. "He's in the United States until the nineteenth. After that, he goes on vacation in Spain for ten days. He won't be back until the end of June."

Nabil had never mentioned that he would be gone for so long. Why the omission? And the way he had spoken the last time Youssef saw him had been so strange, so full of foreboding and sadness. Youssef had a sinking feeling in his stomach, yet he tried to keep his voice level. "So he'll be back in the office on the thirtieth?"

"Yes, sir. If you'd like to give me a phone number, I will make sure he gets the message."

Youssef made up a number and hung up. Although he tried to keep the thought out of his mind, it imposed itself upon him like light upon night: his father had left him. He smoked what remained of his pack of Dunhills while watching young people his age sitting in the café. They seemed so confident, so sure of themselves and of who they were. Just yesterday he might have been able to deceive himself into believing that he, too, was of their world, not just in it.

It had taken a little over an hour to undo all of his life, just as two years ago his life had been turned upside down in the same amount of time. Why was this happening to him? Why did God look on as His creatures went through such pain and not see fit to save them? Youssef felt the last vestiges of faith leave his heart, replaced by hate for Madame Amrani.

And there was, too, along with the hate, the shame that had been waiting at every corner for him, the shame of having failed in his endeavor, of having accomplished exactly what his mother had told him he would—which is to say, nothing. He realized now that he had only played the part of Youssef Amrani, but all along he had remained Youssef El Mekki.

As dusk fell, he began to shiver. He looked around him. Afternoon patrons had left, and now the evening clientele had begun to appear. He felt even more out of place. It was time to leave. But how could he show himself in Hay An Najat again, after everything that had happened? He dropped his face in his hands and tried to suppress his sobs for as long as he could, but it was useless. Soon he became aware of the other patrons' stares, and he quickly wiped his eyes with his napkin. He held the pillowcase full of his belongings and walked, dragging his feet, to the bus station.

❖ ❖ ❖

It was the smell that got to him first. He had forgotten about the stench of garbage mixed with the odor of car exhaust and the stink of old, refried sardines that permeated the street, but as soon as he stepped off the bus, he began to cough uncontrollably. The cart that sold boiled chickpeas still sat around the corner from the bus station, and so did the vegetable stand. Kids loitered at corners, leaning against walls. Discarded black plastic bags dotted the ground, and clotheslines crisscrossed the alleys. The walk from the bus station to his mother's house, which had seemed so short to him when he lived here, now seemed to take forever.

The streets and alleys were full: women getting water, girls carrying shopping bags, drug addicts huddled in groups, merchants peddling their wares from rickety bicycles, teenagers hawking single cigarettes, children playing marbles. Youssef thought that all eyes were on him, that the entire neighborhood had found out about his return and had stepped out to watch the humiliated son return home to his mother. He tripped on a rock and fell down, his things spilling out onto the dirt. Several people stopped what they were doing to watch. Jumping up to his feet, he hurriedly collected his belongings, now covered with red dirt. Someone called out his name in the distance, but he pretended not to hear. He trotted the rest of the way to his mother's house. To his immense relief, the door was unlocked.

He stepped inside and closed the door behind him, finally allowing himself a breath. The smell of mint tea hung in the air. There were dishes drying on the rack in the corner, right on the battered cement floor. Three housedresses in faded colors hung on the laundry line, against walls whose paint was cracked like broken eggshells. The corrugated tin roof over the bedroom was eaten by rust, and the satellite dish mounted on it was covered with bird excrement. The house looked the same as he remembered it.

His mother looked up at him from the divan where she was curled up. She shot to her feet now, and the bowl of sunflower seeds that had been nestled in her lap dropped to the floor. The seeds scattered everywhere. For a moment, it felt to Youssef as though time had suspended itself. He looked at her, wordlessly communicating that what she had warned him against had finally come to pass. She nodded once.

Looking down, he dropped his bag on the floor. She gave him a hug, her head barely reaching his chest. "My son, my son."

After she let go of him, he remained standing in the same spot until she guided him by the hand toward the divan and forced him to sit. She did not ask him the questions he expected — Did he throw you out? What about your school? What about the job? — but instead sat next to him in a silence that resonated with solidarity.

Youssef's throat was dry. His jaw was so tight that he was

unable to speak. He stared at her, and after a while she put her hand on his forehead, then caressed his cheek. He watched her, still immobile. She asked if he was hungry. He did not answer. "Do you want to go lie down, then?" He managed to blink his approval.

She helped him to his bed. He tucked his knees to his chest and turned to face the wall. Chills ran down his arms and legs, despite the blanket with which his mother had covered him. He heard her turn off the TV out in the yard before returning to the bedroom to sit on her bed. As darkness fell, the house grew quieter. He could hear her breathing across the room. He closed his eyes, though he knew there would be no sleep for him tonight.

❖ ❖ ❖

Youssef did not leave his mother's house over the next few days. Although he was due to sit for his final exams, he could not bring himself to go to school. He did little but sleep or stare at the ceiling—counting the dips in the corrugated tin above him, and then counting them again until he fell asleep. He wanted never to wake up. What purpose was there to his existence? If his mother had aborted him, he would have escaped the life that she had condemned herself to, and he would not have had to endure the fate that had been decided for him even before he was born. His anger took many shapes: sometimes it was soft and familiar, like a round stone that he had caressed for so long that it was perfectly smooth and polished; sometimes it was thin and sharp, like a blade that could slice through anything;

sometimes it had the form of a star, radiating his hatred in all
directions, leaving him numb and empty inside.

When the end of the month finally arrived, he called his father.
The line rang, but no one answered. Rather than leave a message,
he hung up. Now he had to contend with the doubts: Had his
father ignored his call, the way he used to ignore his wife's? There
was no other alternative but to go meet him at work. Youssef put
on his nicest shirt, a pair of black pants, and the tasseled loafers
he had bought from a store on rue Aïn Harrouda. He ran up the
street like a fugitive and caught a bus to the west side of town. It
was still early. His father was probably making his morning calls
and getting ready to go out for his rounds—to the factory, the
hotel, a trade conference, or a business meeting. With enough
luck, Youssef might still catch him.

The sun was already high in the sky when Youssef arrived
at AmraCo. The mirrored windows reflected the rays of light,
blinding him. He reached for his sunglasses, then suddenly remembered that he no longer had them; they had been left behind in the apartment. With eyes cast down, he walked inside
the parking lot and stood by the entrance, waiting for his father
to emerge. Cars and cabs fought for space at the semaphore
across the street, starting up in a cloud of dark exhaust as the
light turned green. A policeman whistled at a motorcycle and
then spoke into his walkie-talkie when the driver failed to stop.
A truck stopped by the minimarket up the street and delivered
canisters of gas. It was scorching hot, and Youssef could feel
pearls of sweat forming on his forehead.

Finally the double doors swung open and Omar the driver
came out, followed by Nabil Amrani. Youssef held out the hope

that somewhere in his father's appearance, there would be a hint of Youssef's passage in his life. But Nabil looked exactly the same as ever: harried, elegant, authoritative, in control. Nothing about him hinted at the events that had come to pass.

Omar saw Youssef first. He calmly left the door he held open for his boss, went around to his side of the car, and climbed in. Youssef walked up, standing now face-to-face with his father. "Youssef! What are you doing here?" Nabil asked. He sounded genuinely surprised.

"I came to see you."

Nabil's gaze shifted. "I'm sorry about what happened. My wife and my daughter found out . . . it's complicated."

"Weren't you going to tell them? Why would it be complicated?"

"You wouldn't understand," Nabil said wearily. Then he reached out and touched Youssef's arm. It amazed Youssef how much and how often both of his parents underestimated his capacity to understand. He *did* understand. A small part of him had known, all along, that his dream of a real-life father was impossible, but he had wanted to turn the impossibility into a possibility. Why could *they* not understand that?

"So this is it?" Youssef asked his father. "You don't want to see me anymore?" There was a touch of threat in his tone; he did not know from where it came.

"No, that's not it. I do want to see you. But right now is not the best time." He looked up at the building, as if afraid of being caught. "I am still trying to see if we can reach a compromise. Please be patient."

Promises, again. Youssef was ready for them, though, the

way a traveler in the desert cannot discount assurances of an oasis up ahead; it was better than continuing forth without hope of relief. "Where have you been this whole time?" he asked, his voice softening.

"I was in Los Angeles until mid-June, and then in Spain, and now I have so much work to catch up on, I haven't been able to handle this. But I will." He let his hand rest on Youssef's shoulder once again. "Okay?" He got into the car, closing the door. Youssef jammed his fists into his trouser pockets and stood aside, watching the car ease its way out of the parking lot.

For the first time, Youssef could see why Nabil Amrani never seemed to get emotional when they watched sad movies together in the apartment, or why he never seemed to get angry when he heard news of the war on the radio. The world was the way it was; Nabil Amrani took it as it came and did not think about anything else besides his own existence. Someday, Youssef knew, his father would come to see that life could not be lived like this, that the wider universe had a way of intruding upon people's private world.

TWO WEEKS WENT BY, but there was no word from Nabil Amrani. No matter how often Youssef played images of a future with his father in his mind, he could not bring himself to believe in them anymore. He called his father's mobile phone repeatedly, but his father never picked up. He tried him at the office, but the secretary said he could not come to the phone, and to please stop calling. He even went to the office, but the security guards would not let him go upstairs.

He came to understand that his father had made a choice. Amal was his real child; Youssef was the bastard. He belonged here with all the other young men no one talked about, except every few years when there was a natural catastrophe, a terrorist attack, or a legislative election. He had grown up in Hay An Najat, away from the eyes of the world, and now he became convinced that it would be his grave, too.

A PERFECT CIRCLE

AT FIRST, HIS MOTHER did not ask Youssef why he spent most of his days in bed, staring at the ceiling, but once it became clear his father would not call, the questions began. "Why don't you shave?" she asked. She stripped her bed of sheets and blankets and took them outside to hang in the sun.

"I'm not going anywhere," he said, rubbing his beard.

She watered her potted flowers, started the kettle, turned on the radio. When the tea was ready, she reappeared at the door of the bedroom. "Why don't you come eat your breakfast in the yard?"

The delicious smell of mint and sugar drifted in with her. Still, he replied, "It's too hot out there, a-mmi."

She ate alone without complaint and later brought him a glass of tea and a plateful of fritters. "Why don't you invite Amin to come over?" she asked.

He shook his head. "I don't feel like seeing anyone."

As she was getting ready for work the next day, she told him she would no longer serve meals in the bedroom. "If you want to eat, you will have to get out of bed." He looked at her in despair. Could she not see that he was unwell? He turned to his side and faced the wall, picking at the paint with his fingernail until he heard her leave. When she came home that night, she did as she had promised. It was the same the next day, and the day after that, until hunger drove him to the yard, where he made himself a pot of tea on the Butagaz and ate a piece of bread from the basket under the awning.

In the morning, she shook him awake. "Here," she said, handing him a fifty-dirham bill. "I need you to get some sugar and some oil today."

"I can't," he said.

"Why not?"

"I don't want to go out."

"I don't want to go to work, either, but here I am," she said, putting a blue jellaba over her uniform and zipping it up. From the armoire, she fetched her purse and checked for her keys.

"People will ask me questions. They'll want to know what happened."

"Then tell them." She snapped her purse shut.

"I can't."

"Then don't tell them. Look, you're not going to stay locked up in here the rest of your life."

Why not? Youssef thought. Here, he was safe.

"I have two shifts to do today," she continued, "because Jamila is sick and can't come to work. So I won't be back till after nine o'clock. Get me one liter of oil and half a kilo of sugar."

"Please, a-mmi," he pleaded.

She ignored him, slipped her shoes on, and left. Wrapping himself up in his blanket, he went to the yard, where he turned on the TV. Though he watched the show, his mind was elsewhere. The errand seemed insurmountable, but the thought occurred to him suddenly that it might be possible to do it without being seen. After all, it was only seven thirty in the morning.

He cast the blanket aside and hurriedly put on his shoes. The street was quiet as he walked toward Moha's hanout, on the other side of the hill. Before Youssef had moved out of the neighborhood, he had rarely gone to Moha's, so when he appeared in the store today, no one asked him where he had been. He paid for the sugar and the oil, picked up the plastic bag, and left. He was already congratulating himself on having gone and come back unseen, when, turning a corner, he glimpsed Amin with two street urchins. His heart sank.

"Bellati!" Amin yelled. "A-Youssef, wait!"

Youssef walked faster, keeping his eyes locked on the ground.

Amin and his friends crossed the street. "Can't you hear me calling?"

"Ah, Amin, my brother," Youssef said, trying to do his best impression of his old self. "Forgive me, I wasn't paying attention." Amin wore a jean jacket streaked with dirt around the collar and sleeves. His eyes had that vacant stare they sometimes had when he smoked hashish. Youssef did not recognize the two teenagers standing by his side; maybe they were fresh additions to Hay An Najat from the countryside.

"What are you, deaf?" Amin said, looking at his two friends, who laughed as though he had just told the best joke in the world. "What's this?" he asked, pointing to the plastic bag.

"This? Just some sugar and oil."

"You're running errands for your mother," Amin said, "like a good little boy." And he laughed again.

Youssef shrugged and walked away. Amin followed. "Where have you been?"

"Around."

"What's that supposed to mean?"

"*Around*."

"Leave us," Amin told his friends.

The house was less than a block and a half away now.

"Your father kicked you out," Amin said.

"No."

"You think that just because I live here, I'm stupid?"

"I didn't say you were."

Another thirty meters to go.

"What are you doing here, then?"

"Buying sugar."

"It's a long way to come for sugar. He threw you out, didn't he?"

Youssef didn't answer. He felt his anger sharpen inside him again, taking the form of a blade, ready to strike at his friend.

Ten more meters.

"He threw you out," Amin said. "I told you those people aren't like us. I *told* you. But no, you had to go on pretending you were someone you're not." He was close enough that Youssef could smell cigarettes and hashish on his breath. "I told you!"

"Fine, you told me, O Professor," Youssef said, shooting him a dark look. "Bezza't. Get over yourself."

Five meters.

Amin stopped abruptly. "I should have known better," he yelled, "than to befriend a son of a whore."

THE WORDS TORTURED Youssef all day. When his mother came home from work, he told her he had a migraine and felt dizzy and nauseous whenever he stood up. He gave her such a look of distress that she did not bother him further. But the next day, she brought him painkillers from the hospital and stood over him as he swallowed the recommended dosage. "Now, why don't you go out to stretch your legs?" she suggested.

"I don't feel like going out, a-mmi."

"You don't want to go out and see your friends?"

These were words he never thought he would hear from her. Although he savored the irony, he also wondered how much longer he could avoid seeing Amin. The man was probably parading around the neighborhood with his new sidekicks, telling everyone how his joke had sent Youssef running home—what an intolerable thought.

That afternoon, just before dusk, Youssef went to the Oasis. The Party's building looked better than it had the last time he had been there. Huge flags with the motto THROUGH GOD. WITH GOD. BY GOD hung from the main door, lights outlined the facade, and all the windows were open to let in the cool evening air. Youssef could see young men clustered around the tables in the café. Maati stood guard at the entrance. When he saw Youssef walk up, an expression of shock lit his face. He opened his arms wide. "Long live he who sees you, my brother," he said. "Where have you been?"

Youssef stuck to the story his mother had told the neighbors: a cousin of hers had helped him find a job at a hotel in Marrakech, but now he had been let go. He was grateful for the hug Maati gave him, for the gruff pats on the back that made him feel that things could still be the way they used to be. He scoured the café, looking for familiar faces: Simo was playing chess with Rachid; Mounir was doing a crossword puzzle; Rachid's brother was watching a football match; Hatim was reading the paper, holding it with one hand, while with the other he fingered his green prayer beads. And there, at a corner table, was Amin, with his new friends.

"Go in, go in," Maati said. "Order some tea or coffee. I'll look for someone to cover for me and I'll come join you."

Youssef asked for two glasses of tea at the counter, carrying them to a table at the other end of the café. Before he could sit down, though, Amin cried out, "Look who came here today. He thinks he can come and go as he pleases, like he owns the place, like he's better than us."

Youssef turned around and stared Amin down. The others — Simo, Mounir, Rachid, and his brother — looked up, and they all got up to say hello. While they were still exchanging salaams, Amin approached. "What are you doing here?"

"What do you care?" Youssef replied.

"This is *our* café. You have no business here."

"What's going on, my brother?" Simo asked.

"This is a public space," Youssef said. "I can sit here if I want."

Amin grabbed Youssef's table and shook it from right to left, knocking down the glasses. "Get out," he said. At the sound of the glass breaking, Hatim folded his paper and sat up in his chair. Youssef's other friends looked confused by the argument.

"Look what you've done," Youssef said, his voice trembling. He pushed the shards of glass away from the edge of the table so they would not fall on the floor, where they might injure someone.

"Get out," Amin said between his teeth. In his eyes was a determination Youssef had never seen; he looked like a stranger.

Suddenly, Youssef had the horrible feeling that his coming here had been a bad idea. But now that he had provoked the confrontation, he could not walk away from it. "I'm not going anywhere."

Amin shoved him; Youssef shoved back. Their friends restrained them, but Amin managed to break free and grab Youssef by the collar. Finally, Maati broke through the crowd. "What's going on here?" He held Amin back. "Leave him alone."

"Tell him to get out."

"He's not going anywhere."

Amin lunged at Youssef, but Maati grabbed him by the waist and easily pushed him back. "If you can't control yourself, I'll have to take *you* out. Why don't you just go back to your seat?"

"Son of a whore," Amin said. The insult was not meant for Maati.

Hatim stood up. "Calm down, Amin. There's no use for that kind of language."

"Hadak lehmar," Amin screamed, "he doesn't belong here. Tell him, Hatim, tell him."

Hatim spoke in a steady voice. "I told you there's no use for that kind of language. Either go back to your table, or leave. We don't want any trouble here."

Amin stormed off, followed by his two friends. Youssef took a deep breath of relief, grateful to both Maati and Hatim for having defended him. With a snap of his fingers, Hatim signaled to the waiter to come clean up the mess, and Youssef, still shaking with anger, took his seat at the table. Hatim put a hand on his shoulder. "How have you been? We haven't seen you here in a while."

There was something in Hatim's voice that made it difficult to lie to him, but Youssef had no choice. "I was just staying with my mother's cousin."

"I heard you had a job," Hatim said. "In a hotel?"

Hatim never left this building, it seemed, and yet he, too, had heard the story of the job in Marrakech.

"I did. But I lost my job, so I'm back."

"Meskiin. Did they tell you why they fired you?"

"No."

"And you didn't do anything, did you?"

"No," Youssef said indignantly. He looked up at Hatim now, ready to defend his record, ready to share the madness of what had happened, but Hatim didn't appear to be interested in the details. "I can't tell you how many cases like this I hear about every day," he said. "The injustice in this country boggles the mind. If people only knew what was happening around them — but they don't. This country is like a car going down a ravine, and everyone's asleep in the backseat." Youssef nodded, his pain having found a home in Hatim's words.

13

THE TEST

IT WAS JULY. In other parts of Casablanca, jacaranda trees were shedding their purple blossoms, yielding a soft, sweet smell, but here in Hay An Najat, houseflies thrived, growing bigger and bolder. They grazed on piles of trash, competing with sheep and cows for tea grounds, vegetable peels, and empty containers of yogurt. Mosquitoes appeared, and flying ants, and gray moths, and gnats. Meanwhile, men still sold fish at the market, women still worked in the textile factories, and children still stood at street corners.

Youssef's mother wanted him to return to college in the fall, but he knew it was a waste of time. He had missed classes for most of the previous year, and he hadn't sat for his final exams. "You can repeat the year," she said, chewing on her lower lip. "That's fine. What matters is to stick with it until you get your degree." He tried to imagine what it would be like to return to campus, with new classmates but the same curriculum. It was already painful enough to know that he had made a terrible mistake by dropping out, but going back to school meant being reminded of that mistake every day. He could not bring himself to do it.

Two days later, she came up with a new idea. "Why don't you start over with a different major?" she said. He tilted his head, unsure what to say. What difference would it make if he switched to history, French, or anthropology? His father's friends called universities "jobless factories" for a good reason. Faced with his silence, her suggestion quickly became a plea: "Maybe you could take the schoolteacher's exam?" Youssef did not have the heart to remind her that Rachid's brother had done precisely that, but had been idle since graduation; the Ministry of Education had yet to place him in a school.

At dinner, she persisted. "You could try another college," she said. But Youssef had come to believe that degrees did not matter. Smarter people than he, people with engineering or medical degrees, could not find jobs. They sat in the same cafés as the dropouts and the illiterates. Except for Maati, everyone Youssef knew, every single one of his friends—Amin, Simo, Mounir, Rachid—was jobless. When he pointed this out to her, she gave him one of her wistful looks.

One day she suggested that he sit for the police academy exam at the Royal Institute of Police in Kénitra. After the terrorist attacks of May 16, she said, the government had invested massive amounts of money in security. "This is your chance," she explained. "So many police jobs are opening up that there's no need for connections, just a willingness to work." One of her co-workers' sons had taken the exam and was now an officer in Aïn Diab. If Youssef passed the exam, he, too, would have a state job, which meant a salary, health benefits, and a pension.

He tried to imagine himself in the police academy. Here, in the neighborhood, everyone hated the police — men who never showed up when they were most needed, but were always around when they were least wanted. It would never have occurred to Youssef to apply for a job with them, and his mother knew that. But if what she said was true, then why not? It would be better than sitting at home, watching her worry herself to death about his life. She was as frail as ever. Crow's-feet had deepened around her eyes, and he had noticed what he feared was a nascent hunchback, the result of all those evenings spent on her embroidery. Still, there was dignity in the way she carried herself, a refusal to be bent to the will of others. She had pulled off an incredible act all her life, and she had almost succeeded. In spite of all his disagreements with her, he could not help admiring her. "All right," he said. "I'll take the exam."

"May God bring you success," she said. She rolled up her shirtsleeves to start preparing their meal. He wanted to ask her why she had never married, but the usual sense of propriety stopped him. He had never heard anyone discuss the topic of a mother's romantic life, and even if he could, he would not find the right words in his vocabulary to speak of such things. Mothers were mothers: they cared for children, sacrificed for them, worried about them. It was in the order of things, as old as the world itself. Yet the way he had treated his mother was not in the order of things. He had met her love with denial, and her pleas with contempt. He had gone searching for a father instead. A crushing feeling of guilt descended upon him. He promised himself he would not let her down any longer.

"We're running low on water," he said, getting up.

His mother lifted the lid off the jar and looked. "No, we still have some."

"It's all right. I'll go get some now."

❖ ❖ ❖

Because it had been some time since he had taken a test, Youssef read each of the questions on the police exam several times before writing an answer. Compounding his hesitation was his knowledge of the basic unfairness in the exercise; many people paid a bribe to guarantee a passing grade. Whenever he came across an unusual phrase, or an unexpected premise, or even a typographical error, he worried that it was a trick, designed to fail the maximum number of applicants. Still, by the time the proctor stood up to collect the papers, Youssef felt surprisingly poised. The exceptional care he had put into his responses somehow filled him with hope. He would pass. He would start over.

Walking down the peeling halls of the Kénitra institute, he saw framed photographs of the interior minister and of high-ranking officers, men whose vulturine features radiated authority. However odd the idea had seemed when his mother suggested it, a career in law enforcement started to make sense. The uniform would give him a stake in the world. Instead of getting nervous whenever a policeman looked at him at a traffic light, Youssef would salute and go about his business. In any case, it was time he tried out some of his mother's suggestions, since he had been so incapable of making his way in life on his own.

Afterward, he took the train back from Kénitra to Casablanca, and then a packed grand-taxi that careened down Boulevard Zerktouni at dangerous speed. Turning away from the sweaty popcorn vendor sitting next to him, he looked out of the passenger-side window. Young people dressed in sharp suits stood outside the Twin Center, smoking cigarettes; a teenage boy lowered the window of his Range Rover, slipping a bill to the policeman who had stopped him at a red light; a middle-aged woman spoke on her mobile phone while her driver stuffed shopping bags into the trunk of her car.

Why? This was the question that tortured him unrelentingly. Why had his father taken him in, told him he was the son he had always wanted, only to throw him out? Over and over, Youssef played back scenes of their time together, trying to understand where he had gone wrong, and each time he came up with nothing. He had trusted his father so much that he had forsaken everyone and everything for him, but now he had no friends, no degree, no job. Resentment and shame mixed afresh in his heart, so that by the time the grand-taxi dropped him off, he yearned once again for his bed, for sleep.

The stench of burning garbage made it hard to repress the tears, and he let himself go. Someone grabbed him roughly by the elbow. Youssef jumped as if he had been bitten by one of the malevolent dogs that roamed the neighborhood in packs. It was Amin. "What's wrong?" he asked.

"What do you care?" Youssef said, wiping his eyes with the back of his sleeve.

"You're crying."

"It's just the smoke. That's all."

Amin put his arm around Youssef's shoulders, the gesture taking Youssef by surprise. "Look," Amin said, "about that night at the café. I don't know what happened. I was angry." It was unlike Amin to apologize for anything. "You have to understand," he went on, "you disappeared. And you stopped returning my calls. You have to admit, you did me wrong, my brother."

"It's true, I did," Youssef said. With this acknowledgment off his chest, he felt he could finally take an unlabored breath. Amin looked at him with what seemed like compassion — or at least what Youssef desperately wanted to believe was compassion — in his eyes.

"You want a cigarette?" Amin asked, pulling one from behind his ear. He lit it and then handed it to Youssef. "So where were you coming from?"

"The police academy in Kénitra," Youssef said, taking the cigarette. "I took the exam."

"Aw? You're not at university anymore?"

"I stopped going."

An old man carrying a burlap bag on his head walked hurriedly past them, followed by a group of children arguing about something.

"I flunked, too. By two points — two miserable little points."

Youssef's eyes widened. "What are you going to do?"

"I don't know," Amin said, pulling on his cigarette and exhaling through his nostrils. "I don't know what I was doing in college, anyway."

"You're not going back?"

"What for? It's not going to make a difference."

They had come to an intersection, and instinctively Youssef stopped. Amin stood for a moment with his hands hanging by his side, then leaned against the wall. "When do you find out about the exam?"

"A couple of weeks, I think," Youssef said. He did not mention that he felt good about his chances, for fear that he might bring the evil eye upon himself.

"When you get a job with the police," Amin said, "tell them to start patrolling around here. We could use some cleaning up." He laughed, and although Youssef joined him, he was not sure if his friend was laughing with him or at him. "You want to go play a game of chess at the Oasis?"

"What happened to your friends?"

"Hamid and Mustapha? They're in school right now. They're just kids. So you want to come?"

"Not now. I need to check my e-mail. But I can meet you tomorrow, insha'llah," Youssef said. "If you like."

"All right. But get ready to lose the game, my friend. I've had a lot of practice while you were gone."

❖ ❖ ❖

Youssef went to meet Amin at the Oasis immediately after Friday prayers. He took a long time to decide on each one of his moves, in part because he had not played chess in a long time, and in part because Amin had sounded so confident of his victory. Surely, even if Youssef could not win this match, he could win the next, or the one after that. Not even Amin was infallible

at this game. Hatim came in, carrying his usual load of newspapers and magazines. He took a quick look at the board as he
passed them. "Careful with your king," he said, patting Youssef
on the shoulder. Good point, Youssef thought, and moved a
pawn to protect his piece.

Hatim sat down at a table nearby. A moment later, he leaped
to his feet. "This is unbelievable!" he shrieked.

Youssef and Amin looked up with alarm from their game.
Hatim had gone pale; a thick vein throbbed on his forehead.

"What's wrong?"

"Look at this," Hatim said, holding up *Casablanca Magazine*.
On the cover was a slightly out-of-focus picture of Hatim in an
elegant blue suit, shaking hands with a man Youssef did not
recognize. The two smiled widely, as if they had just concluded
an agreement. Under the photo, a caption in big red letters
read, THE PARTY'S MONEY.

"You're on the cover?" Amin said, standing up to take the
magazine from him. "That's great!"

"You're famous!" Youssef added. For some reason he could
not explain to himself, he felt envious.

"No, no, no," Hatim said impatiently. "This is another one
of Benaboud's attacks."

When he heard the name, Youssef stood up to read the article over Amin's shoulder.

A slogan like "Through God, by God, with God" may sound catchy,
but it doesn't pay the bills. And there are many: health services, a
community center, even a summer camp for children. How does the
Party fund its social programs? An exclusive investigation by Farid
Benaboud.

PYRAMID SCHEME

Like any self-respecting grassroots organization, the Party relies on member donations. But rather than wait for members to reach into their pockets, the Party does it for them. Each member has to contribute 3 percent of his monthly salary via direct deposit, a sum that is increased to 10 percent in the months of Eid. With this money, the Party has already set up its headquarters at the site of an abandoned warehouse. The Party encourages its members to recruit people into the organization. If a mutahazzib—a Partisan—has brought in three new Partisans, he no longer has to pay a monthly contribution. This expanding base of activists provides the Party with a respectable amount of resources for daily expenses. Still, it can't cover big projects.

FOREIGN DONORS

This is where foreign donors (typically from Saudi Arabia) come in. They contribute Qur'ans and religious books, which the Party resells in its establishments or through individual retailers, pocketing the profits. A Qur'an received for free and resold at 20 dirhams can net the Party as much as 18 dirhams. New Partisans, especially, are encouraged to contribute to the coffers of the Party by helping to sell religious materials. The Party receives occasional cash donations as well. For instance, the summer camp in Tétouan last year was entirely paid for by a wealthy Saudi friend.

FRIENDS IN LOW PLACES

However distasteful the Party's methods may seem, they are legal. But Hatim Lahlou also has friends among the Tangier and Tétouan drug barons. The Party has recruited heavily in the two cities. A security source who spoke on condition of anonymity told me that the Party counts among its followers Ahmed Achiri (alias Ad Dib), one of the most notorious drug lords the state has ever had to contend with.

WHO IS HATIM LAHLOU?

Unknown just three years ago, the 35-year-old Hatim Lahlou has quickly garnered a following in the slums of Casablanca. Born in Rabat and educated in private schools and later at Lycée Descartes, Lahlou studied engineering in France before starting a doctoral degree at NYU. Then, at age 28, he left New York abruptly and traveled to Egypt, where he studied for four years.

Before Youssef could finish the rest of the article, Hatim took the magazine away and leafed through its pages again. "Benaboud does a cover story about me," he said, "and he doesn't even bother to talk to me. So of course this article is full of fabrications. He says our Qur'ans are from Saudi Arabia, as if it were a crime to receive donations of the holy book. He says I studied at the Lycée Descartes in Rabat, when in fact I studied at a public school right here, in one of the poorest parts of Casablanca. He repeats the rumor that I fixed up this building using cement stolen from the houses of Moroccans working abroad. This is an outright lie; I bought it at the cement factory. All these lies!"

Youssef remembered the gentle, polite man who had come to Nabil Amrani's apartment, invoking principles and asking for support, and he had trouble reconciling the impression he had of the accomplished journalist with the sloppy reporter Hatim complained about now. "Why don't you write him a letter?" he suggested.

"That man is on a mission to destroy me," Hatim said.

"But he has a Letters to the Editor section in the magazine. It's for cases like this—"

Amin interrupted. "He won't publish it."

"Or how about if you write your own counterarticle," Youssef offered, "in *At Tariq*?"

"Look at this," Hatim said. He seemed locked in a conversation with himself, hardly hearing those around him. "Here is an ad for vodka, right underneath an article on Hajj. Look at the photos with this article on Agadir—all these women in bikinis. And this—now, *this* you won't believe: an interview with the filmmaker Mehdi Mimouni, who talks about being homosexual as if he were talking about something normal. Benaboud has no shame." Hatim dropped the magazine on the table. "He calls himself a Muslim. But he is not a Muslim. He is *nothing*."

He collected his papers and went upstairs to his office. Youssef and Amin returned to their game, but Youssef let his finger hover over his knight, unsure whether to move it. How odd it was, he thought, to read an article and hear directly from the person about whom it was written. It was the kind of piece that would get a lot of attention. People would lend the magazine to their friends; journalists at competing publications would try to write similar articles. Youssef could not imagine that Benaboud would print lies. After all, some of the claims he made came from the police themselves. Still, Hatim was right:

Benaboud should have spoken to him first. And the line about the Party's headquarters being in an abandoned warehouse — it proved that Benaboud had never set foot in Hay An Najat. Hatim was right to be angry.

❖ ❖ ❖

The following Monday, Youssef rose with the sound of the muezzin and crept out of the bedroom. The dawn prayer was his favorite because the chant was pure, uninterrupted by the honking of motorcycles or the ringing of school bells or the cries of children. The alley was quiet, and if he stepped outside now, he could almost forget the ugliness that was still hidden under a cloak of darkness. He washed up in the water closet and got dressed. Today he would deliver new job applications, written in his best Arabic penmanship, asking the human resources manager of this administration or that ministry to consider him for a state job. Each letter invariably closed with respectful salutations and was signed, sincerely, by Youssef El Mekki.

His mother was already making breakfast by the time he was ready to go. She served the bread and tea directly on the cane mat — the small, round table that was used for the main meals was still propped on its side against the wall. Her blue jellaba was folded next to her purse, ready to go. "Where are you going today?" she asked.

"Two ministries in Rabat, Foreign Affairs and the Interior. Then I'll get back on the train to Casablanca and drop off another application at the National Office of Fisheries."

"May God open all doors for you."

"Amen."

IT WAS JUST after 9 a.m. when Youssef arrived at the Interior Ministry in Rabat. He was directed to the human resources department, on the second floor, where a middle-aged man with a thin mustache and thinning hair sat at a desk right on the landing. The expression on the man's face was familiar to Youssef: an immediate appraisal, categorizing him as another supplicant.

"Good morning, sir."

"Good morning."

"I am here to deliver a job application."

The man took the letter from Youssef, gave it a quick look, and then added it to a pile on his right-hand side. He fixed his eyes upon a distant spot behind Youssef.

"When might I hear about it?"

"The director has to read it. Come back in two weeks."

And so it went with every other government body he tried that day. He was running out of places to try, having exhausted the list of state agencies he had found in the phone book.

On the train home, a wave of panic washed over him. What if he could not find another job? What would become of him? For a while his life had seemed to open up, allowing him to see a path for himself, a future, but now the darkness was closing in again. He wanted out of this miserable existence. The pain was so acute that he could feel it, just under his ribs, with each breath he took. When he got off the train, he stopped by the news kiosk to buy *Le Matin*. The job advertisements were the usual calls for applications from computer engineers and MBAs, but he saw a two-line ad for a receptionist at a cybercafe and another one for a helper at a copy shop. He called the first number. An angry café owner answered, barking at him that he regretted having placed the ad—he had received more than one hundred calls and had spent all day on the phone, turning people down. And yes, the position had already been filled. Youssef dialed the second number and got a busy signal. He kept trying for fifteen minutes without success. At last he left the station to catch the bus home.

For lunch, his mother had made a plate of couscous garnished with a few carrots, a small piece of meat, and a lot of sauce. He ate the couscous, but left her the meat, refusing to take another bite of food until she ate. They were drinking a glass of verbena, listening to the news on the radio, when the mailman knocked on the door to deliver the letter that informed Youssef that his application for the police academy had been rejected.

14

DREAMS

YOUSSEF STARTED GOING to the street corner again with Amin. There, he watched people come and go, and sometimes listened to or repeated new gossip. Did you hear that a teenager from Douar Lahouna stole twenty kilos of copper wire from the railway line? The commuter trains from Rabat to Casablanca had to be stopped for several hours while the ONCF made repairs. The boy sold the spools of metal and made enough money to buy a motorcycle. And did you know that Simo was mugged while coming home the other night? The greaser put a razor right here, at the base of Simo's neck. And did you see the way Sawsan dresses and carries herself? That girl had better watch out; she is looking for trouble.

By early afternoon, Youssef and Amin usually tired of standing at the corner and went to the Party headquarters to see Maati, keeping him company by the entrance. They sat on the white plastic chairs outside and shared his coffee and cigarettes. Sometimes, Maati would tell them one of his new jokes. "Did you hear the one about the police?" he asked. When they both said no, he continued. "The heads of security services from

Morocco, France, and the United States meet at a conference, and they make a bet about who is the best at finding criminals. So they come up with a challenge. They release a rabbit into a forest and they each have to try and find it. The Americans go in. They set up a huge command center. They hire informants; they spy on all the animals; they harass the ones that look rabbitlike. After two months, they issue a report saying that rabbits do not exist in that forest. The French go in next. They investigate for two weeks. They can't find the rabbit. So they burn parts of the forest and make no apologies. It was the fault of the rabbit; he should have turned himself in. Then the Moroccans finally get their turn. They come out two hours later with a battered and bloodied fox. The fox is yelling: 'Okay! Okay! I *am* a rabbit! I *am* a rabbit!'"

Everyone burst out laughing. Youssef loved hearing Maati's jokes, but it frightened him how quickly he fell back into this routine with his old friends, standing around with nothing but words to occupy them. It was as if he had never left the neighborhood, as if his life had never been interrupted.

One day, Amin told Youssef about the lawyer. Maître Chraibi had immigrated to the United States many years ago, had a law practice in New York, and now had an office with a brass nameplate on Chari' Al Massira. His online ad boasted that he could get green cards to all those who entered the visa lottery through his firm. *Most of the applications filed with American immigration services are improperly filled out, the ad warned, so directions must be followed exactly. Why deny yourself an opportunity? Let me take care of the paperwork.* All you had to do, Amin told him, was fill out a form and provide a photo, and the lawyer would take care of the rest. The service cost one thousand dirhams, half up front and half after the applicant was called for the consular interview.

"Are you going to apply?" Youssef asked, turning to look at Amin. They had come into the cybercafe after an afternoon of playing chess at the Oasis.

"Not this year," Amin said, barely taking his eyes off the computer screen. "I don't have the money."

Youssef considered this for a moment. "I have enough for both of us."

"Aw? Where did you get the cash?"

"The money I made from my job. I have enough for both of us. We can both apply."

Amin pushed the keyboard away and looked incredulously at Youssef. "You would give me the money? Really?"

"Of course." Youssef said, quickly averting his eyes. He did not want to explain that this was his way of atoning for how he had treated Amin. Maybe this lottery would give them the chance they had been waiting for. It would take both of them out of Hay An Najat this time, and for good. Youssef pictured palm-lined beaches, white picket fences, giant hamburgers, baseball matches, fast cars—it was a dream that came, fully formed, in stereo and in high definition, into his mind. All he had to do was replay scenes from the films and television shows beamed into his home by satellite, and insert himself into the story.

They sent in their lottery applications the next day. Now, all they could do was wait. They spent their days together, shuttling from the street corner to the Oasis, from the Oasis to the cybercafe, and back again. Sometimes, one or the other of them left Hay An Najat to inquire about a job listing, but such occasions seemed more like formalities than possibilities, their names and addresses having already disqualified their applications.

Their routine was disrupted when Amin's girlfriend Soraya got married — to a store security guard, at a ceremony to which neither Amin's family nor Youssef's mother was invited. Amin stopped coming to the street corner in the mornings. He was too depressed to want to leave his house, and when he reappeared, it was mostly at the cybercafe, reeking of hashish. Youssef started going there, too, taking a seat next to him at the computer station. Most of the other customers were looking at porn photos or Islamic Web sites, or both, but Amin was addicted to online chat. He was trying to start a romance with a foreign woman. He was worried that the American consul would deny him a lottery visa because he didn't speak English very well. He was ready to go anywhere: somewhere in Europe or America was best, but he did not mind the Gulf or Australia, either. He had created different nicknames for different chat rooms in different countries: for the West, he was Ash; in the Middle East, he was Ashhab; and Down Under, he was Heb.

Soon, Amin mastered the bizarre abbreviations made necessary by the bandwidth of his Internet connection. In one window, he typed, "What r u up 2?" while on the other he was waiting for an answer to his message "T où, là?" On yet another window, he used a latinized spelling of Darija to chat with a

French Algerian girl: "Finek a zzin?" Amin had no trouble conversing, half-literately, in three languages. He was determined to be a mail-order groom.

"How do you keep them straight," Youssef asked him, "all these different people you claim to be?"

"You get used to it quickly," Amin said. "Playing a role, I mean."

Staring at the screen over Amin's shoulder, Youssef saw that Katia from Oslo had just asked where he was from. "Casablanca," Amin typed. A smiley face appeared in the tiny window of the chatting software, but nothing else. Still, that little emoticon was enough to give Amin hope, and he said he would try Katia again in a few days, see if he could get her to talk.

Amin's belief in his chances was steadfast, and therefore it was infectious. Watching him type with two fingers, Youssef was tempted to consider the idea of an Internet love match for himself—but he could not bring himself to create a fake identity. He was tired of the masquerades. He was Youssef El Mekki; he was his mother's son, a child of Hay An Najat. He no longer had any wish to be someone else.

He often thought that Maati had outsmarted them all. Three years ago, when he had flunked out of high school, he had seemed to have the least chance of making it. Yet now he was the only one among Youssef's friends bringing home a salary, the only one who had not wasted his time at the university. Already he had saved up enough to help his parents with his sister's wedding. Youssef could not help feeling pangs of envy every time he saw Maati at the Oasis.

And the worst of it was: Youssef was luckier than many others he knew. Around the neighborhood, young men from Senegal and Mali and Niger had begun to settle, sharing shacks, eight or ten to a room. They had come looking for Europe but had run out of money on the way and had stayed here in Casablanca. They worked as vendors, porters, or beggars. At any moment, they risked getting picked up by the police or harassed by thugs. But their fate did not raise concern in Youssef, for *he* was going to America, and surely, surely, such things did not happen there.

Whenever he was turned down for a job interview, he simply returned to the dream. "Just imagine—," Youssef would say to Amin, unable to control a smile, "imagine how it will be when we get the visa."

"Everything will be better," Amin concurred.

America was different, its movies told them; it was a place where one could go to escape tyranny, poverty, or both—and succeed. Once, as they were walking near the French lycée, on their way back from another pointless interview, a zealous cop stopped them and made them turn out their pockets for no discernible reason. When the search was over and they were let go, Youssef found refuge in the fantasy. "This would never happen in America," he said with unwitting conviction. He had watched suspects on TV shows being read their rights: *You have the right to remain silent; anything you say can and will be used against you in a court of law; you have the right to an attorney; if you cannot afford an attorney, one will be provided for you.* He knew the warnings by heart, and foolishly he believed them.

But the dream ended, as all dreams do, when rumor spread that the American Consulate had already interviewed those who had been selected. Frantic, Youssef ran across town to check with Maître Chraibi at his office. There was a FOR LEASE sign on the door. Youssef had failed, once again, and now the money was gone.

PART IV

The way of even the most justifiable
revolutions is prepared by personal
impulses disguised into creeds.

JOSEPH CONRAD, *The Secret Agent*

15

SECRETS AND LIES

APPEARANCES ARE DECEIVING. Rachida had understood this simple fact long ago, so she was often surprised to come across people who fell for artifice and good looks, for sweet words and appealing facades—for lies. Just that morning, at the market, the artichoke vendor had told her his son had found a job with a naval company based in Dubai. After the customary congratulations, she asked about the company's line of business. "I don't know, exactly," the vendor said. "Something to do with tourism." Lowering his voice to a whisper, he added, "The salary is fifteen thousand dirhams. My son paid the fee for the medical exam, so he's just waiting to hear about when he will start."

"He paid money to get the job?" Rachida asked, but the vendor did not catch her hint. He weighed the artichokes, giving her an extra 150 grams for free; she could not bring herself to tell him his son had been deceived.

Now she sat cross-legged in her yard, pulling the scales off each artichoke to get to its core. Every once in a while she ate the fleshy top of a leaf, letting its tartness linger on her tongue. She was planning on making a tagine of meat and artichoke hearts, one of Youssef's favorite dishes. Perhaps it might entice him to eat. Ever since he had lost all his money to the immigration lawyer, he had had little appetite. She had warned him that it would be a scam, but he hadn't listened, of course. Boys these days were like dandelions: the lightest of winds could blow them away. Yesterday, when she had returned home from work, she had found him lying supine on his bed. Twice she called to him before he heard her. "Are you hungry?" she asked. "Should I serve you dinner now?" He looked at her as if he could not see her, then shook his head no. She wanted to tell him that he would find his way someday, but he looked so distant that she doubted her words could penetrate his world.

There was a knock on the door. Rachida set aside the artichokes and went to answer. On her doorstep was a young woman in a sleeveless white shirt and blue pants, her right arm clutching a large red handbag. She had on diamond earrings and a turquoise necklace, which made Rachida worry for her safety. She was obviously not from the neighborhood. Rachida wanted to put her arms around her to protect her—she had the look of someone for whom the world had not yet taken off its mask.

"Good morning, a-lalla," the girl said. "Is this Youssef's house?"

"Yes, it is. Who's asking for him?" Rachida said, leaning forward to take a closer look at Youssef's friend. Could she be an old classmate from university? Perhaps Rachida could enlist her help in convincing Youssef to go back to college.

The girl seemed to hesitate. She turned to look up the street, as if expecting Youssef to magically appear from that direction, then said, "My name is Amal Amrani."

Rachida felt her stomach drop. Here she was, worrying about getting her son back into university, back to the life he had before his father appeared in it, and who should show up on her doorstep but one of his people? The only thing that kept Rachida from closing the door in Amal's face was that look of hesitation and vulnerability. It tugged at her instincts.

"May I come in?" Amal asked softly.

Almost despite herself, Rachida opened the door wide. Amal walked in and sat down on the divan in the yard. She let go of her handbag, but it balanced precariously on her lap, so that the slightest movement could make it tumble forward. She looked around—at the pot of artichoke hearts, the washtub full of dirty laundry, the water closet with the broken lock—taking great care not to let her eyes rest on any single item for too long. "I think perhaps you know who I am," she said.

Rachida had begun to warm up to this strange girl, but now she was irritated with her. Was arrogance passed down from father to daughter? "No. Who are you?"

"I'm sorry," Amal said. She looked searchingly at Rachida. "I thought Youssef might have told you about me." She waited for Rachida to say something. When nothing came, she drew her breath: "I am his sister."

Something about the way she spoke those words made it seem that they had crossed her lips for the first time. Hearing them, Rachida felt a visceral need to turn around, to walk away from the reality to which even her best approximations, her most convincing lies, could not compare. All she had ever wanted was to give Youssef a family he could call his own. She had created stories and memories to which he could relate, so when he told her he had met his father, she had been dumbstruck; she did not understand why the comfortable world she had created had not been enough for him. But now, with Amal in her living room, quietly saying she was Youssef's sister, Rachida saw clearly that her words had been powerless against reality.

"I wanted to talk to him," Amal said.

"He's not here," Rachida repeated, her voice coming out hoarse. She cursed herself for having let Amal in. What if Youssef came home now and found her here? It would inevitably send him into another fit of questions about the past, about his father, or, worse, about his father's sudden change of heart. "What did you want to tell him?"

Amal's face fell. She seemed not to have considered the idea that people were not going to be waiting for her when she needed to talk to them. Again, Rachida felt sorry for her—such ignorance, such innocence. Many years ago, when Rachida had arrived in the Amrani family home near Fès, she, too, had been ignorant and innocent. She had let herself believe that Nabil Amrani was in love with her. Love was new. Love was intoxicating. Love gave license to the ultimate of taboos: sleeping with a married man, a married man whose pregnant wife was on bed rest. When Rachida herself became pregnant and Nabil Amrani's mother ordered her to get an abortion, Rachida had refused and had returned to the orphanage with nothing but her dashed dreams and a baby growing inside her. Nabil's reputation had been safeguarded; her life had been ruined.

"I just wanted to meet him," Amal said. "I didn't know about him until last June, when my mother came to visit me in Los Angeles."

Rachida looked away at the mention of Malika Amrani. Did Amal know anything about Rachida's visit to the mansion in Anfa? Surely, Malika would not have been so foolish as to talk about their conversation on the terrace that warm afternoon. Rachida had worn her best clothes—a navy blue jacket with matching pants, her only pair of gold earrings—and had come to the door of the Amrani house. She told the maid she was the nurse who had watched over Malika's pregnancy twenty-two years ago, and that she was here about an urgent matter. Malika Amrani recognized her immediately, kissed her cheeks, welcomed her in, and ordered tea to be served outside. She looked at Rachida with patient eyes, waiting for a favor to be asked. Why would she think otherwise? Favors were commonly asked of a woman of her station. Although Malika was older than Rachida, she looked younger. Her hair was expertly cut, her face was carefully made up, her nails were manicured, and she seemed at ease with all the comforts around her. Rachida kept her chapped hands on her lap, hidden by the tablecloth. She spoke as softly as she could. The truth was hard to speak and—she knew—to hear.

The words formed short, simple sentences, but the propositions beneath them were filled with urgency and purpose: your husband has my son; take back your husband; give me back my son; and we can go back to the arrangement I made twenty-two years ago, with your husband's mother, the other Madame Amrani. What mattered to Malika Amrani was what mattered to Rachida Ouchak: each wanted to protect her family. The two of them had come to an understanding because they had a common interest. All the other details were best forgotten, slipped under the rug of memory.

And all of it was Nabil Amrani's fault, as far as Rachida was concerned. He should not have taken Youssef away and turned him into someone she barely recognized. She remembered walking into the back office at the hospital and finding Youssef standing by the detergent shelf, tall and handsome. He wore a polo shirt with the insignia of the Royal Golf Dar Es Salam, and a pair of fancy leather shoes. His posture had changed, his speech was peppered with words she was not used to hearing on his lips, and he had a new set of mannerisms, as if he were imitating someone. He was slipping away from her grasp. She might have been able to live through this loss if she had been sure he was going to make something of himself. But when he said he had stopped going to school, an animal rage awoke in her. She had worked so much, and for so long, to see him graduate from college, and now he had thrown it all away for the promises his father had made him. She had to do something.

Getting Youssef back had been the easy part; it was keeping him that turned out to be difficult. Although he tried not to let on, he was still yearning for his father, Rachida knew, and his sister's visit would only heighten that feeling. She looked at Amal, at this girl who could have been her own, had the world been different. "I know you didn't know about Youssef's existence. But there isn't anything you can do now."

"And I think my father didn't know, either."

Why did she have to make excuses for Nabil Amrani? She seemed like a smart girl, a nice girl, but she was trying to defend the indefensible. Not only had Nabil Amrani known but he had also offered Rachida the same alternatives as his mother. Her choice had changed everything: she could go back to the orphanage, but she could never go back home, to Sefrou. When her mother had died, her father had placed her with the Franciscan nuns at Bab Ziyyat, and although he rarely visited her, it was understood that she would stay there to get an education, train in a profession, and then return home. Soeur Laurette, the head nun, had decided that Rachida would become a midwife; it would be a most useful profession in the village.

There was no question of going back home once she became pregnant. She would dishonor her father and bring shame upon his household. Just as Madame Amrani had safeguarded her son's reputation, so, too, did Rachida Ouchak safeguard her father's. She had not told him of the pregnancy and had chosen instead to disappear. She had to create a new life for herself. So it was that she became the orphan. She gave up her home; she gave up her father and her aunts and her cousins; she even gave up the language, for how could she explain to people that she spoke Tamazight? She was simply an abandoned girl raised by nuns, and she could only speak the languages of the city, not the idiom of her village.

"How could he not have known?" Rachida asked Amal. "Youssef is his son. He knew."

"He told me he didn't know."

"And you believed him?" Rachida snickered and then looked

down, slightly embarrassed at her reaction, for when she looked into her heart, she found her own lies to her child taunting her. Who was she to judge Amrani's lies to his daughter?

There was another long silence as Amal appeared to think carefully about what to say next. "I wanted to tell Youssef," she said finally, "that I was sorry about what my father did, and about what my mother did. About everything."

All these years, Rachida had hoped for apologies, even prayed for them, but she had not expected that they would come from the most innocent of the Amranis, the one person who had nothing to do with what had happened. The apology was touching, but it was irrelevant, coming as it did from someone who had not wronged her. The universe had an odd sense of fairness; it took away things one did not want to give up, and then gave things one did not ask for. Rachida reached out and touched Amal's hand. "Does your mother know you're here?"

"No."

So Malika Amrani had kept her promise. A relief. "Why did you come here today? Hasn't it been a few months since you found out about Youssef?"

"I'm sorry. It took me a long time to . . . ," Amal said. "I just wanted to talk to him."

Rachida did not want to do this, but it was necessary. "My daughter, that is impossible."

"Why is that?"

"Because he left for Tangier three weeks ago, and from there he went to Spain to find work." She delivered this line with what she thought was conviction, but she was not sure she had succeeded until she saw the expression on Amal's face—she looked like someone who had been running to catch a train and then missed it just as it left the platform.

Amal grabbed her heavy handbag with what seemed like reluctance. "If he calls, could you tell him I came to see him?"

"Insha'llah, my daughter," Rachida said, getting up. She did not point out that she did not have a phone line.

Amal left, and Rachida finally allowed herself to take a deep breath. She waited a few minutes and then quietly unlocked the door and peeked outside, to make sure that Amal was gone. The noon sun glazed the whitewashed walls, and everyone's door was shut. The laundry lines were filled with already-dry shirts and trousers, stiff like sentinels. The street was empty, thank God. Rachida closed the door and returned to her artichokes. Youssef would be home soon, and she thought about what she would say to him.

She needed to come up with a new plan for him, even though these days he seemed convinced he would fail at everything. The way he looked at her—those eyes, so painfully reminiscent of his father's, boring through her—always made her feel she had failed at something. Although he never blamed her, he somehow managed to make her feel that everything was her fault. What did he want from her? Yes, it was difficult to make it out of Hay An Najat, but some people did manage to find decent jobs and move out, so why not him? He already had some work experience. Surely he could find something else. He needed to get away from that Oasis café, away from those good-for-nothings Maati and Amin. It was time he made something of his life.

• • •

RACHIDA WAS IN the bedroom when she heard the door creak. She listened for Youssef's noises — the soft pop when he took off his shoes, the clopping of his slippered feet as he walked to the bathroom, the water running as he washed up, and finally the heavy thud when he flopped down on the divan. Amal's visit had shaken her and she was worried she might betray herself. Still, she went into the yard and sat down on the divan next to her son. "I made a tagine of artichoke hearts."

"I'm not very hungry."

She said she would not eat, either, unless he ate, but that did not seem to have the intended effect on him. He just stared into space, lost in his thoughts. She watched him: the faint lines along his cheeks, the ashen complexion, the slightly trembling hands. He was in such obvious pain, and yet she felt powerless to help him. He drew his legs under him and lay back against the cushions.

In that position, he reminded her of her father, Hammou, how he would sit on the rug-covered seddari in the living room of their house in Sefrou with his pipe in hand, a bluish cloud of smoke rising above him. How she had missed her father. She was angry with him for placing her in the orphanage, even though he had told her repeatedly it was for her own good. The orphanage had been the beginning of her troubles. It had set everything in motion. She could still feel his presence sometimes, the way an amputee can feel the pain from a phantom limb. He would be sixty-five this year, if he was still alive. Had he ever looked for her after she disappeared? Did he remarry and have children? Did he still live in their old house overlook-

ing the green fields? She caught herself—she was about to fall
into one of her melancholy moods. Now was not the time for
those questions about what should have been. She had to stay
focused on Youssef.

"What's wrong?" she asked him.

No answer came, but Rachida did not move. She sat on the
divan in the yard for an hour or two or three, waiting for him
to share his pain, waiting to help him. She had started to doze
off when he spoke. "A-mmi, can I ask you something?" His
voice trembled. She said nothing, intending for her silence to
signify her agreement, but then he did not say anything, either,
for a long time. At length, he continued: "Wouldn't your life
have been easier if you had gotten rid of me? You would have
started over, gotten married, and had a good life. Why did you
have me?"

She looked at him, startled by his question. He had never, in
their worst arguments, asked her this. He wanted to know why
he was alive, but who knew why any of us were? He wanted
answers she did not have, and yet she had to try, because
the moment demanded it. For the second time that day, she
called to mind the moment she had gotten pregnant. When
Nabil Amrani had suggested the abortion, she considered it,
of course, but she also thought of the ten years she had spent
alone in the orphanage, and how much she missed her mother,
her father—her home. The baby inside her could give her that.
Youssef could give her the home she had always wanted, and
she could give him a home, too. How could she explain all of
this without revealing the truth about herself to Youssef? Her

son had suffered enough as it was without being burdened with more stories about his birth. "Yes," she said, "it would have been easier, but it would not have been right. Besides, I *wanted* to have you."

The answer seemed to satisfy him, for now at least.

16

THE MISSION

YOUSSEF WAS READING the newspaper while his mother, seated in a patch of sunlight, put henna on her hands. Using a syringe filled with the dark green paste, she pressed the plunger to draw thin lines on her hands. Starting on her palm, she outlined a fern whose leaves climbed up each finger in turn. It was a rare but welcome sight for Youssef — his mother making herself look pretty. She had been invited to a neighbor's betrothal, and she had gone to the hammam early in the morning and spent the rest of her day primping.

Someone knocked on the door. It was Moussa. "Hatim wants to see you," he said.

Youssef ran his fingers through his messy hair. "Right now?" he asked, then went back inside to put on his shoes. Syringe held up in the air, his mother asked, "What does he want?"

"I don't know," he said. "I'll find out."

She sucked her teeth in response. She never attempted to disguise her dislike of the Partisans. Youssef liked Hatim, but out of respect for his mother he said, "I'll be back as soon as I can, a-mmi."

When they arrived at the Party's headquarters, Youssef noticed that the Oasis was closed. He asked why. "We just wanted
some quiet today," Moussa replied, "because we have a lot of
work to finish."

It had been three years since the building that housed the
Star Cinema had been turned into the headquarters for the
Party. Walking through the lobby, Youssef could barely remember what the old theater looked like; it was part of a world that
had been destroyed and that he no longer mourned. It seemed
now as if the Party had been here forever.

"Let's go. Hatim is waiting for you."

The waiting area upstairs was bare, save for a clock in the
shape of Al Aqsa Mosque on a corner table and the Qur'anic
verses embroidered on black velvet, which hung ostentatiously
on every wall. They knocked on the door.

"Come in."

Hatim sat at a large desk, leafing through papers. The computer hummed to his right; to his left a glass of coffee with milk
gave out a faint steam. When he saw Youssef, he threw the sheaf
of papers into a folder, which he held shut with a paperweight.
Youssef was startled to see that it was the silver trinket he had
sold to the bric-a-brac dealer. It was the last thing he expected
to find here — one of his father's knickknacks, another useless
ornament, an object that could barely fulfill the function for
which it was designed.

"You wanted to see me?"

"Yes, yes," Hatim said. "Please, have a seat." He walked
around the desk to sit across from Youssef, leaning with his
elbow on the armrest of his chair. Moussa stood by the door

as if he were keeping guard. "My son," Hatim began, giving Youssef a deeply concerned look, "I don't need to tell you how difficult things are for our neighborhood. Our men have no jobs. Our women are loose. Our children have turned to sin. They drink alcohol; they fornicate; they sniff glue; they listen to filthy, disgusting music; they watch filthy, disgusting movies." He opened his palms. "Ya'ni, they have fallen."

Youssef was taken aback. He had been called from home in the middle of the day, and *this* was what Hatim wanted to tell him? The sermon seemed no different from the ones he regularly delivered downstairs.

Hatim continued. "And things have only gotten worse since the attacks of May 16. The government promised that it would deal with unemployment, fight poverty, and increase safety and security. But look around you. Do you think anything has changed for the better? Even the so-called Islamic parties in Parliament play the political game, like all the other politicians. The Party is different, as you know. We Partisans are the only ones who *chose* to come here and help. Since we have set up our headquarters here, we have tried our hardest to provide for the material and spiritual needs of our people. The first-aid services, the Ramadan dinners, and the after-school programs have been good steps. Oh, and the soccer field—I think you've used it a few times, haven't you?—it turned out quite well. All this is just the beginning; there is so much yet to be done."

Hatim deserved credit for the work he had done around Hay An Najat, though it surprised Youssef to hear him point it out. Ordinarily he kept quiet about the Party's past work and spoke instead about his goals for the future.

"If we are to truly succeed," Hatim went on, "we must first return the community to the state of purity it has lost. That way, we can reform our society from the bottom up. Our morals have become completely muddled by our blind love for the West. They have to become *unmuddled*. We have to regain the purity we have lost, and we can do that through the Islamic values we have neglected. Until we can return to the roots of our faith, until we can apply the precepts of our faith to every single aspect of our life, we will never be able to rise above the sin, the poverty, and the misery that have befallen us."

Youssef thought about what Hay An Najat could look like in a few years: real houses, good schools, safe roads—a new world in which someone like him might even have something to do and a place to call his own.

"But," Hatim yelled, raising his finger upward and bringing Youssef back from the vision he was entertaining, "our problems run much higher. Our community's fall into disgrace started with our political leaders. Oh, and what leaders! They promised to build schools and hospitals, create jobs for the young, and improve our economy. Of course they did none of that. The years come and go, governments follow one another, but our literacy rate stays the same, our hospitals remain ill equipped, and our economy still depends on agriculture and tourism. Like sheep, our foreign-educated elite want to do whatever France or America wants them to do, without regard for whether it is good for the rest of us. And in the process they waste or steal our money. They are a small number of people, those decadent few, but they are the real obstacles to progress. So you see, our society is rotten from the bottom up, but also from the top down. And only by purifying it *at all levels* will we be able to make tangible progress.

"Now, as you know, our efforts at reforming our society have been met with a lot of resistance. We expect this struggle. In fact, we welcome this struggle. After all, God is on our side, and He will not fail us. The battle between the forces of good and the forces of evil is upon us, and it is time, my son, for each one of us to choose sides. Are you with us? Will you side with the fallen, those who promote the mixing of the sexes, cast their hungry eyes on women, listen to filthy music, watch indecent movies, and drink the forbidden drink? Will you side with those who line their pockets with our taxes, steal from the poor to give to the rich, falsify election results to suit their purposes, brutalize and torture everyone who dares stand up to them? Or will you side with your brethren, those who promote virtue and forbid vice, avert their eyes when they see women, and protect children from licentious magazines and television shows? Will you side with those who help the poor, give to charity, spend their time in prayer, and work for a better tomorrow?"

Youssef stared, unsure what to say. Was this why he had been called—to pledge allegiance to one side or the other?

Hatim looked at him impatiently. "Let me make it simpler for you, my son. Do you want to stand side by side with the people of Hay An Najat, with your friends and neighbors, the people you see every day? Or would you rather side with the people of Casablanca? Lord, I hate that city, that place of filth and sin, where men and women walk hand in hand in plain view, where our daughters prostitute themselves to foreigners, where the Jews control our businesses, where the rich are taking advantage of the poor." He cleared his throat. "You must choose, my son. Are you on the side of your mother or your father?"

"My father?" Youssef said breathlessly. Only one thought raced in his mind now: Amin told him about me, Amin betrayed me. "What would you know of my father?"

Hatim gave him a quick smile. "I know more than enough about Nabil Amrani, my son. I've known for a long time." The Al Aqsa clock suddenly went off, broadcasting the call to the afternoon prayer, but Hatim, leaning forward in his chair, stared unblinkingly at Youssef. "Well? Are you on your mother's side, or your father's?"

"My mother's," Youssef whispered.

Hatim sat back in his chair and smiled. "Of course. How could it be otherwise, when you look around you, when you consider what the others have done to us?" he said, thumb pointed at his chest. "I know what you have gone through. You have studied, you have worked hard, you have played by the rules, and all for what? Here you are, jobless, with no prospects, no way to support your mother or to start a family of your own. Meanwhile, those who are responsible for what happened to you are sitting in their fancy houses in Anfa. Do you think it is right that your father should live in a mansion and you and your mother should live here? How long can we tolerate this kind of injustice? How long before we rise up and *demand* that things change?"

Youssef had still not recovered from the shock of hearing his father's name on Hatim's lips. He was mesmerized, unable to stop his anger toward his father and his father's world from kindling in his heart once again. This time it was taking the shape of a star, and he had trouble keeping it from radiating in all directions.

"I have been thinking for a while about how this senseless situation in our community is allowed to continue. And I have come to see that it is all because there is no *perception* about what is going on. I read a lot of these papers." He pointed to a pile of newspapers and magazines on the floor beneath the window. "And I am always appalled at how journalists conduct their business. They do not report the truth. They may promote the views of the government, or the views of their parties, or the views of the West. But they always lie. They never give us voice. They don't listen to our grievances. They ignore what we have to say about how we can reform our ways through our faith. They want to keep God out of everything. Let me tell you something: they can't. So the time has come to send them this message: Enough of your lies!" He slammed his fist on his desk, spilling some coffee on the papers.

Hatim's words were like a labyrinth in which Youssef was losing his way. His anger blinded him; he could not find the exit on his own and instead began to take each turn that presented itself without question. When the Al Aqsa clock broadcast its second reminder, he was so startled that he stood up. "The call to prayer," he said. "You will be late for prayer."

Hatim pulled him back down by the wrist. "Prayer can wait, my son. There are times for prayer, and there are times for action. We are having an important conversation. Moussa?"

Moussa came around the desk to the computer. With a few clicks of the mouse, he had connected to a video-sharing Web site and was already playing a clip, made up of still photographs, grainy and unfocused. An unseen man read a long series of names of students and activists, men and women, young and old, who had been killed in prisons and torture centers during the Years of Lead. "You are told," Moussa said, "that Derb Moulay Cherif and Tazmamart belong in history, that you're living in a new age now. But watch this." He played another video clip. This one had hidden-camera footage of riot police beating demonstrators on a campus in Meknès, customs officers stopping cars on the freeway in order to get bribes, judges rendering sentences on hundreds of young bearded suspects at once. It was true, Youssef thought. Too little had changed in the country.

Afterward came images of thugs beating up student pro-testors. For a moment, Youssef thought that this was another sample from a campus somewhere in the heart of the country, but when one of the men spoke ("ana ma 'amiltish haga") he realized the demonstrators were Egyptian. Suddenly he felt a new kinship with the young people of Egypt, whose struggles were so similar to his own.

Then Palestine: people waiting in line for food in Gaza, fam-ilies walking single file down a rocky hill in order to get to a checkpoint, the burial of a twenty-day-old baby with a gunshot wound to the head, an officer slapping a toothless old man in the West Bank. The images were no different from those shown on any given day on twenty-four-hour news channels, and usu-ally they would have stirred feelings of anger in Youssef. Today, though, the anger was already there, and the images merely sharpened it.

The last series of photographs were from Iraq. Men, naked

and barefoot, without faces or names, their hands cuffed to beds, rails, and doors, standing in their own urine or sitting in their own feces. Their heads were covered with black sandbags or with pink, frilly women's underwear. One stood on a box, wires taped to his hands, his arms spread out in a crucificial pose. Another was made to bend, as if he were in ruku', while a soldier sat on a chair in front of him. Men were piled like stones in pyramids of varying heights or dragged on a leash like animals.

The horror gave rise to fury, and suddenly Youssef felt unable to decide what to do with himself. Cry out in pain or stay quiet? Stay here in this musty office or run as far away from it as possible? He put his fingers on his temples, trying to follow each thought to its conclusion, but each one vanished before he could.

"The point that Brother Moussa is trying to make," Hatim said, "is that our stories are the same. We get injustice, repression, and torture, and somehow we're supposed to stay quiet? To say please and thank you?" He shook his head. "Not us. We say no."

Youssef had walked into that office preoccupied only by his own troubles, but after hearing Hatim's words and seeing Moussa's pictures, he felt as though he were losing touch with himself, becoming part of something much bigger. The injustice he had suffered was small and insignificant compared with these others, yet they were all made of the same fabric, the same disregard for human dignity.

"Everyone knows we are at war," Hatim continued, "but the Party doesn't fight the war with the same weapons. Some people think that strapping themselves up with explosives and killing fifty people is a good way to win, but I think that's inefficient, not to mention outdated. Any fool can blow himself up. A smart man has to worry about winning the image war, too. We want to hit very specific targets that will have maximum effect. This is why we set our minds on Farid Benaboud—you remember him, I'm sure. He wrote the first article denouncing our work here, and of course many of his colleagues have since followed him, like the Ben Oui-Ouis that they are. In the past, he has defended the whores who were caught with foreign tourists and has even suggested we must stop teaching religion in schools. Enough, I say. It is time we send a message to him and to those of his kind, to let them know we will not be intimidated, that we will continue our work regardless of their efforts to stop us. Imagine what eliminating him will do to the rest of his useless class of writers and journalists! The time has come for an operation against him."

"An operation?" Youssef repeated. The radiating star inside him numbed all other senses, so that his own voice sounded faint, as if it came from a faraway place and not from his own mouth.

Hatim placed his fingertips together in a steeple. "Nabil Amrani owns the Grand Hotel, which we have been monitoring for quite a while now. You are familiar with it since you worked there for a year. It is a place of filth and sin, so it is perhaps fitting that it turned out to be Farid Benaboud's favorite place to get a drink. We will conduct the operation there, so we can strike two birds with one stone." Now Hatim picked up the silver paperweight and turned it around in his hand. "My son, I think you know where I am going with this. You have been chosen for this operation—a great honor for you and your mother. Your people's future is on your shoulders. The question is, What will you do? How will you choose?"

"But why Benaboud?" Youssef managed to say. "He doesn't deserve this."

Hatim chuckled with incredulity. "So you think he is innocent? What about *you*? Are you not innocent? Do you think that you deserved what happened to you?"

Youssef drew his breath, but he had no response to that question. He *was* innocent. What had he done? He had been condemned to a life of poverty and alienness, and those who had pronounced the sentence were not even aware of his existence. Why should innocence belong only to those on the other side?

Hatim raised his eyebrows. "My son, think of this as a big play. We all have a part in it. Your mother. Nabil Amrani. Farid Benaboud. Me. You. All the actors have taken their places, and now it is your turn. Will you do it?"

Youssef had not thought there could be a way out of the labyrinth of words; his anger had imprisoned him there, but now Hatim was leading him to the exit. He was at once exhausted and relieved to see it. "Yes," he whispered. "I will do it."

Hatim exchanged glances with Moussa, who left the room at once, closing the door behind him. "I always thought you were smart, Youssef. You have not disappointed me. Now, listen to me carefully. We'll set up a meeting with Benaboud at the Grand Hotel, and we'll drive you there on the appointed day. Your job is to slit his throat. It's not as hard as it sounds. Have you ever slaughtered a chicken or a sheep? It's not that different.

All you have to do is aim for the jugular vein, right here"—he pointed to his neck—"and make a neat, unhesitating cut. It's quick and effective. He will barely feel anything."

From a desk drawer, he pulled out a knife so small it could easily be hidden in a sock. He demonstrated its sharpness by running its tip against a piece of paper, cutting it neatly in half, then gave it to Youssef to hold in his hand. Until this moment, Hatim's proposal had remained theoretical, maybe even hypothetical, but the cold knife in Youssef's hand turned the theory into practice, and the plan into plot.

"After you complete your mission, I want you to leave the hotel through the back doors, where the car will be waiting for you. Do you understand me?"

"But people will see me. They'll recognize me."

"They won't," Hatim said, "because we'll provide you with a disguise. No need to worry about that. Frankly, my biggest concern is discretion. We have two weeks to set everything up, and a lot can happen in that time. I don't need to tell you about the gossip in this town. I know you're not the type to talk, but all the same, I have to stress that you cannot speak to anyone—not your mother, not your friends—about the mission. The only people who know so far are the people in this room. We have to keep it that way."

Youssef nodded. Not long ago, he had asked his mother why she had not aborted him, why he was alive. Now it seemed to him he had finally found the answer to that question: to stand up to all those who had wronged her. This, at last, was the purpose of his existence.

"I want to warn you that we'll also be using one other person for this operation."

"Who?"

"Who doesn't matter. What matters is why. The reason we're using a second person is that we can't leave anything to chance. Think of it as a contingency plan. For example, what if Benaboud tries to get away? We want to make sure we get him the first time around. This is just a backup plan, nothing for you to worry about. All you need to worry about is your own part."

17

HEAVENS AND HELLS

IN THE END, it came down to one word. One word thrust Youssef to his fate. One little word: Mmi. *My mother.* The choice was forced upon him, but once it was made, it brought a strange sense of order to everything: he would leave his mark on his father's world, his mother would start over without the burden of supporting him, his own struggles would be over. Lying on his bed that night, he thought about the images he had seen in Hatim's office. What could one man do against all the injustices of the world? It was too awesome a task, but Hatim had shown him that trying to change everything at once was futile; it was better to focus on small acts of great significance. Youssef turned the idea around and around in his head, seduced by its brilliant simplicity.

His mother's voice came to him from far away. "I brought some sweets," she said. "Do you want some?" She had returned home from the neighbor's betrothal, and he had not even heard her come into the room. Mmi. Mmima.

"I'm not hungry," he said.

He would do this for her — for all those who were victims of people like his father. He turned to face the wall. Hatim was right. One man could restore some balance to this imbalanced country. Youssef would be that man.

❖ ❖ ❖

On weekdays, Amal was able to distract herself with work—her duties at the company, the dinners and cocktail parties she had to attend nearly every night, the occasional trips to Paris and Madrid for supplier conferences—but Saturdays and Sundays stretched themselves out before her, long and uncertain, like a treacherous river she had to cross. She never knew if she would be able to make it to the safety of Monday, to the numbing comfort of her desk. The slatted light fell on her bed, but she turned away from it and tried to go back to sleep. Weekends were hard, and this was one hardest of all.

Today marked the anniversary of their meeting, at a symposium in the Geography Department at UCLA, which she had attended not because of any particular interest in the study of the earth, but because *The Daily Bruin* had said that the event would feature a Lebanese buffet lunch. Fernando had seen her pile her plate with stuffed grape leaves and pita bread, and he leaned in and whispered that there was an even better buffet in the History Department that week. She had been too embarrassed to say anything, and she mumbled something about having to catch her 2 p.m. class and walked out. Of course she had run into him the next day, when he was escorting one of the guest speakers out, and she had been mortified to be seen hovering over the food, once again. Weeks went by. One day, she bumped into him at an antiwar rally on campus. He asked whether she wanted to get a cup of coffee, and she said yes, if she could pay for both of them — after all, it was thanks to him that she had found the treasure trove of buffets. On the way over, he asked about the paperback that poked out of her purse. "*Imaginary Homelands,*" she said.

"I love the part about growing up kissing books and bread," he said, running a finger on the spine.

They went on their first date the next day, decided to move in together two years later, and shortly after that, she left him behind, trading his love for the love of father and mother, the love of country, the love of home. She had been told to make a choice, and though she still had no idea why, she had chosen. On the way from the airport to the house, she had lowered her window and stuck her head out. "I invoke God," her mother shrieked, pulling strands of her no-longer-perfect bob from her eyes, "what are you doing?"

"I'm smelling the city," Amal said, taking a long, deep breath — but it was hard to detect anything over the powerful odor of diesel gas and the particles of dust and soot.

"It's cold," her father complained. "Close your window."

Amal pressed the button and sat back in her seat. Maybe her olfactory senses were weakened by her jet lag; she was dehydrated; she was getting a cold. That was why Casablanca did not smell to her like it used to, like a cocktail of odors: tea and coffee, sea breeze and fritters, fresh bread and cigarette smoke, human urine and animal excrement. As she settled back into her old life, everything struck her as different about the city — the unbreathable air, the constant sound of construction, the ubiq-

uity of mobile phones and pickpockets, the luxury-brand stores
on all the major streets. Foolishly, she had expected Casablanca
to remain as she had left it, as if it had been frozen in time in
her absence. But the city had grown: Parts of it had flourished;
others had festered, afflicted by the combined cancers of greed
and corruption. (Or were those things there all along, and she
had never noticed? She did not know.)

The few friends she saw, those who had never left to study
abroad, teased her that she acted differently now. When she
tried to pay for her own ticket to the movie theater, the response
would quickly come: You think this is America? I invited you;
I'm paying. When she complained that the company driver who
picked her up from the train station in Rabat to take her to a
business meeting was late, she was told with a chuckle, Wasʿi
khatrek. This is Morocco, not America. When she expressed
outrage at the threats made against Farid Benaboud after another article denouncing corruption in the government, she was
scolded: The trouble he finds himself in is his own fault. Where
does he think he is? Home was Morocco. America was away.
And there was not much more to it than that. You are back
home now, they said, everything will fall into place soon.

Over time, though, it seemed to her that the different loves
to which she owed an allegiance were being tested against reality. Her parents fought more than ever before—not about
important things, but about insignificant ones, like who sent an
invitation to Madame Ilham, that insufferable bore; who was
always hidden behind a newspaper; who bought another painting without consideration for where in the house it would go;
who preferred to watch a movie rather than talk to his daughter.

Amal grew tired of keeping score. She wondered why her parents chose to stay married when all they did was bicker.

It took her several months to gather up the interest and the courage to find her brother. She had to coax Omar to tell her what he knew. ("Not much, lalla Amal. I once heard him say something about Sector Five. I don't know that area very well. You should not go. It's not safe there.") She had driven around Hay An Najat until she found the right sector, parked in front of a hanout, and asked the proprietor for the right block number. She had given him twenty dirhams to watch her car and headed out to find Youssef El Mekki's house. As she came to a bend in the road, she noticed a white two-story building with huge flags that flapped in the wind. On them were the words, THROUGH GOD. WITH GOD. BY GOD.

A bearded young man was keeping watch outside the building, and when she passed him he started to follow her. "What are you looking for?" he asked, coming up close. She turned around to face him, noticing at once that inquisitive, confident, even cocky look she sometimes saw on plainclothes police officers at the airport. His eyes twinkled with curiosity.

"What business is it of yours?" she asked.

"I just wanted to make sure you found what you were looking for."

"Don't worry, I will," she said, feeling her cheeks flush. She wondered all of a sudden if he was a thief, if he had been after her purse, so she slid the strap down her arm and held her bag tightly with both hands.

She started to walk up the hill, toward the tin-roofed houses where thousands lived. There was poverty here the like of which she had never seen, and she averted her eyes as if she were looking at the most private, the most intimate of sights. How was it possible to live like this? The thought quickly vanished when she saw number 10, a little whitewashed house with a blue door. She knocked, and a middle-aged woman appeared. Her eyes widened in surprise at seeing Amal. "Are you lost, my daughter?"

"No. I am looking for Youssef El Mekki. Is this his house?"

The woman nodded. "Yes, it is. Who is asking for him?"

"I am Amal Amrani." Upon hearing the name, the woman looked as if she was about to close the door in Amal's face, until Amal placed her hand on the jamb and said softly, "May I come in, please?"

They sat in the yard, on an old, hard divan that was pushed up against a peeling wall. Youssef's mother stared at Amal with such intensity that Amal grew uncomfortable. She did not know how to begin. The best she could manage was, "I think you know who I am."

"No, I don't," Youssef's mother said. "Who are you?"

Amal was taken aback by the question. It was as though Youssef's mother wanted to force Amal to say the words out loud, like a confession. "I am Youssef's sister," Amal said. As the words parted from her lips, she could feel a shift in the air, like a sigh of relief after someone has managed to pull out a painful splinter, but she was not sure whose pain was relieved by those four words—hers or Youssef's mother's. "I wanted to talk to him."

"He's not here."

When Amal had found out about Youssef, she had been jealous

of him for taking so much of her place in her father's heart. In time, jealousy became anger and anger turned into shame and shame became sorrow—for what could have been and never was. Now, sitting in his house, she felt she had to explain her absence. "I didn't know about him until last June."

Youssef's mother sat up, as if she had suddenly decided that this meeting was taking too long. "It doesn't matter."

But it does, Amal thought. I want to meet him. "My father didn't know, either."

"And you believed him?"

Amal let the sarcasm slide. She continued with her penance. "I wanted to say I was sorry about what my mother did. But you have to understand what it was like for her, finding out about all this."

"Did you come here to apologize for them?"

Youssef's mother was becoming impatient; it was time to get to more pragmatic matters. "I want to meet him."

"That won't be possible. He left for Tangier three weeks ago. He's going to start over in Europe."

It was over before it had even begun. There would be no relationship with Youssef, and life in Casablanca would continue in the same way it had before. Sometimes, Amal felt like a fish that had been taken out of water and put back; she was finding it difficult to breathe. Her mother and father quarreled; her brother was gone; several of her friends were still abroad, finishing degrees or starting new ones. In a city of five million, she felt unaccountably, incredibly alone. What was left? *Who* was left?

The alarm clock on Amal's nightstand showed that it was 9 a.m. already, which meant it was about midnight on Friday in Los Angeles. She imagined Fernando getting home from an evening out, alone or with friends. He would drop his keys in the metal bowl in the hallway, slip his shoes off, toss the mail on the kitchen counter. Maybe he would make himself dinner. Maybe he would just go to bed. Maybe he would think of her. They had called, e-mailed, and written, but she always said she needed more time.

"Time for what?" he would ask.

"I don't know," she would say.

It will pass, child, her mother said, it will pass. But it had not. It was love. It was still there, throbbing with life, and no amount of distraction seemed to have any effect on it. It was like a language she had learned to speak; how could she learn to unspeak it? Amal could still remember the way Fernando's lips tasted, the heft of his arms around her shoulders, the sound of his voice when he laughed, his breath against her hair at night. Weekends were hard, and this one was hardest of all.

Once, she remembered, they had gone to a fancy restaurant in Santa Monica, where they were meeting some friends for a birthday dinner. Fernando had worn a black jacket and Amal was in a cocktail dress, and they stood on the sidewalk under a green awning, chatting with their friends, waiting to be seated. An old man pulled up in a luxury car and, leaving his door open, walked up to Fernando and handed him the keys. It took a few seconds for everyone to realize that the old man thought Fernando was one of the parking valets. There was contrite laughter, and the old man, teasing his false teeth with his finger, looked around him, suddenly noticing the real valets in red vests.

"That was strange," Amal said when the man was out of earshot.

Fernando shook his head. "Not really. He's just used to brown people waiting on him."

Even though he had shrugged the incident off, Amal could see that Fernando had been upset by it. It was one of those little things that seemed entirely insignificant in isolation but over time made you feel you did not belong. She knew the feeling well. After all, her race had been the biggest signifier about her in America. "Are there many Arabic women who go on to study in college?" one of her TAs had asked. Amal did not know whether it would be too impolite to point out that Arabic was a language, not a people. "But you don't look Arab," a middle-aged school registrar had said upon finding out that Amal was from Morocco — and she said it in a tone that suggested it was a compliment. When Amal had sold her car, the used-car dealer had asked if the trunk was empty. "Yes," she said. "No explosives or anything?" he replied, and laughed and laughed and laughed. These words added up over time, like grains of sand in a glass jar, telling her she did not belong. So she knew. She knew what it felt like, and she held Fernando's hand and pressed it and said nothing.

Home and away. She had known both; found good in both; loved and hated both. She did not want to have to choose one or the other, because in every choice something is gained but something is also lost. And in any case, why was home thought of as a place? What if it were something else?

❖ ❖ ❖

Youssef had never read Farid Benaboud's *Casablanca Magazine* with much regularity, but two days after his meeting with Hatim, he went out and bought a copy from the newsstand. It contained the usual offerings—news, cartoons, reviews. There was an in-depth report about a bank buyout, an article on infighting ahead of a local party's national convention, a column about the national team's chance in the next World Cup, an interview with a popular hip-hop band. Then there was Benaboud's editorial, in which he wrote about the failure of the latest literacy campaign to make significant gains. The picture that accompanied his piece showed him at his desk, his reading glasses perched on his nose, his chin resting on his palm.

Youssef remembered Benaboud's visits to the apartment, the first time for an interview about the tourism business, the second to ask for help with the libel suit brought against him by a government minister. He had asked good questions about how Nabil Amrani ran his businesses, he had brought up the salaries of his employees, he had even defended the Party against Nabil's accusations. What if the roles had been reversed, and Youssef had been the journalist while Benaboud had been the bastard son? Would Benaboud have agreed to Hatim's plans, too?

At the headquarters of the Party, it had seemed natural to agree that Benaboud was a part of Nabil Amrani's world and that he represented the worst it had to offer. But the more Youssef thought about Benaboud's visits, the more difficult it became to think of him as a symbol of everything that was wrong with the country. What about everyone else—government ministers, political activists, industry heads, union leaders, university teachers, college students—what had they done for the country?

It was true that Benaboud should have been more thorough in his article. He should have spoken to Hatim; he should have visited Hay An Najat; he should have tried to see things for himself. On the other hand, was it not enough for Hatim that he had *At Tariq,* where he could write what *he* wanted? If he disliked what Farid Benaboud had to say, why couldn't he respond in the same way?

Walking back from the kiosk, magazine tucked under his arm, Youssef had the feeling of being watched. The enormity of what he had agreed to do began to settle upon him.

❖ ❖ ❖

Many years later, Nabil would still remember it as an ordinary day, a Saturday like any other: Amal ate breakfast, answering with shoulder shrugs and rolls of the eyes whenever he addressed her; went to the gym to work out; came back and then disappeared into her room; played some music on the stereo. Around lunchtime, as Nabil was trying to convince Malika to change their evening plans, Amal came down the stairs, dragging a suitcase behind her. He thought she must have been confused about the date of next Saturday's meeting of the Association of Moroccan Hoteliers in Marrakech; he was going to make a joke that she had a worse memory than her mother. But then she turned toward them, he saw the expression on her face, and he understood. She was lost to him. She was going back to that man.

Nabil knew it was useless to stop her, but he tried anyway. He got up from the plush armchair and in five quick paces he had crossed the living room and was standing at the bottom of the staircase. He noticed at once that she was still wearing the turquoise necklace that man had given her. She looked so young, so innocent, so full of a kind of hope he had long forgotten, and he wanted to take her in his arms and hold her and never let go.

Behind him, Malika asked her chirpily, "Are you going to Marrakech?"

"No, Maman," Amal said, moving slightly to the right so she could better see her mother. "To Los Angeles."

"You're not going," Nabil replied in his sternest voice. "You belong here. In your country, with your family. What will you do there?"

"I will be with him."

There it was, her choice. He wished he could go back in time and unhear those words, but it was like wishing the sun had not come up that morning.

His wife stepped up. "The Royal Air Maroc flight for the U.S. has already left. You have to wait till tomorrow," she said. She sounded like someone who was bartering with the grocer, trying to get a better deal on a kilo of potatoes. Maybe she thought that one more day with Amal would make a difference and she could change her daughter's mind, once more.

"I'm flying through London," Amal replied.

Malika put her hand over her mouth.

"You will break your mother's heart if you leave," Nabil said, though he meant his own heart but could not say it.

Amal glanced at her mother, then bit her lip. "I'm sorry, Maman. I'm not leaving you; I just have to be with him. We'll still see each other."

Malika started crying, which at once irritated Nabil (did she always have to be so emotional?) and delighted him (surely the tears would affect their daughter and make her reconsider?). But nothing seemed to matter; nothing broke Amal's resolve. She gave her mother a hug and went out to ask the driver to bring the car. When she came back for her suitcase, he took it away from her and grabbed her by the hand and tried to pull her toward the living room.

"Let go of me," she said.

It was useless. In another minute, she was gone.

Nabil let himself slide into the armchair. He closed his eyes, and the first images that came to him were of a trip to the beach with Amal when she was five or six. It was a father-daughter weekend—Malika had gone to visit her mother. Amal sat in the backseat and sang songs and asked questions and kicked the passenger seat with her shoes. They were approaching Moulay Bousselham when a piece of gravel hit the windshield, cracking it into a cobweb of glass. Nabil stopped the car to inspect the damage. They were only fifty meters from their destination, so he decided to continue on; he would call the repairman from the house. Just as he parked the car in the driveway, the windshield gave in and a million pieces of glass fell, like rain, on the dashboard, on his arms, on his lap.

That was how he felt now, as if his already-fractured heart was at last and irremediably broken. It could never be put back together the way it was before. Amal had left him behind for the sake of that man, just as he had left Youssef behind for her sake. How could it be that he had given up the son for the daughter, and now he had neither the son nor the daughter? People always said that life was unfair, but maybe it was not. Life had caught up with him and dealt him a sentence of unendurable fairness.

He had betrayed all those he loved. When he had heard about Amal's American boyfriend, he had yelled at her, stopped paying for her school, and pretended to give her up. He had wanted to win her back by force. The deal he had made with his daughter may have been unspoken, but it was firm; it was final: she had to apologize and return to the old ways, or she would lose his love. What he had not counted on was that she was proud and stubborn, just like him. She had refused the deal. Once she was on her own, it had been easy for that man (what kind of a name was Fernando?) to prey on her and take her away.

Youssef had appeared at AmraCo in the middle of all this, like an answer to a prayer. Nabil thought he had been given another chance. He had taken care of Youssef, tried to groom him, prepare him for his entrance into the Amranis' world—not through the main door, of course, for there were still appearances to keep up, but through the side door, perhaps—get him to meet Amal and Malika, maybe have him come for dinner every once in a while. Then Malika found out, told Nabil's brothers, and Nabil had to make another bargain. He gave up the son in order to keep the wife and daughter. He had not realized that the pain would hit him as sharply as that piece of gravel striking the windshield. For as long as he lived, he would never forget the look in the boy's eyes when they stood by the car outside the company's headquarters. The look of a child begging you to love him, and all you did was turn away.

Now even Malika would leave him. She had no reason to stay any longer. He had made a fool of her over the years. She had never cared because she had always believed that they were a family and family was more important than *des affaires de cuisses*. But today everything had changed. Her only daughter had left. She was standing by the window, staring outside at the road, as if she could still see Amal's car in the distance. She had stopped crying. Her hands were folded over her chest. "Malika," he said. She did not respond, did not turn, did not show any sign of having heard him. "Malika, we can get her back." Nothing. It was as though she was no longer in the room with him. A kind of loneliness such as he had never known before entered his heart. If he did not have a daughter, or a son, or a wife, then who was he, in the end?

Over the next few days, he tortured himself with thoughts of a happier past, a time when he would never have made the bargains he made, a time when he still stood for something. What had happened to his world? When did things fall apart? Men of his generation were children of '56, children of the independence. Like them, he had signed petitions for the release of Saida Menebhi, written articles for *Lamalif*, spent hours in Rafael Levy's smoky living room discussing Frantz Fanon or Mehdi Ben Barka, closed down his law office during general strikes, denounced the imposition by the World Bank and the IMF of a structural adjustment plan, called these institutions "tools of neocolonialism *par excellence*," collected money for the families of those killed during the bread riots of 1981. Those were years when he still dared to dream, when he was still full of love for his country.

Some of his friends—journalists, professors, writers, artists—were forced into exile, in Cairo or Paris or Madrid. He knew people who had been imprisoned and tortured. One of his colleagues was made to disappear. Bit by bit, he began to lose hope, betray his ideals, trade his love of country for the comfort of home. By the time he was twenty-nine, he had given up. He told himself he was married, with a child on the way, that his wife—fragile as she was—would not be able to take care of Amal if something were to happen to him. He could no longer take the risk of wanting change. He started working for his father in the family business, like his father before him, and had been content to think of politics as something that was discussed every once in a while over a glass of whiskey or during a game of golf. Whatever happened in the nation or the world was not his concern any longer.

Now Nabil sat in his office in AmraCo, staring out the window at the city, with the minaret of the King Hassan Mosque at one end, the Twin Center towers at the other, and the vast, the incredible sea of homes and apartment buildings in between. What had he done with his life? The pain in his chest made it difficult to breathe, and in order to distract himself, he turned his office television on, watched a young journalist chatter on about the imminent danger of Islamic fundamentalism. He turned the TV off, tossing the remote on the desk. Young people these days seemed to have no idea what country they were from; they talked of Morocco as if its history had begun ten years ago, as if the issues they were facing had just appeared on the scene, lacking any provenance, devoid of any context.

He was overcome now by a feeling of shame at having turned away Farid Benaboud when he had asked for support. He had heard from a friend that Benaboud was in trouble—and not just the usual harassment, like slashed tires, or tapped phones, or stolen mail, but something else altogether, something far more sinister. How long before Benaboud gave up and he, too, made politics the occasional subject of a game of golf? He would close down the magazine; or worse, he would keep it open and turn it into a sounding board, against which the praises of the most beautiful country in the world could be sung and amplified.

There was something in Benaboud that Nabil recognized—a part of his old self, a part of the past he had long betrayed. And it was in order to save that sliver of himself, in order to be loyal to that past, that he picked up the phone and called to say he would write a statement of support. He knew this would anger his friends in government. But it would make others like him pause, and perhaps they could help Benaboud's magazine survive. This time, at least.

❖   ❖   ❖

Youssef was lying on his bed when he heard his mother crying. Immediately alarmed, he ran to the yard. "Yak labas?" he asked. She pointed to the television screen; she was watching *The Nightingale's Prayer*. "You startled me," he said, his hand on his heart.

"It's nothing," she said. She wiped her tears and shook her head, embarrassed to have been crying over a movie.

"It's all right," he said softly. He sat down next to her, watching for a few minutes. *Nightingale* was not his favorite film by Henry Barakat — he preferred his earlier work. But the performances by Faten Hamama and Zahrat El 'Ola made it worth watching.

"Tell me," she said, clearly wanting to change the subject, "were you going out?"

"Oh, no. No, I wasn't."

"You've been staying home a lot."

He couldn't tell her why. Even if he could tell her, he would have been ashamed to.

Why had he agreed to Hatim's plans? Even now, days later, he did not have a simple explanation.

His troubles had started when he had left Hay An Najat. He wished that he had never left the neighborhood, never dropped out of college, never said yes when Moussa came to the door to ask him to meet Hatim, never heard of Hatim's plans. Hatim had given him the impossible task of choosing between his mother and his father, and in his shock at realizing that his secret was no longer a secret, he had found himself cornered and forced to make a decision. The words had escaped his mouth before he could weigh their meanings or their consequences. Hatim had seemed satisfied because that answer meant Youssef would agree to the operation.

But Hatim did not know what Youssef's mother was like, or he would not have invoked her. Youssef's mother hated politicians, people who showed up in Hay An Najat only in election years. She made no distinction between the Party and the others, saying they all cared about the same things. If she had been in Youssef's shoes, she would already have reported Hatim to the police. How could he betray her now by doing the very thing she would never agree to?

Then there was Hatim's insistence that the mission was part of a bigger plan, where each person had a role. Youssef was tired of playing a role; he wanted, for once—for just this once—to be himself: Youssef El Mekki, son to a loving mother, college dropout, movie fanatic, perpetual loser at chess. But there was no going back. He had made a choice, and if he recanted it now, Hatim would kill him—or his mother.

He was a coward. He was letting an innocent man be killed for fear that his own innocent mother would be murdered. Night after night, he lay on his bed, stared at the ceiling, willed his mind to be blank. It was the only way he had found to convince himself that nothing he could do would change the course of things, that nothing was under his control. The plot would be carried out with or without his involvement.

When on Saturday the new issue of *Casablanca Magazine* came out, Youssef was stunned to read Nabil Amrani's article. He had come forward to support Farid Benaboud, to say that the intimidations had to stop. The old man has finally grown a backbone, Youssef thought, and despite himself he felt pride. Nabil Amrani's support would surely help Benaboud, but how could it save him from Hatim? On his way back home from the newsstand, Youssef once again had the feeling of being watched, and he hurried home, where he would be safe, and silent.

❖ ❖ ❖

Rachida had not meant to eavesdrop. In fact, she would not have paid any attention to Maati and the older man with whom he was talking if they had not switched from speaking Darija to Tamazight when they noticed her walking behind them. She was in a rush to get home to catch her Mexican soap opera, and the lane was narrow, so she had come up behind them at a quick pace, expecting they would step aside to let her pass. But instead they switched to Tamazight. Without knowing why, she slowed down and listened.

Maati's companion asked him about the Party.

"Two men came to see Hatim yesterday," Maati replied. "One of them is tall, about one meter eighty. Completely bald. Long beard. First name is Reda. The other one is about my height. Dark hair. Brown eyes. He has a lame leg. I don't know his name."

"We're familiar with Reda, alias El Mdardag. I think I know who the other man is, but find out his name."

They arrived at a fork in the road, and Rachida had to turn and head toward her house. She did not dare look back, though she kept listening to the sound of Maati's flip-flops until it faded away, down the other road. Maati! The high school dropout, the failed boxer, the good-for-nothing whose smile made her wonder whether any thought had ever entered his head. She would never have guessed he was a police informant. Appearances were deceiving—and how.

Over and over, she had told Youssef to stay away from Maati

and Amin, from the Party, from that cursed Oasis. If the police were monitoring Hatim, then something terrible was brewing, and there was no telling what would happen. She quickened her pace, eager to get home and tell Youssef.

She found him lying despondently on the divan. For the past few days, he had been like this—quiet, pensive, lost in a world she could not enter. "Youssef," she whispered. He turned to look at her, and her expression must have betrayed her because he sat up immediately. "What's wrong?" he asked.

She pointed to the bedroom. They went inside. She told him what she had heard, her right hand over her chest as if to still the beating of her heart.

"You're sure it was Maati?" Youssef asked.

"Of course I'm sure it was him, my son. I've known him since he was ten years old."

Still, he looked incredulous, unable to accept the idea that one of his closest friends was an informant. He paced in front of her, his fingers touching his temples, as if he could not contain all the thoughts that raced around inside his head. Then he made her repeat, word for word, the conversation she had heard. "But isn't it strange," Youssef said when she was finished, "that they spoke of such things openly, even though you were right there? Are you sure they weren't just pulling a prank?"

His tone suggested absurd hope, and so Rachida realized that the only way to convince her son was to tell him the truth. She would never be able to save Youssef from Hatim and his people if she did not, at long last, tell the truth. "They spoke in Tamazight."

"You understand Tamazight?"

She nodded. Tamazight belonged to a time when she still had a family, she began.

"A family?" Youssef asked. His face grew pale, and he sat on his bed and watched her with disbelief, his pupils dilated in the half-light of the bedroom. He seemed to her again like a child, no longer a grown man but just a child, and she wanted to wrap her arms around him and run her fingers through his hair and tell him that everything would be all right in the end. But there was no getting away from the truth this time. She told him first about her mother, Izza, whose face she could no longer recall after so many years. Rachida did remember, though, the shape of Izza's body as she came through the doorway of their house, backlit by the bright mountain sun. She remembered the feel of Izza's hands as she brushed and plaited Rachida's four-year-old hair. She remembered the weight of the stones when they played marbles together. She remembered the smell of lavender on Izza's bed, even at the very end, when she was too sick to leave it.

A few months after Izza died, Rachida's father, Hammou, had sent Rachida to the orphanage in Fès, where she could attend school. It would be good for her, he said, better than climbing trees and running around in the fields, picking daisies. In all her time at the Bab Ziyyat orphanage, Rachida's father had visited just three times, and when he did, it was to marvel at how much she had grown and how well she could read. "He gave me up to the orphanage and told me it was for my own good."

Rachida was in her first year of training to be a midwife when the head nun told her she would be working for Fatema Amrani, who needed someone to attend to a pregnant woman on bed rest. Rachida had taken care of Fatema's daughter-in-law Malika Amrani, carefully noting her weight, temperature, and blood pressure in a notebook, and spent the rest of her time on the veranda, working on her embroidery or reading a magazine.

This was how she had met Nabil Amrani, who always spoke with passion, whether it was about music or movies or, especially, politics. His eyes sparkled with curiosity whenever he looked at her. He smiled at her every time she passed him in a corridor, brushed against her when she brought a tray for his wife, asked whether it was true the nuns at the orphanage had chartered a bus to go see Nana Mouskouri in concert in Casablanca.

His wife had never suspected anything, but his mother, Madame Fatema Amrani, had found out and had thrown Rachida out of the house. She had not even given her time to pack her suitcase. Nabil had entered her life and changed it for the worse, but also for the better, for had he not given her Youssef?

Rachida had to start over in a new place. She was no longer Rachida bent Hammou ben Abdeslam ben Abdelkader Ouchak. She was merely Rachida Ouchak, a widow and mother, living in the city, away from the mountains of her childhood, away from the orphanage of her adolescence, away from the mansion of her youth.

The relief of sharing a story she had waited so long to tell was intoxicating. She could not stop, now that she had begun. Her father came from a long line of horsemen. He owned land and was respected in all the villages in the area. To go back to him pregnant would mean the end of him. So she stayed away from him and took her baby to Casablanca, where everyone could start over.

As she spoke, she watched Youssef's face for hints of his reaction. Would he believe her, or would he, once again, look at her with his heartbreaking skepticism? There was a time in his life when she could read the emotions on his face. Once, when he was eight years old, he had come home, his right hand bleeding, saying that he fell on a rock. She inspected his hand; he had a deep cut, in the shape of a paperclip, and she immediately set about disinfecting it. As she worked, she noticed the way his lips quivered when she pressed him for details, and she knew he was lying. "I told you not to play with the neighbor's bicycle," she said sharply. "You fell on the handle, didn't you?" His eyes widened in terror and he confessed on the spot.

But all that was long ago. He had changed so much in the past three years that she could not claim to know what went on inside his head. She expected he would be angry with her, and she would not blame him if he were. What she feared, though, was that he would accuse her of hiding something — she had lied to him so often in the past — and that he would ignore her pleas to stay away from Maati and from the café. She *needed* him to believe her. She took a deep breath, and when she released it, she spoke in the language of her childhood, in Tamazight, the words rolling on her tongue like a declaration of love. "Hati lmaaqul aktinigh, aywi, amni."

At the sound of this new language inside their home, the lines on Youssef's forehead disappeared. His jaw relaxed. He spoke in a whisper. "It is true, then," he said.

"It is," she said, and put her hand on his. "Now do you believe me?"

"Yes."

"Will you stay away from Maati?"

"Yes."

All of a sudden, her knees felt weak and she sat down on her
bed, across the room from Youssef. It seemed that he was listening to her this time, not just hearing her words and reluctantly
speaking his own. But then he lay on his bed and stared at the
ceiling, lost in his thoughts.

❖ ❖ ❖

Youssef had wanted nothing more than the truth; all his quar-
rels with his mother had been because of it. Now she had delivered it, and as it sank in, he began to see what it might mean.
He was an Ouchak from Sefrou on his mother's side, and an
Amrani from Fès on his father's side. He was half-Berber and
half-Arab; he was a man of the mountains, and a man of the
city; a man of the people and an aristocrat; a full-blooded Moroccan, with the culture and the history of a thousand years—a
rich identity, of which he could be proud.

But this truth was as invisible as air, as fleeting as breath
itself. The real truth was what everyone around him saw: he
was a slum dweller, the son of a hospital clerk, a man with no
illusions about his place in society. Youssef had yearned for a
father, and the yearning had led him on a journey to find him.
His father had deserted him. His friend Amin had betrayed

him. His friend Maati had spied on him. What was left? *Who* was left?

The only constant in his life was his mother. She had played the role of the widow, when she had never had a husband; the role of an orphan, when all along she had had a father. She had done it for him. She had lied her way through his life, and yet she had also given him the only certainty in it—her love. In the end, she was his only home.

It was an inexpressible relief to find out the whole truth, but suddenly it did not seem to matter as much as it once had. Farid Benaboud's life hung in the balance, and that was more immediate, and far more critical, than any story Youssef's mother could tell. Benaboud's troubles, Youssef thought, began and ended with the truth, too. He had angered government ministers with his articles about the "bonuses" they received for privatizing state companies; he had engaged in a public battle with Parliament members over their corruption and dereliction; he had persistently criticized the Party for taking over the social life of Hay An Najat; he had exposed Hatim's murky finances. He had written the truth, or at least what he thought was the truth. Now he would pay for it with his life.

Youssef was taken out of his reflections by his mother's voice. It was best to do nothing, she said. To just stay away from the Party. Stay away from the Oasis. Stay home with her. The police were watching Hatim, and someday very soon they would arrest him for one crime or another. It was important not to be at the wrong place at the wrong time.

If the police knew about the assassination of Farid Benaboud, then they would stop it before it happened. For three glorious days, that simple hope numbed Youssef's guilt at having stayed quiet, and silenced his concern about Farid Benaboud. He watched satellite news channels constantly, expecting to hear news about an arrest. Then the eve of the "operation" came, and nothing had been done. Despite having an informant inside the Party, maybe the police did not know of Hatim's exact plans, since Hatim had been so discreet. Youssef began to wonder whether anything, or anyone, could save Benaboud.

THE DAY OF THE MURDER

THE BOULEVARD WAS HEAVY with traffic. Drivers strained
to make their way through the single open lane, while workers
in blue uniforms fixed a billboard advertising a music festival.
The sound of exasperated car horns abated at the roundabout,
where the water fountain ran and where flocks of pigeons came
to drink and rest in between their peregrinations. At the top of
the street, the Grand Hotel sat, its gigantic glass doors closed,
reflecting the rays of the sun. Standing on the pavement across
from the building, Youssef was blinded by the bright light.

He had left the house early, quietly closing the door behind
him. Moussa had given him the knife and the disguise — a
woman's flowing jellaba and veil — and then taken him downtown by car, dropping him off two blocks from the hotel.
Youssef had to walk the rest of the way. Periodically he looked
behind him; he was sure Hatim had sent someone to follow
him all the way to the door. As he neared the hotel, he watched
carefully for signs of the police, for signs that his silence would
not cost a man his life.

Now, raising his hand to shield his eyes from the sunlight, he surveyed the scene carefully. Four men were seated in a parked Peugeot. The two in front wore dark sunglasses and turned their heads back, listening to one of their companions in the back. Youssef thought—he hoped—that they were plainclothes officers, but after a few minutes the driver started the engine and eased his car out of the parking spot and onto the street. In another minute they were gone.

He grew light-headed. Fear and hunger gripped his stomach like a fist—he had not eaten anything all morning. He retreated under the shade of a big oak tree and placed his hand on its trunk to steady himself. He took several deep breaths, inwardly repeating the mantra he had held on to for the past few days: Everything will be all right. He turned to watch the street once again. Time passed. Then a white van with no discernible logo pulled into an empty space on the right corner. The driver sat still, and no one came out of the vehicle. With each passing minute, Youssef became more convinced that it was the police. He was jubilant. This is it, he told himself. With the police here, everything would be all right. Farid Benaboud would be safe.

Just then a young man in a black suit walked up the street on the left, heading for the entrance of the Grand Hotel. Something about the way he carried himself seemed familiar. Youssef stepped out from under the tree to get a better look, his eyes straining against the white sunlight. As if realizing that he was being watched, the man in the black suit glanced back. It was Amin. Youssef's hand covered his mouth, muffling a gasp that would attract attention. Amin had been persuaded to carry out Hatim's plans, too. He was the second assassin.

There was a moment of silence and stillness, when even the wind seemed too afraid to blow through the trees. Youssef felt a bead of sweat travel down his spine, until it lodged itself in a hollow between his skin and the inside of his waistband. He felt it dissolve against the fabric, just as new beads were forming on his forehead, under his armpits, on the back of his neck, and between his toes. He was assaulted by these sensations and upset with his body for registering them at such a moment. He needed to think, but he could not focus under the glare of the sun and in the oppressive heat.

Instinct made him cross the street and run inside. He did not know what he wanted to do, but he knew he could not let Benaboud die, any more than he could let Amin kill. Coming in from the sun, he was momentarily blinded. He stood in place, waiting for his eyes to adjust. He took in the cool, air-conditioned air. He tried to find his bearings. The reception desk was on the right, the cashier was on the left, and there, past the lobby, was the café, Chez Momo. He walked through the lobby in quick steps, afraid one of his former co-workers might recognize him in spite of the jellaba and the veil.

The café smelled of steamed milk and cigarettes and cut flowers. At a table by the window, a handful of socialites smoked and spoke in loud voices. A couple whispered in a corner. Under the gilt-framed mirror, three men in casual clothes sipped coffee. A woman sat by herself, reading the newspaper. And at a table at the other end of the café, almost hidden from sight by a potted plant, sat Farid Benaboud. He was talking animatedly with an older man, a bald fellow who sat back in his chair, his legs spread far apart.

Scouring the café, Youssef saw no sign of Amin. Where had he gone?

A waiter brought an ice cream sundae for Benaboud and an espresso for his companion. Benaboud's friend reached for the cup and knocked it over, the black liquid spilling on the table. Gasping audibly, he blotted the coffee with his napkin and steadied the cup. Benaboud offered his napkin, but his friend waved his hand and got up to go to the bathroom. Now alone, Benaboud slid his spoon into his ice cream, scooping out the cherry on top. This little man, who had spoken so forcefully and seriously about the country and its problems, seemed child-like now, completely lost in the simple pleasure of a goblet full of ice cream.

The door to the bathroom swung open again, and out came Amin. Without looking around him, he walked over to Benaboud's table.

"Amin," Youssef called.

At the sound of his name, Amin turned, but he did not show any sign of surprise at seeing a tall figure in a white jellaba and veil. It was as though this interruption was part of a script. He took two more steps and pulled out a knife.

"Wait!" Youssef yelled.

All the café's patrons turned to look at Youssef. Amin stuck the knife in Benaboud's neck, the sound of it so soft that no one heard it. Then the dark jet of gushing blood caught the attention of the woman reading the newspaper, and she screamed and pointed. Everyone turned to look. In the middle of the confusion, one of the three men at the table nearby pulled out a gun and shot Amin. Screams of terror erupted as blood and bits of brain spattered on the walls. People stampeded out of the café.

For a moment, Youssef remained in his spot, paralyzed by the horror. Then he ran out of the café, too, through the lobby, and out the double glass doors. Just as he appeared outside on the steps of the hotel, an officer tackled him and pushed him roughly against the wall. "Wait," Youssef cried out. "You don't understand."

YOUSSEF SAT ON THE CURB for what seemed like days but what he would later learn was just two hours. His hands were cuffed behind his back, and beside him on the ground were the jellaba and the veil. An officer stood across from him, watching him. Youssef felt as though he were dreaming, as though he were still lying on his bed in the little house in Hay An Najat and he would wake at any moment. Yet there was no relief from the nightmare. "You have the wrong man," he said for the hundredth time. "This is a big mistake."

"No mistake," the officer said.

"I had nothing to do with it."

The officer chuckled. "You people always say that."

"I came here to stop them from killing Benaboud," Youssef said. His throat was parched and he felt his blood thumping in his ears.

"You can tell this to the Commissaire, although I wouldn't advise it." The officer laughed, as if the thought of Youssef's convincing the police chief of his innocence was somehow irrepressibly funny. Now the officer stretched his hands above his head and cracked his knuckles. He had the look of a man satisfied with a good day's work.

Another officer came by. "We're getting close," he told his colleague. "We can take him in as soon as the Commissaire gives the OK."

It occurred suddenly to Youssef that his innocence was irrelevant. It served no purpose in the overall plot and, what was worse, it complicated matters for the police. This realization hit him with the full force of revelation. He could see clearly now that he had been a small actor in a big production directed by the state.

What terrified him was that he had not even been aware that he had played a role in the assassination of Farid Benaboud. Naively, he had believed he was acting like a concerned human being, maybe even a hero: he had tried to stop a murder. But now he had discovered that the part that had been reserved for him by the state was that of the failed terrorist, the one who gets caught, the one who makes the police look good because his arrest proves that the state tried to protect the inconvenient journalist.

Amin had received a simple role, a role that required no lines. He had killed Benaboud, out of anger, despair, resentment, a broken heart, a belief that his life was not worth living, or for another reason altogether. He was dead now, having traded his life for whatever the Party had promised him. It was Maati who had received the best part. He had fooled everyone. Youssef had considered Maati to be a simple man, someone who was not fit to be a confidant to his secrets, when in fact he had been trusted with far heavier secrets, and he had delivered them to the police. Appearances are deceiving, Youssef's mother always said.

The Commissaire finally arrived on the scene and was immediately surrounded by aides who briefed him on the investigation. He listened, nodding a few times, and then his eyes came to rest upon Youssef. "This is him?" he asked.

"Yes, sir," one of his assistants replied, pointing. "His name is Youssef El Mekki."

Acknowledgments

I am grateful to the Hedgebrook Foundation for providing me with space in the spring of 2005 in which to work on this novel; to Oregon Literary Arts for financial support in 2006; to the Fulbright Commission for funding my stay in Casablanca in 2007. I am also thankful to the Multnomah County Library and the libraries of the University of California at Riverside.

The neighborhoods of Hay An Najat and Qubbet Jjmel are fictional, as are the Star Cinema, the Grand Hotel, and the publications run by Hatim Lahlou and Farid Benaboud. In transliterating Moroccan Arabic expressions I have tried to be as phonetically correct as possible without resorting to diacritical marks. For proper names, however, I have used standard Moroccan spelling.

I am indebted to Antonia Fusco, Kathy Pories, Brunson Hoole, Rachel Careau, Michael Taeckens, Courtney Wilson, Craig Popelars, Kendra Poster, Ina Stein, Elisabeth Scharlatt, and the entire team at Algonquin for their work on behalf of this book. Many thanks to my amazing agent, Ellen Levine, who believed in it from the beginning.

I thank my parents and siblings for their patience and continued indulgence with me. Thank you to my daughter, Sophie, who came to me at the same time as this book and brings me the kind of joy it cannot. As always, my thanks to Alexander Yera, my husband, my partner, my best friend, my first and last reader.